"What are you hiding from, Zach?" Jamie asked.

Even in the darkness, she felt the force of his glare. Then, without a word, he turned on his heel and walked inside.

Jamie sucked in a breath. Obviously that question had struck close to home. But maybe she should ask it of herself. What was *she* hiding from?

Suddenly realization dawned, and with it a unique, intense pain. She reached up and touched her cheek. Stunned, she brought her fingers to her lips and felt the moisture there. She was crying.

And then she knew. She hadn't rescued Zach because she owed him. She'd come here because, even after seven years, she'd never been able to forget him. She'd never let go.

She'd come here because she still loved him.

Dear Reader,

Welcome to another month of powerhouse reading here at Silhouette Intimate Moments. Start yourself off with Lindsay Longford's *Renegade's Redemption*. Who doesn't love to read about a rough, tough loner who's saved by the power of a woman's love?

Move on to Susan Mallery's *Surrender in Silk*. This sensuous read takes a heroine whose steely exterior hides the vulnerable woman beneath and matches her with the only man who's ever reached that feminine core—the one man she's sure she shouldn't love. Alexandra Sellers plays with one of the most powerful of the traditional romantic fantasies in *Bride of the Sheikh*. Watch as heroine Alinor Brooke is kidnapped from her own wedding—by none other than the desert lord who's still her legal husband! In *Framed*, Karen Leabo makes her heroine the prime suspect in an apparent murder, but her hero quickly learns to look beneath the surface of this complicated case—and this fascinating woman. Nancy Morse returns with *A Child of His Own*, a powerfully emotional tale of what it really means to be a parent. And finally, welcome new author Debra Cowan. In *Dare To Remember* she spins a romantic web around the ever-popular concept of amnesia.

Read and enjoy them all—and then come back next month for more of the most exciting romantic reading around, here at Silhouette Intimate Moments.

Yours,

Leslie Wainger
Senior Editor and Editorial Coordinator

Please address questions and book requests to:
Silhouette Reader Service
U.S.: 3010 Walden Ave., P.O. Box 1325, Buffalo, NY 14269
Canadian: P.O. Box 609, Fort Erie, Ont. L2A 5X3

SURRENDER IN SILK

SUSAN MALLERY

Published by Silhouette Books
America's Publisher of Contemporary Romance

ISBN 0-373-07770-X

SURRENDER IN SILK

This edition published by arrangement with Harlequin Books S.A.

Printed in U.S.A.

Books by Susan Mallery

Silhouette Intimate Moments

Tempting Faith #554
The Only Way Out #646
Surrender in Silk #770

Silhouette Special Edition

Tender Loving Care #717
More Than Friends #802
A Dad for Billie #834
Cowboy Daddy #898
**The Best Bride* #933
**Marriage on Demand* #939
**Father in Training* #969
The Bodyguard & Ms. Jones #1008
**Part-Time Wife* #1027
Full-Time Father #1042
**Holly and Mistletoe* #1071

*Hometown Heartbreakers

SUSAN MALLERY

makes her home in the Lone Star State, where the people are charming and the weather is always interesting. She lives with her hero-material husband and her attractive but not very bright cats. When she's not hard at work writing romances, she can be found exploring the wilds of Texas and shopping for the perfect pair of cowboy boots. Her last Intimate Moments, *The Only Way Out*, was a finalist for the Romance Writers of America RITA Award for best Romantic Suspense novel for 1995. Susan writes historical romances under the name Susan Macias.

To James, who believes in home,
family and staying married forever.
You're the kind of man we write about in romances.
When you find that special woman
and she tells you how wonderful you are,
don't forget you heard it from me first.

Prologue

Two rescue helicopters swooped down and broke the silence of the night like noisy birds of prey. Spinning blades kicked up sand, dirt and debris, swirling them into a blinding tornado. The powerful military engines were loud enough to wake the dead.

Worse, they would alert the enemy, but everyone expected that.

Zach Jones crouched behind an abandoned shack, his automatic weapon ready to fire. He squinted against the darkness and the cloud stirred up by the choppers, then made a beckoning motion with his left arm.

"Now," he called to the dozen men waiting behind him. "Get going."

They moved as one. A low, dark shape—men hunched over to provide a smaller target—slipping like a snake toward safety.

The first burst of gunfire came from the north end of the compound. Zach spun in that direction and pressed his finger on the trigger. Instantly the gun jerked to life, spitting bullets faster than the eye could see. His men sprinted quicker, lower, then broke ranks when one of their own was shot. Zach couldn't see who had gone down. Damn. They'd already lost too many men on this mission.

"Grab him and get moving," he yelled, still firing toward the enemy, giving his men protection as they scooped up their fallen companion and continued their escape.

The first helicopter had nearly reached the hard-packed earth, with the second close behind. The deafening noise had a life of its own. The power of the engine, the whipping of the blades, and the sharp, staccato bursts now coming from the tower at the far end of the compound.

"Dammit all to hell," Zach muttered. He'd known there would be trouble on this mission. He'd planned for it. Just not well enough. Their intelligence information had underestimated the size of the enemy force by nearly a hundred. They'd had to abort and call in the helicopters early. His group of sixteen men had already been reduced by two. He glanced at the injured man being carried toward the first helicopter. Make that by three.

He touched the radio transmitter in his ear. "All right, Albatross, how bad is it?"

There was a brief scratching of static, then a voice said, "Bad. Three trucks of reinforcements just pulled up. I'll do the best I can from up here."

"The hell you will." Zach stepped out of the protection of the shack and sent a quick burst of gunfire toward the tower, then ducked back to safety. "Get down here now. The choppers are going to be leaving pronto."

"I can take out at least one of the trucks."

Zach swore. "They're bringing in Stinger missiles. If they aim one at the choppers, we can kiss our ride home goodbye. Albatross, move it. Now!"

"Yes, sir."

But Albatross never made it. Seconds later the southern

wall where Albatross had been hiding exploded in a brilliant flash of fire and heat. Zach turned away, as much to protect himself from the blast as to save his night vision. The smell of helicopter exhaust, sand, dust, ash and burning wood flooded him.

He spared a quick glance at the first helicopter. All the men were inside. He pressed another button on the transmitter. "Get the hell out of here," he said.

"Yes, sir." The first chopper lifted off immediately and quickly climbed into the night.

There were more bursts of gunfire, followed by muffled shouts. The enemy was organizing. Zach eyed the distance to the second chopper, then wondered how many bullets he would take between here and there.

"Sir, we've got you covered," a voice from the chopper said in his ear. "Anytime you're ready."

"Now," Zach said, and took a step forward.

He never got farther than that. Something fast slammed into the exhaust pipe of the helicopter. The bird exploded.

Fiery debris flew through the night, knocking Zach down, cutting through his clothes and burning his skin. Despite the pain, he tried to crawl away. But his leg wasn't working. It hurt too damn much to be gone, but he knew he'd injured it badly. He'd hurt something else, too. Maybe his head. The night sky started spinning as the ground rushed up to meet him.

Just before he lost consciousness, he saw several pairs of military boots surround him. The bastards were going to get him alive and they were going to make him pay for what he and his men had done this night. As the darkness claimed him, Zach Jones knew Albatross was the lucky one.

He'd had the good sense to die.

Chapter 1

"You can't leave him there," Jamie Sanders said, then shoved her hands into her jeans pockets so no one would see that she was shaking. She wasn't sure if it was caused by rage or fear.

Probably a little of both.

"Zach Jones is dead," Winston Danville III stated calmly.

"You don't know that. According to the men who got away, he wasn't in the second helicopter when it exploded."

Winston leaned back in his leather chair and stared at her. Jamie had always thought his combination of pale blue eyes and white blond hair made him look like a Hollywood casting director's idea of the perfect villain—cool, confident, in control. Winston's reputation did nothing to dispute that image.

"Three weeks, Jamie," Winston said softly. "Three weeks in one of their prisons, being tortured several times a day. If Zach Jones wasn't dead, he is now."

Her stomach rolled at the thought. She desperately needed him to be alive, but the thought of him having to endure that kind of suffering was more than she could bear. The word *torture* wasn't just a casual phrase to her. She was intimately familiar with the inhumanity of deliberately inflicting pain on prisoners. Surely death would be a kinder fate.

But Zach wasn't dead.

She crossed the richly decorated room and sank into one of the leather chairs opposite her boss's desk. She stared at him, meeting his cold gaze with an equally determined stare of her own. She'd trained at the hands of a master. She knew how to intimidate as well as anyone in the agency.

Surprisingly Winston looked away first.

Before she could pounce on her unexpected advantage, there was a quick knock at the door. Winston's pretty, young assistant stepped inside and brought them each a mug of coffee.

Jamie accepted the cup with a muttered "Thanks" and took a sip. The assistant glanced at her, then left. Jamie knew she looked out of place. The worn jeans, scuffed athletic shoes, faded tank top and the flannel shirt she wore instead of a jacket didn't fit the dress code of the office. She had never been the suit-and-high-heels type. She filed away the feeling of discomfort, knowing she would deal with it at another time. All that mattered now was Zach.

"He's not dead," Jamie repeated.

Winston raised one eyebrow. "How do you know?"

"I just do."

"I see. Well, fine. I'll write up the report and quote your intuition as the source. I'm sure the director will be convinced."

Jamie set the coffee on the desk and rose. "I'm going in, Winston, with or without your permission."

"No, you aren't. You still work for me and you'll do what I tell you." He paused and raised his pale eyebrows. "Unless you plan to resign. Isn't that what you've been talking about?"

He was right. She *had* wanted out. The last mission was supposed to have been her final one. She even had the letter of resignation typed up at home. But she hadn't turned it in. A voice inside of her, a voice Zach had taught her to listen to, had whispered to wait. Now she understood why.

"That was before I knew about Zach."

Winston motioned to the chair. Jamie hesitated. Since finding out what had happened to Zach Jones, she'd been on the move. She'd flown directly to Washington on the first flight she could get. Once in the capital, she'd made a few phone calls and come up with a plan. All she needed was Winston's cooperation.

Sitting down felt too much like giving up, but her boss was stubborn enough not to talk to her if she didn't at least pretend to go along with him. Grudgingly she perched on the edge of her seat.

He reached for his coffee and took a sip. "I wasn't aware you and Zach were so close."

Jamie grimaced. "You know we aren't. Zach took me through training and my first assignment. He made me the best. I owe him for that."

There was more, of course, but Winston didn't need to hear about it. Their boss prided himself on knowing every detail of his operatives' lives. This was one detail he hadn't been able to claim. Not that it mattered. Seven years was a long time for anyone to remember. She was reasonably sure Zach had been able to forget, even if she hadn't.

"According to my records, you've never worked with him since. That's a long time to carry a debt," Winston said.

She shrugged.

"Interesting." He leaned back in his chair. "And touching. But the answer has to be no."

She was on her feet in an instant, her hands braced on his desk. "Listen to me, Winston. Short of arresting me, you can't keep me from going after Zach. You can make it easy or you can make it hard, but I'm doing this." She glared at him, ignoring the frosty look in his icy blue eyes.

"You'll end up just as dead as he is."

"I'm willing to take the chance."

"Then you're a fool."

"Maybe, but I'm a determined fool. Besides, if you're right and I do get killed, how are you going to explain my body?"

"Terrorists don't send bodies home."

"What if they do this time?"

His thin lips twisted in disapproval. "I'll handle it the way I've handled other problems."

"I'll leave a letter with my lawyer explaining everything and exposing the agency."

"Don't threaten me, Sanders."

She knew she was playing with fire, but she didn't have a choice in the matter. She *had* to convince him. "I have a better chance of surviving with your help than without it," she told him. "But it doesn't matter what you say or do. I'm going in after Zach and I'm going to bring him home."

"I suppose you're just going to walk in there and take him from under their noses," Winston said. He reached for his mug and cradled it in both hands.

Jamie sank into her seat. "Exactly."

He stared at her for a long minute. She couldn't tell what he was thinking, but she refused to let the silence make her squirm. She was an expert at waiting. She had to convince him. Winston was her only hope. She would go in without agency assistance, but without the backup, the odds for success were almost zero.

Finally he nodded briefly. ''Explain.''

Relief crashed through her. She had him. He was going to agree. Once he heard her plan, he would be convinced—she knew it!

She pushed aside the momentary flush of victory and concentrated on the task at hand. She grabbed a pen and the blank legal pad poking out of the pile of papers on his desk. Working quickly, she made a sketch of the compound, based on the aerial photographs she'd seen and what she knew about the area.

She drew the low, one-story building where Zach was probably being kept. A quarter mile away was their munitions storage.

When she finished, she slid the paper toward Winston. ''Zach is here,'' she said, trying to sound as if she really knew where he was being held instead of just guessing. ''It's not a main training facility, which is in our favor. Also, Zach's men were there less than a month ago. The debriefing information should still be accurate. The plane will drop us off about thirty miles away, and we'll drive until we get within sight of the perimeter.''

''We?''

She nodded, trying to act casual. ''Rick Estes is coming with me.''

Winston was a pro. He might wear expensive suits and silk ties, but there had been a time when he'd been the best field agent in the agency. Not by a flicker of his pale lashes did he give away what he was thinking.

''Why Estes?''

''He owes Zach, too.''

''I wasn't aware Agent Jones inspired such loyalty.''

She didn't bother commenting on that one.

After a few moments of silence, Winston shook his head. ''It won't work.''

"But we—"

"No, Jamie. I'm not the heartless bastard you think I am. I didn't abandon Zach to those animals. He's a good man and a friend. I've already sent in a team. Half the group couldn't get close, the other half suffered fifty percent casualties. Enough people have died. I'm not risking any more just to bring home a corpse."

She hadn't known. She could feel the blood draining from her head. The room tilted, but she didn't give in to the weakness.

She swore under her breath. "We have a better plan."

"Backed by that famous intuition of yours?"

She ignored the sarcasm. "You sent in a team. This time there's just going to be the two of us. Rick will create a diversion, and I'll get Zach out. We'll rendezvous at the jeep, then meet the plane."

"Sounds simple. Why didn't we think of that?" He glared at her. "Jamie, you're not stupid. What do you think you can do that hasn't already been tried?"

"We're going to blow up the munitions."

That got Winston's attention. He leaned forward in his executive leather chair. "Are you crazy?"

"I'm aware of the potential problem."

"Problem? Problem? We don't know what's there, Sanders. That's a hell of a lot more than just a problem."

For the first time since entering Winston's office, she was the one to look away. She and Rick had discussed this in detail. Blowing up the terrorists' ammunition and weapons would be a terrific diversion. There was only one catch. No one knew exactly what was stored there. If their intelligence was correct, then Rick could safely blow it up. If the intelligence was wrong—if the terrorists had more-powerful bombs and explosives—then the blast would not only take out the stash, but Rick, Jamie and everyone else in the vicinity, including Zach.

"It's a calculated risk," she said softly. "One Rick and I are prepared to take."

Winston glared at her. He punched a button on his phone. "Get Estes in here." He broke the connection without waiting for a reply. "I assume he's lurking around waiting to hear the outcome of this meeting."

"Yes."

Winston swore. "You're putting me in a difficult position."

She drew in a deep breath. The relief was as tangible as the chair she sat in. "I'm sorry for that," she said.

Winston glanced at her. "No, you're not."

"I know."

"You'll need a transport plane, a jeep. I assume Estes already has his supply list ready."

She nodded.

"You really think Zach is still alive?"

"I know he is."

"You could be risking your life for a dead man."

"It's a chance I'm willing to take."

There was a knock at the door.

"Come!" Winston called.

Rick Estes entered. Jamie looked up at him and smiled. "We're in."

The cell was twelve-by-twelve, but Zach Jones couldn't appreciate his spacious accommodations. The chain that ran from the floor to the metal collar around his neck was so short, he couldn't stand without choking. Not that he had the strength to stand anymore.

He leaned against the wall and closed his eyes. At least he could lie down if he wanted to. When he lost the will to do anything else, he collapsed onto the dirty straw in his cell and listened to the rustling of unseen creatures.

By his figuring, he'd been a prisoner for about three weeks. He could be off by as much as four days. Some of the "sessions" with his captors left him unconscious, and then the rising and setting of the sun went unnoticed and unmarked. The days they left him alone slipped by easily, aided by the feverish sleep that claimed him. The days they came for him were endless hours of pain and suffering as he struggled to maintain a slim hold on sanity. He'd surrendered his humanity the first time they'd beaten him with the chains. Now he just wanted to live long enough to get out.

A fly buzzed nearby, but he ignored it, as he ignored the scabs on his face and his cracked lips. He hadn't had any food or water for over twenty-four hours. He knew what was coming. They starved him to the point of weakness and dehydration, then they beat him. They came when his reserves were at their lowest. Then they left him to heal just enough to endure the torment again.

Every inch of him was bruised and bloodied. He didn't think they'd broken any bones. At least, not yet. He'd called upon all the training he'd been given in order to survive this ordeal. He hung on to the fact that it wouldn't continue forever. Either he would be rescued or he would die.

There was no middle ground.

After three weeks of being chained, his swollen, beaten muscles had become so weak he couldn't walk. He could barely feed himself. The fever came and went. Several sores were infected. He was in bad shape. If they didn't get him out in the next few days, they might as well not bother.

In his lucid moments, he thought about the various plans they might employ to rescue him. He figured teams had already been sent in and failed. He knew Winston would weigh the cost of his life against the risk to other operatives. Zach didn't know how much his boss would think he was worth. Maybe that line had already been crossed.

Maybe no one was coming.

He opened his eyes and stared at the small window on the other side of the cell. From his seated position, he could only see a rectangle of blue sky. The cell faced south. If he inhaled sharply, he could catch the scent of the outdoors, a flower of some kind, the hint of warmth in the air. Today it was enough.

He didn't mind dying. Sure, he had regrets, who wouldn't? But he could live with them. He'd known it would come to this. Warriors always died in battle. But, dammit, he would like to go out with a weapon in his hand.

In the distance, a door opened. Despite his desire not to react, he stiffened when he heard the faint laughter of the guards, followed by the metallic clinking of the chains. They had returned to punish him again.

He cleared his mind, forcing himself into a deeper place. One untouched by pain and blood. His breathing slowed, as did his heartbeat. His superior strength and training had kept him alive this long. It would keep him alive a little longer. Sometimes he was pleased, but most of the time he cursed his inability to find release in death.

Jamie checked her utility belt for the fourth time. She knew exactly what was there, but the ritual made her feel better. More relaxed. Pressure built in her ears. She swallowed to relieve it, then glanced out the window. They were descending.

"Nearly show time," Rick Estes said from the seat across the aisle. "You ready?"

"Of course."

Rick touched the heavy backpack next to him and grinned. "Me, too."

Jamie studied him. She and Rick had been recruited into the agency within a few days of each other. They'd gone through training together, under the watchful eye of

Zach Jones, then had gone with him on their first mission. They'd been green and scared. When things had started to go wrong, Zach had saved both of them.

Seven years ago. She and Rick had changed. He'd been a gawky, awkward young man with a gift for explosives. She'd been the only woman in a class of eight. Zach hadn't given her a moment of special consideration and had nearly flunked her for not having the upper-body strength to complete the obstacle course.

Now Rick had filled out and matured. He spoke about timers and fuses as if they were intimate members of his family. His red hair was still worn short, but the innocence was gone from his eyes.

Jamie knew she'd changed, too. The last time she'd tried the obstacle course, she'd beaten every man in her group. She'd honed her body into a lean, muscled machine. It had required hours of dedication, but she'd been determined to be the best. As soon as she and Rick got Zach to safety, she would resign from the agency and have to face the question of what to do with the rest of her life. But for now there was only the mission.

As the plane slipped toward the ground, Jamie double-checked the contents of her backpack. She had food and water, along with medical supplies. Her knowledge of first aid was limited to crisis management. Her gaze moved past Rick, to the far end of the plane. A medical team sat together, talking in low voices. The doctor had already briefed her on what to expect if Zach was still alive. Dehydration, infection, possible broken bones. All she had to do was get him back to the plane. The team would take care of the rest.

There was a slight bump, then the engines jerked into reverse as the plane taxied to a stop. Jamie and Rick were already up and moving. By the time the plane came to a stop, they were in the jeep, prepared to back out into the desolate countryside.

Jamie wasn't sure how they'd gotten permission to use this private airstrip and she wasn't about to ask. Winston knew people everywhere. He pulled strings, called in favors, paid whatever sum was necessary and everyone looked the other way. As long as the job got done, the director was happy.

"Ready?" Rick asked.

When she nodded, he started the engine. The rear of the plane opened slowly; the floor behind them lowered into a steep ramp. With a salute to the medical team, Rick put the vehicle in reverse, then backed onto the tarmac.

Brilliant sunshine blinded her momentarily. Jamie grabbed her sunglasses and put them on. It was late March, and the Middle Eastern desert temperature was pleasant. At least Zach hadn't had to suffer through the summer heat.

Rick checked his compass, then hit the gas. Within five minutes, they were driving due north and the plane was out of sight.

"Once we leave the jeep, I'm going to need an hour and fifteen minutes," Rick said, going over what they'd planned.

"I brought a book to help pass the time."

He glanced at her and grinned. "Loosen up, Sanders. It'll take a lot more than these guys to kill Zach. You know that. They don't come any tougher than him."

"I know."

She tugged her cap lower over her forehead. If their luck was good, no one would see the jeep speeding along the dirt-and-sand-coated paved road. They would get to the compound, blow up the depot, get Zach and be gone. If their luck was bad—

Jamie refused to think about that. She'd known the risks involved when she'd stormed into Winston's office. Being obliterated by the depot explosion was the least of her concerns.

She shifted on her seat, then reached over her shoulder to pull her long braid out of the way. As she fingered the end, she remembered the first time Zach had told her she had to cut her hair before she returned to class the next day. She'd spent the night studying regulations and had reported back that short hair wasn't one of the rules. They weren't in the military, after all. The agency's purpose was to quickly protect U.S. interests abroad—by whatever means necessary.

She felt her lips curve into a smile. Zach had been mad enough to spit nails. For a second, something had flickered in his gaze. She'd wanted to believe it was respect. He'd leaned so close, she'd felt his breath on her face.

"Your damn hair is going to get you killed, Sanders," he'd roared, still inches from her.

Although she'd been shaking so hard she'd barely been able to stand, she hadn't backed down.

"It's a risk I'm willing to take, sir."

He'd grabbed her braid and pulled it around her neck. Hard. "What about the risk to the team?"

She hadn't had an answer for that question. She couldn't risk the others because of her pride.

He'd given her a cruel, mocking smile and walked away. So much for respect. That night she'd cut her hair. In the past few years, she'd let it grow back.

Zach. It was always about him.

Rick slowed down. Up ahead was an outcropping of rocks.

He parked in their shadow and climbed out. Jamie followed. She checked the sun, her watch, then pulled out her compass.

"Two miles that way," she said, pointing northeast. "Try not to get lost this time."

Rick grinned. "Are you ever going to let me forget that one?"

"Never."

They walked together in silence. Thirty minutes later, they parted company. Jamie could see the compound in the distance. High fences should have shielded the inside from curious eyes, but most of them had recently been blown away. There were several buildings, trucks and dozens of armed men. Her heart started pounding in her chest. Dammit, they didn't have a prayer of making this work.

Then she forced herself to slow her breathing. Gradually her muscles relaxed.

The terrorists had chosen this spot specifically. There weren't a lot of trees or plants, so it was difficult to approach the compound without being seen. She found a shallow depression in the warm earth and again breathed a prayer of thanks that it wasn't summer.

Her camouflage uniform was the color of sand and dirt. With her cap and smudged face, she would be difficult to spot unless she did something stupid. She slid off her backpack, then reached for a bottle of water. After taking a sip, she settled down to wait. An hour and fifteen minutes until Rick blew the depot. *If* he blew it.

"Don't think like that," she told herself. "Everything is going to be fine."

She grabbed her binoculars and rolled onto her belly. She could just make out the details of the buildings. She focused on the section to the left. A low, one-story structure with small windows. According to their intelligence information, Zach was in there. Possibly chained. She had small but strong cutters in her backpack. If he was there, she was going to get him out.

"Just an hour and twelve minutes now, Zach," she said softly, scanning the area around her. No one had seen them arrive. All they needed was a little luck. "Hang on. Just hang on."

She lowered the binoculars and took another sip of water. Her shoulder began to ache. She shifted, remembering the first time she'd lain flat on her belly to scan the enemy's position. It hadn't been the desert then. Seven years ago, she'd gone to the Central American jungle. She'd been as green and soft as a ripe avocado, and just as effective. She would have died in that jungle if it hadn't been for Zach Jones.

That's why she was here today. To pay that debt. And maybe, just maybe, to get a few questions answered.

Chapter 2

Seven years ago

Jamie sucked in a breath. She could feel the snake crawling over the backs of her thighs. Zach had already glanced at it and dismissed it as harmless. Her entire life experience with crawly things had been seeing one dead rattler at the end of the block the summer she'd been ten. Even then, the sight of the squashed, dead reptile had been enough to make her shudder. Being this close to a live snake made her stomach churn.

I'm not going to throw up, she told herself firmly, ignoring the clamminess of her skin. The prickly feeling of heat and dampness had nothing to do with her nerves and everything to do with the temperature and humidity of the jungle. She'd spent the first twenty-one years of her life in Arizona. This was like visiting another planet.

Slowly, trying to move without making a sound, she raised the binoculars to her eyes and peered into the darkness. It wasn't night, but the thick, lush foliage and tall trees didn't let in a lot of sunlight. She studied the path twenty feet in front of them, and the clumps of greenery. She lowered the binoculars and shook her head.

Zach stared at her. His dark brown eyes bored into hers, until she felt as if he were digging down to her soul. A muscle in his cheek twitched.

Look again, idiot.

He didn't say the words. He didn't have to. She could clearly read his irritation.

Once again she raised the binoculars and stared at the trees, then the plants, then the path. There wasn't anyone there.

She wanted to elbow Zach Jones right below his rib cage. She knew where and how to do it, too. High and hard, so all of his air rushed out and his diaphragm convulsed a couple of times before relaxing enough to let him suck in a breath.

Her track coach had shown her how, her sophomore year in high school. She'd run cross-country with the boys' team because there hadn't been enough interested females to form a girls' team. Those long bus rides would have been impossible if she hadn't known how to take care of herself. She'd learned quickly. It wasn't difficult. She was a jock by nature, preferring a pickup basketball game to shopping or attending dance class.

But she knew if she tried to elbow Zach, he would get her in a headlock that would cut off her air so fast, she would see stars. Besides, as annoying and hurtful as she found him, he wasn't the enemy. He was in charge of the mission.

When she'd scanned everything a third time, she lowered her binoculars and shook her head again. Zach's mouth twisted with impatience. He clamped his hand on the top of her head and turned her until she was staring to the far left. He pointed to a tree that had broken in half.

The charred trunk looked as if it had been struck by lightning. Or a bomb.

He gave her a quick, painful squeeze as if to say, *There, you dumb recruit.*

She stared hard, then bit back a gasp. Leaning against the trunk of the tree, nearly hidden by the shadows, was a man. Zach had found him without the benefit of binoculars. Geez, he was better than everyone had said, and the rumors made him a living legend. She wanted to scream with frustration. Just once she would like to impress Zach and have the last word.

Zach motioned for her to slide back. She worked her knees and forearms, crawling along the ground, trying not to think about creepy or slithery things. Thick air swirled around her, making her sweat. A drop fell into her eyes, and she blinked away the accompanying burn.

They slipped silently through the jungle. When they were about two hundred feet from the man, Zach stood up. Before Jamie could scramble into a standing position, he grabbed her by the backpack and pulled her upright.

"I don't need your help," she said as she staggered a step or two to find her balance, then dropped the binoculars around her neck.

"Yeah, right."

He dismissed her as easily as he'd dismissed the snake. It had been like that from the beginning. Zach Jones had told her the first day of training that he believed women were smarter than men, that they thought faster on their feet and they followed orders better. But that didn't mean they made good field agents. Women didn't have the gut instinct to kill. It had to be taught. And more times than not, they hesitated before ending a life. That hesitation was expensive, for them and for the team. If anyone hesitated, everyone might die.

She'd stood before him then, arms stiff at her side, her chin raised. "I won't hesitate, sir," she'd said firmly.

"You won't be here long enough for it to be an issue."

But he'd been wrong about that. She'd survived the six-month training course. She'd mastered weapons, communications, map reading and an assortment of electronic and computerized equipment. She was one of the best trainees the agency had ever had. She'd worked hard to build her upper-body strength, but she hadn't known how to develop her killer instinct. She knew it, and Zach knew it.

He was good-looking enough to tempt a statue. She'd developed a crush the first week of training, then had tried to bury it under hard work. She'd done everything Zach ever asked and more, but he'd never acknowledged her effort. Or her. Occasionally he'd gone for a drink with the guys, but she'd never been invited. She was done trying to make Zach notice or like her. Jamie had been looking forward to seeing the last of Zach Jones. After graduation she'd gotten her first assignment. With him.

Zach plowed through the jungle. When she would have stopped to study her compass, he moved quickly, as if the path were familiar. She didn't even see a path.

Life was all around them. Plants, bugs, snakes, small creatures that rustled the leaves on the ground. Only the birds were silent, alert and watchful. She wasn't fond of the jungle. Why couldn't insurrection happen in the desert, which she was familiar with, or better yet in the mountains? She'd always wanted to go to the mountains.

She pictured a cool stream washing over shiny rocks. Unfortunately, at the same moment, she stopped paying attention to the path in front of her. She tripped over a half-hidden tree root and tumbled toward the ground.

Zach caught her before she fell. He jerked on her backpack, pulling at her shoulders. With his other hand, he grabbed her arm. His fingers bit into her sore muscles.

"That one *is* poisonous," he said when he released her.

She glanced in the direction he pointed and saw a brightly colored snake slither away.

She looked up at him. Good manners dictated that she thank him. No matter how hard he made it, he'd just saved her life. Her heart pounded loud and fast in her chest. Her breathing was labored. The physical reaction was as much to seeing the deadly snake as to the exertions of hiking through the killer heat.

The hell with good manners. "If you dislike me so much, why didn't you ask to have me transferred to another assignment?" she asked.

"I requested you, Sanders."

Of course. It made sense. "So you could drum me out." It wasn't a question.

Jamie was nearly five-nine, but Zach was a good six inches taller than her. He outweighed her by fifty pounds. He was as friendly as an iceberg and as animated as a building. He was good-looking enough to never lack for female companionship, but Jamie knew that inside, Zach Jones was nothing but a black hole. Which made the slightly romantic feelings she had when she was around him even more frustrating. The man obviously hated her.

"I don't think you have what it takes," he said.

"You told me I wouldn't graduate and you were wrong."

"Now we're out in the real world. No second chances."

She flinched, knowing he was referring to her appeal on failing the obstacle course. "I see. And you wanted to be here to watch me blow it."

"I'm here to get the job done, Sanders. Nothing more. Quit trying to make it personal."

"Requesting me specifically *is* personal."

They stood there, staring at each other. She could feel sweat collecting on her face and dripping down her back. Zach looked cool and comfortable. If she thought she could have gotten away with it, she would have elbowed him in the midsection and left him for snake bait.

His dark gaze searched her face, then he gave her one of his mocking smiles. "Why don't you find camp for us?" he said, and stepped back to let her lead.

"My pleasure, sir." She pulled her compass out of her pants pocket and glanced at it. Then she checked the sun. Her stomach was acting up again. She knew it was from that last encounter with a snake. It had to be. She refused to be affected by Zach Jones's low opinion of her.

Jamie found their base camp without a problem. Once there, she slipped off her heavy backpack and poured herself a glass of water from one of the plastic containers they'd brought with them.

Their mission was simple. Collect information on certain known bands of guerrilla soldiers, including their whereabouts and numbers. They were not to confront or interact. They had four days, then they would be picked up by the same large, unmarked helicopters that had dropped them here.

Two more days, Jamie told herself. She would survive because she had something to prove. And because this was what she wanted. She'd known early on she wouldn't make a good cop, like her dad, but this was close. She could still make a difference.

She checked the damp ground for bugs and snakes, then sank down and leaned against a thick tree. She closed her eyes and willed herself to relax. She was running on nerves. She hadn't slept well in a week, and the strain was starting to get to her.

"How's it going?"

She opened her eyes and saw Rick Estes standing in front of her. As the only woman, she'd taken a lot of ribbing at the beginning of class. By the second week, the seven men knew she wasn't kidding and she wasn't a typical female. All but a couple of them had kept their distance, not wanting to risk a friendship with a woman who Zach Jones was trying to get rid of.

She hadn't asked for special treatment then and she wouldn't accept it now. She'd earned everything through hard work and determination. If she hadn't had so much trouble with the obstacle course, she would have graduated at the top of her class. If not for the one or two friendships she'd made, that six-month training course would have been miserable. Rick had been one of the friends. She was glad he was on the assignment with her.

She shrugged. ''It's going okay.''

Rick sank next to her and grinned. ''Jones still riding you?''

''Constantly.''

On her good days, she told herself Zach Jones went out of his way to make her life miserable because he thought she had potential. He was determined to make her tough enough to survive and be the best. On her bad days, she figured he was nothing but a misogynist bastard who deserved to be horsewhipped, staked to a fire ant hill and left to slowly die. She told herself she didn't need his approval or his friendship to survive. But in her heart, she wanted both.

Worse, she wanted more.

''See anything?'' he asked.

''Someone on patrol.''

Actually she hadn't seen him—Zach had. She might know all the theories and have a thorough understanding of field work, but she was quickly learning that was very different than actually living through it.

''Oh, I saw a poisonous snake, too,'' she said.

''Cool. What kind?''

''I don't want to think about it.''

Rick made a fist and gave her a mock punch in the upper arm. ''Chin up, Sanders. It'll get easier.''

"Thanks."

She thought about pointing out that he was as green as she was, but figured this was male posturing. No doubt Rick also lived in fear of making a big mistake. Out here you didn't fail a test if you messed up; you risked dying and taking everyone on the team with you.

Rick stood up and headed for one of the small tents they'd pitched. Jamie studied the camp. There were six operatives assigned to this mission. She and Rick were the newbies. Each of them had a senior officer who watched over them. She didn't know if it was just fate or punishment sent down by an angry God, but she'd drawn Zach Jones.

Two of the men stood over a small metal folding table. Maps were spread out and examined. Zach strolled over and joined the discussion. He wasn't the tallest of the group, nor was he the loudest, but as soon as he spoke, everyone paid attention.

Her gaze flickered over him, noting the broad shoulders, the strong muscles. He worked hard to stay in shape. She'd seen him running through the forest by the training center on the mornings she'd gotten up early to work through the obstacle course.

She'd known from the beginning that her lack of upper body strength was going to be a problem. Running track had given her endurance, but not muscles in her arms. As soon as she'd been recruited by the agency, she'd started a training regime. Three mornings a week on the obstacle course, three mornings on weights, one day of rest.

About the third week of training, Zach had run through the forest and caught her on the overhead ladder. He'd startled her so much, she'd lost her grip and fallen on her butt in the mud. She'd thought he might give her a hand up, but instead he'd just stared. As usual, his expression hadn't given anything away.

"I know this is a weakness, sir," she'd said nervously. "I'm determined to pass."

He'd jogged away without saying a word. Three days later, he'd shown up in the gym ten minutes after she started her circuit. They'd worked out together, sweating in a silence punctuated only by grunts and curses through the last repetition. After a couple of weeks of not talking, he'd offered to spot her so she could work with free weights and barbells.

She smiled slightly. There was something unnerving about lying flat on her back, staring up at a man's thighs. But she'd done it because getting through was all that mattered. She'd worked hard and gotten stronger. Not that Zach had noticed.

Jamie finished her water and set the empty glass on her lap. Zach pulled off his cap and ran his fingers through his dark hair. Everything about him was dark, she thought. His hair, his eyes, his expression. If she pictured him in her mind, it was always a night scene, which was ridiculous. Except for a week spent on night maneuvers, she'd never seen the man in anything but daylight. Still, that was how she thought of him—dark and dangerous. As if he were second cousin to the devil himself.

A rustling in the bushes caught her attention. She turned toward the sound, then stiffened. It was definitely coming from something large. There was supposed to be one man on patrol. Had something happened?

Jamie glanced at Zach and the other two men. She needed to alert them, but she didn't want to call out and risk giving their position away. Rick was on the far side of camp. He wasn't going to be any help.

Quickly she glanced at the ground and found a small rock. She picked it up and took aim. The rock sailed toward Zach and hit him square in the back. He spun toward her.

She'd already pulled her pistol free and crouched by

the tree. When she had his attention, she pointed toward the noise. Instantly the other men pulled their weapons, as well.

The rustling grew louder.

"*Puta Madre!* Where is your *pinche* camp?"

Jamie glanced at Zach. He smiled and lowered his pistol, then motioned for her to do the same.

"Ernesto, over here, amigo," he called.

Jamie eased back into a sitting position and watched as a man of medium build broke through the brush and stepped into the small clearing. He glanced around, raising his eyebrows when he saw her, then walked to Zach and held out his hand.

"Ah, Major Jones, so pleased to see you again."

Zach slapped the man on the back. "Last time you called me General Jones."

"Last time I had just been paid by your agency. Now it is three weeks until the next check. So you are simply a major."

"Makes sense." Zach pointed to the map. "Tell me what you know, Ernesto."

Their voices lowered, and Jamie couldn't hear what they were saying. She walked over to get another glass of water, then returned to her seat by the tree. Ernesto kept glancing at her over his shoulder. She grimaced. Obviously he wasn't used to seeing an American woman in the middle of the jungle.

A small lizard jumped from the tree and landed on her lap. She prided herself on only jumping slightly and not screaming at all. The creature stared at her for several seconds, flicked its tongue, then scurried off her and into the underbrush.

Definitely the desert, she thought. Next time she wanted an assignment in the desert.

Jamie, Rick and Nick Havers left on patrol at dawn. Jamie knew it was dawn because the total darkness lightened to only semi-darkness. They had simple instructions. Check the north end of the shallow valley to make sure there weren't any soldiers camping out. According to Ernesto, their informant, the area was clean, but Zach wanted to double-check. Havers was along to make sure she and Rick didn't get into trouble. His instructions were to observe, but not interfere. Which meant she and Rick could make fools of themselves *and* have a witness.

"Don't screw this up," she muttered under her breath. She pulled out her compass and then glanced east, searching for the sun.

"I'll lead," Rick said, moving in front of her and heading northeast.

"Why?"

He tossed her a grin over his shoulder. "Because I've got the *real* directional equipment. It's a guy thing."

She rolled her eyes and glanced at Havers, who was waiting for them to pick a route. "I thought that only helped you find women."

"It has other uses."

"I'll be sure to mention that in my report," Jamie told him, and fell into step. If Rick felt walking in front of her made him a man, let him. She was more interested in surviving this assignment. Havers walked behind her.

Last night had been a total failure in the sleep department. She'd barely managed to relax, then it was her turn for night duty. She'd paced around the camp, trying not to think about which creepy crawlies were trying to attach themselves to her. When Benton had relieved her, she still hadn't been able to sleep. The skin on the back of her neck prickled. Not from the heat or the bugs, but from a feeling that wouldn't go away. A feeling that something bad was going to happen.

After a few minutes, she glanced at her compass. "You're straying too far east. We're supposed to go due north for a mile or so, then head east. On this course, we'll miss the whole northwest end of the valley."

She glanced at Havers. He grinned but was silent.

Rick ignored her and kept walking. "Men," she muttered, and continued to check her compass. She noted their position and the movement of the sun. They were coming out of the densest part of the jungle, and she could actually see patches of blue sky overhead. Sweat poured down her face and back. It had to be nearly a hundred degrees with close to ninety percent humidity.

Two hours later, Rick stopped and took a drink from his canteen. Jamie pulled out a small piece of paper. She'd made a hand-drawn copy of the map on the table.

"We should have reached the river by now," she said.

"I'm taking a different route." Rick didn't meet her gaze.

"You're lost," she said flatly, then sighed. She should have taken charge the first second he'd stepped off course. "At least it's not a big valley."

She glanced at Havers. The tall man sipped from his canteen. "How long were you going to let us wander around lost?" she asked.

Havers shrugged. "Another couple of hours."

"Do you know where we are?"

"Of course."

"Great." She exhaled sharply, then glanced up at the sun. If she didn't want to be completely humiliated, she was going to have to figure this out herself. At least they weren't in any real danger.

"We've been heading too far east," she said. "If we go due north, we should find the river."

Rick glanced at her. "I make the decisions, Jamie."

She felt as if she'd been slapped. "What's going on with you? We just spent six months training together, and all of a sudden you're going to act like a guy?"

"I—" He paused, then smiled sheepishly. "Dumb,

huh? Sorry. You're right. I guess being out here in the open has—"

Suddenly Havers motioned for silence. Jamie stared at him. She'd heard it, too. A whisper of conversation. A crackling of movement. Who else was out there?

Havers motioned for them to get in line behind him, then pointed back the way they'd come. That feeling at the back of her neck returned.

The blast of a single gunshot cut through the jungle. Birds took flight, unseen creatures screamed and Nick Havers crumpled to the ground.

Instantly Jamie was at his side. She rolled him over and saw the single hole in the center of his forehead. She didn't have to check his pulse to know he was dead.

"What the hell is going on?" Rick asked in a heated whisper.

She heard the panic in his voice and felt terror building inside her chest. Before she could move or even breathe, a voice broke the silence.

"Come, come, *chica*. This way, pretty lady. Your boyfriend, too. We'll take good care of you."

A dozen men broke through the thick green foliage. They were all in camouflage and heavily armed. Some had rifles, and a couple were carrying automatic weapons.

Fear exploded in Jamie's belly. Her heart pounded and her breathing increased. But she refused to let them know she was afraid.

The man in the middle, broad and a couple of inches taller than her with a scar on one cheek, approached. He took her pistol and slipped the knife from her utility belt. She stared straight ahead, forcing herself not to react or even speak. The man cupped her chin, forcing her to look at him.

"Very nice," he said, his accent heavy. He released her, then spoke in Spanish, ordering his men to tie them up.

A few minutes later, they were once again on the move. Havers's body had been left where it had fallen. A man walked closely behind Jamie, prodding her with the tip of his rifle. He kept up a steady stream of conversation. She understood Spanish well enough to know he was detailing exactly what he planned to do with her that night. When it was his "turn." She forced her mind away from the images invoked and willed herself to focus on survival.

The camp was large and well organized, with makeshift huts instead of tents. Jamie and Rick had been secured in the center of the cleared area, tied to poles about six feet apart.

Everyone watched them. Even if she'd been able to loosen the ropes at her wrists or ankles, there was no way to escape. They would be spotted in seconds. Several soldiers spoke English, so communicating with Rick was futile. They were well and truly trapped.

She glanced up at the sun and figured they had about an hour of daylight left. Despite the crude threats made on the way to camp, no one had approached her. She wondered if they were going to wait until dark or if the words had simply been a cruel trick to frighten her. If it was the latter, it had worked perfectly. She didn't dare close her eyes. If she did, she saw Havers falling to the ground again and again.

She was dying of thirst. Neither of them had been given any food or water all day. She didn't dare ask. She didn't want to draw attention to herself. As she sat on the hard ground with her hands tied behind her and her bound legs straight in front of her, she tried to be calm. To think. What would Zach do?

That thought helped her survive the rising panic. She recalled all of her training and searched for a piece of information that would assist her. When it didn't materialize, she told herself Zach Jones had pushed her harder than any other recruit. She was smart and, thanks to him, she was tough. She would make it. She ignored the voice that whispered no matter how hard she trained, she was still a woman...and therefore was vulnerable in ways a man rarely understood.

A small jeep drove to the edge of the compound. Jamie glanced up and caught her breath. Ernesto stepped out and spoke with one of the men. Why was he here? He was supposed to be working for the Americans.

Okay, maybe he was collecting information, she told herself. He had to have something to sell. But the prickling she'd felt last night got worse. Something was wrong.

Ernesto spotted her and strolled over. He squatted in front of her. "Jamie, here you are. I'm so glad they found you."

He leaned forward and touched her face. She jerked her head free and glared at him, but didn't speak.

"Such fire. I sensed that right away." He stood up and smiled. "Soon, Jamie. Soon."

He walked away.

She sat there trembling until the sun had set and the temperature began to drop. Night creatures took flight. The scent of flowers and the sickly sweet smell of decaying foliage was replaced by the smell of cooking food. Her stomach growled. Most of the men disappeared into the largest building. Only a few were left on patrol.

Now, she told herself. This was her moment to escape. There was only one problem. She couldn't free her hands. She'd tried several times. The ropes were tight enough to scrape off layers of skin. Her fingers were nearly numb.

"Jamie, can you get free?" Rick called from behind her, speaking for the first time since they were captured.

"No, can you?"

"Uh-uh. They've got me tied tight. Don't worry. Our team will come after us."

"You, maybe," she muttered. "Zach will be thrilled to

have me done in by the enemy. It will prove all his theories correct."

They sat in silence. She tried not to think about how hungry she was. Or the fact that she had to go to the bathroom, or what would happen later.

In the distance, she heard an odd, high-pitched shrieking. It wasn't a bird, yet the sound was familiar. A heartbeat later, something slammed into the largest hut and exploded. The noise was deafening. Had she been standing, the explosion would have knocked her off her feet.

A stun grenade.

Men on patrol staggered around, obviously disoriented. Seconds later three dark shapes slipped into camp. There was a blur of movement, then the guard fell to the ground unconscious. The rescue team separated. One of them ran toward Jamie.

She recognized Zach. Relief brought tears to her eyes, but she blinked back the weakness.

"Havers is dead," she said quickly as he reached behind her and cut through the ropes. "They shot him in the jungle. There are about two dozen men in the big hut. Another dozen on patrol. Ernesto is here."

Zach glanced at her then. He wore a close-fitting black jumpsuit and a black cap on his head. There were smudges on his face. A hundred or so feet away, someone fired a gun.

Zach finished with her legs and pulled her to her feet. The rush of pain almost made her sick. He held her for several seconds as she breathed in slowly. Blood filled her numb limbs. She shook her feet, then flexed her fingers.

When she could stand on her own, Zach handed her the knife and a pistol. Then he did the strangest thing. He touched her cheek. Just once. His dark gaze met hers. She caught her breath. There was another gunshot. Zach turned away. "Get Rick," he said, and was gone.

By the time she got to Rick, men were spilling out of

the large hut. They staggered around, covering their ears and their eyes. The wind carried the scent of tear gas. Sporadic gunfire cut through the night.

When Rick was free, she helped him up. Her legs and hands still burned, but it was getting better.

Rick swore. "This hurts like a son of a bitch."

"Tell me about it. Try walking anyway. We've got to get out of here."

They started inching toward the edge of the compound. The men were still stunned and staggering. Jamie kept an eye on them. Dark shapes slipped around, taking care of anyone who regained his senses too quickly.

One of their rescuers grabbed Ernesto. She was too far away to hear their conversation, but she knew the man in black was Zach. She watched closely. Then a flicker of movement caught her attention. Something in the brush. A shadow. A glint of a rifle aimed at Zach's back.

There wasn't time to do anything but act. She pushed Rick out of the way and raised the pistol. As she squeezed the trigger, she reminded herself that her still-stinging arms wouldn't be able to handle the recoil. She willed herself to stay strong and fired three bullets into the soldier. The man sank noiselessly to the ground.

Across the compound, Zach's dark gaze found hers. He'd been wrong about her inability to take a life. She'd just taken her first. The thought should have thrilled her. Instead of celebrating, she took two steps, bent at the waist and vomited in the bushes.

Chapter 3

Three days later, she was still being debriefed.

"There was no warning before Nick Havers was shot?"

Jamie stared at her boss. She'd met Winston Danville III briefly, when she'd been accepted as a trainee. The man had white blond hair and icy blue eyes. There was something ominous about him.

He wore a gray suit with a white shirt and navy-and-red-pin-striped tie. He should have looked like an executive. His office was plush, his chair leather, his desk big enough to serve as a runway for small aircraft.

"No, sir," she said firmly, although inside she was shaking.

He flipped through the file in front of him. "It says here you were the best recruit we'd hired in years. So why'd you act so irresponsibly?"

Jamie glanced to her left. She could see Zach sitting on a chair against the far wall. He'd accompanied her to all her debriefings, except for the one with the agency psychiatrist, and now he was silently observing her conversation with Danville.

Best recruit? Who had told him that? "Sir?"

"Rick Estes got the three of you lost. Well, the two of you. I doubt Havers was lost. Why'd you let Rick take charge if you knew he was wrong?"

Jamie grimaced. "You're right, sir. I should have said something. He'd never acted like that before. It threw me. I kept track of our course. I was pretty sure about where we were. I'd drawn a map and—"

"You had a map?" Danville asked.

"Yes, sir. We weren't given one, and that seemed odd. I didn't think the point was for us to get lost." Now she wasn't so sure. "Was it?"

Danville didn't answer the question. He shuffled a couple of papers on his desk. "According to your file, you've never expected special treatment because you're female. You've pulled your weight. Why this sudden shyness around Estes? You sleeping with him?"

Jamie raised her chin slightly and met Danville's chilly gaze. "Intimate relationships between agency operatives aren't forbidden, sir. But, no, Rick and I are friends. I let him because—"

She hesitated. Dammit, she hated that she'd messed up, and on her first assignment, too. As for why she'd behaved so foolishly...she wasn't sure she wanted to tell him the truth. She sneaked another quick glance at Zach. His impassive features didn't give her much in the way of advice on the situation. She drew in a breath and figured she might as well risk making a fool of herself.

"I hadn't been sleeping well. Nerves, I guess. I was tired and not a hundred percent. In addition, I couldn't shake this feeling."

"What feeling?" Zach asked, speaking for the first time.

His low voice made her shiver. She didn't know what

he was thinking, which was probably a good thing. But oddly, instead of resenting his presence, she drew comfort from him. He was the devil she knew. His brand of justice was swift. He wouldn't torture her. If he thought she screwed up, he would just let her go.

"I had this prickling at the back of my neck." She lowered her gaze to her hands and stared at the raw sores encircling each wrist. The ropes had rubbed away her skin. "I felt that something bad was going to happen. That's why I made a copy of the map. I didn't want to be unprepared." She stiffened her shoulders and waited for his laughter.

"Why didn't you report this feeling of yours?" Zach asked.

She turned to look at him. "What?"

"Obviously something bad *did* happen. If you'd reported your misgivings, we might have been able to prevent Havers's death and the kidnapping."

"By not sending me, you mean," she said, and returned her attention to Danville. "I know Ernesto came after me because I'm a woman. I put the mission in danger."

Zach swore.

"Don't be ridiculous," Danville said. "Oh, I'm sure the fact that you were female pleased him. Ernesto knew that we would be bringing in two recruits. He arranged for the kidnapping, because he knew we'd pay to get you and Rick back and he wanted the money. You two wouldn't have the training to survive. Not to mention the fact that it wouldn't look good for the agency. Havers was an experienced field agent. That's why they killed him."

She stared at him and blinked. "You mean it wasn't about me?"

"I told you, Sanders," Zach said. "You make everything personal. It's a big mistake. You're going to have to get over that or you'll never make it in the field. Ernesto had turned on us. He didn't think we knew, but we were onto him."

She opened her mouth, but no words came out. Nothing made sense. She tried to remember Ernesto's brief visit to the camp. He'd been friendly with everyone. She'd had no idea.

Danville closed the file. "You may keep the hotel room here in town for a couple of days. Report to the agency on the twenty-second to get your next assignment."

Jamie stared at him, then at Zach. "That's it? I'm still in?"

Danville smiled. "You're still in, Ms. Sanders. Congratulations."

She shook his hand, then hesitated, not sure what to say to Zach. He ignored her, so she left. On her way to the elevator, she ran the brief conversation over in her mind. Danville hadn't wanted to yell at her. She hadn't been fired. She'd made it!

The elevator doors opened. As she stepped inside, a voice called, "Hold them, please."

Her index finger hovered over the Close Door button, but at the last minute, she pressed Open. Zach walked in.

Instead of facing front like a normal person, he leaned against the side wall and stared at her. She glanced at him, then quickly turned her attention to the row of lights above the door. They flashed one after the other as they rode down toward the ground.

Her skin got prickly. She chalked that up to excitement and leftover nerves. Seventy-two hours before, she'd been in the middle of a Central American jungle, held prisoner by the enemy.

The elevator stopped on the twenty-first floor and let in three women. They were all dressed in suits, stockings and high heels. They dismissed her with a quick glance, while Zach became the focus of their attention.

Typical, Jamie thought with a trace of irritation. No one

cares what a man wears, but a woman's clothing is all-important. Well, not for her. She was off duty and she planned to spend it the way she always did—in jeans and a sweatshirt. Zach wore the same casual clothing, but while she looked messy, he looked...wonderful.

She grimaced. His sweatshirt, soft from countless washings, hugged his shoulders and emphasized his narrow waist. Worn jeans had faded to white in the most interesting places, including the seams by his hips and crotch. With his smoldering dark eyes and lean good looks, he was temptation incarnate. Assuming she was in the mood to be tempted.

She swore under her breath. She thought she'd gotten over her crush months ago. Oh, sure, she found the man attractive. Who wouldn't? But it wasn't about a man-woman thing. She wanted him to say *Good job, Jamie. Well, done.* She wanted him to like her.

Quit wishing for the moon, she told herself, even as she recalled the feel of his hand against her cheek when he'd rescued her. Why had he touched her like that?

When the elevator stopped on the ground floor, she quickly stepped into the foyer of the large office building. She hurried to the wide glass doors and stepped out in the crisp fall afternoon. A taxi had pulled up and emptied its passengers. She waved to get the driver's attention, then jogged across the sidewalk.

"The Hyatt," she said, as she slid onto the back seat.

"You don't mind if we share, do you?" Zach asked, appearing at the door.

The driver glanced at her. She shrugged and moved to the far side of the bench seat.

They rode to the hotel in silence. Jamie could feel her tension increase with every mile. She clasped her hands together and stared out the window, refusing to acknowledge his presence or the odd heat in her belly. When they arrived, she handed the driver a twenty, muttered for him to keep the change and tried to make her escape.

It didn't work. Zach followed her onto the elevator and, when she reached her floor, he stepped out behind her. She turned toward him.

"What do you want?" she asked.

"We have to talk."

"No, we don't. You're not my training instructor anymore. You can't punish me or humiliate me or tell me I'm not good enough. I made it, *sir,* despite your attempts to keep me out."

He stared at her, his dark eyes as unreadable and bottomless as the road to hell. "Who do you think told Danville you were the best recruit we'd hired in years?"

"Wh-what?"

He grabbed her elbow. "Which room?"

"801."

He steered her down the wide, silent hallway, then waited while she fumbled with the plastic card key.

The corner room was a mini-suite with a king-size bed, a sitting area and a wet bar. She'd been told not to expect this kind of treatment during all her stays in the capital, but this time was special. She'd graduated and survived her assignment. This was her reward.

Once inside, Zach led her to the sofa in the corner. She sat down, still trying to absorb his words. He'd told Danville she was the best recruit? *He'd* told Danville? No way. It wasn't possible.

"But you hate me," she said, glancing up at him.

One corner of his mouth turned up in a decent facsimile of a smile. "Yeah. More and more each day. That's why I rode you so hard, Sanders. To make you drop out."

"Well, *wasn't* that the reason? You said women make crummy agents."

"I said women had problems they had to overcome.

You only heard what you wanted to hear. You made it personal, Sanders. You always do."

Moving with the liquid grace she'd always admired, he sat on the edge of the coffee table in front of her. They both had long legs. Her knees were together; his were apart. If she slid to the edge of her seat, her knees would brush against his inner thighs. The intimacy of their positions startled her. Suddenly it was difficult to breathe.

Zach didn't seem to notice. He leaned closer and grabbed her right hand. He stared at the raw sores on her wrist.

"Hurt?" he asked.

"Yeah. They gave me a medicated cream. It should help me heal pretty quickly, and I probably won't have a scar."

His touch was surprisingly gentle...as it had been in the jungle. His fingers brushed against her skin, sending a powerful current humming up her arm. She felt her eyes widen and she glanced down so Zach wouldn't see.

No, she told herself. She wouldn't make a fool of herself in front of him. He must never know that she admired and respected him, and that she had spent countless hours of training seminars staring at his butt.

He released her hand, and she nearly whimpered in protest.

"I wasn't pleased about having a woman in my class," he said. "I'd had them before. Too much work and trouble. They slept with all the guys and stirred up resentments. Besides, only one had ever passed the obstacle course in the time allowed."

"I almost didn't."

"You worked your butt off for it, Sanders, and I respected that. You know when I knew you were going to make it?"

He respected her? The elation was powerful enough to make her giddy. She kept her gaze firmly on the small square of carpet visible between their feet and struggled for control.

"No, sir," she said quietly.

"When I came out of the forest on a run one morning and saw you practicing. Sleep is a premium during training, but you gave up some so you could practice. Why do you think I helped you in the gym?"

She looked at his face. "You helped me? On purpose?"

He shrugged. "You had determination. I wanted you to succeed."

"But you were so hard on me."

"I was hard on everyone, Sanders. Who do you think granted your appeal on the obstacle course?"

She stared at him. Had she been misreading him the whole time? She thought for a moment, then voiced the question that had troubled her for days. "Did you really request me on the mission?"

"Yes, and I'm glad I did."

He stood up and in the blink of an eye, the pleasant man she'd been speaking with disappeared. He placed his hands on his hips and glared down at her. "What the hell were you thinking? You let some snot-nose macho kid take charge when you *knew* he was wrong?"

His quick change in personality left her gasping. "I...I..."

"Well? Explain it. You're smarter than most of the agents. They're not going to like you for it, Sanders. So what? Get over it. Do your job. You're no good to the agency if you're dead."

She sprang to her feet. "I made a mistake."

"You're not allowed mistakes. Why did you do it?"

"I thought I could keep track of where we were."

He leaned toward her. "Why did you do it?"

"Because I—" Her eyes began to burn. Dammit, he wasn't going to make her cry. "Rick's a friend of mine. I didn't want to make him feel bad, okay?"

"Not okay." He grabbed her shoulders and shook her. "Never okay. If you know you're right, be right. Follow your instincts. When the skin on the back of your neck crawls, do something about it. If Rick or any other man is heading in the wrong direction, speak up. Use your brain, your intuition and every other ability you've been given. Because if you don't, you die."

She swallowed hard. "I was confused. I didn't know why he was acting like that."

Zach leaned closer, until she could feel his breath on her face. "He acted like a jerk because I ordered him to. It was a test and you failed."

She brought her hands up and knocked them against his forearms, pushing his hands off her shoulders. She stepped back because the alternative was to slug him high and hard in the rib cage, just as her track coach had taught her. One part of her mind noted that Zach let her break his hold. She knew he could have taken her easily.

"Bastard," she said, her voice low and angry. "Who gave you the right to play games with my life?"

"My job. I suspected this would be a weakness for you. You failed the test this time, Sanders, but you'll never fail it again."

She was speechless. Betrayal, pain and anger all swirled together. He'd set her up. Worse, he'd used a friend to do it, damn him.

"Get out," she ordered.

"Not yet. There's one more piece of business we have to discuss."

"I have nothing more to say to you."

"Don't blame Estes."

She glared at him. "I don't blame Rick. I blame you."

She turned away and walked to the window. From here she had a view of the capitol, but she couldn't see the historical building or even the traffic snarling below. She couldn't focus on anything except the fact that Zach had set her up.

She wasn't mad at Rick. He'd just been following orders. But Zach. She'd hoped for something else from him. She grimaced and stared at the view. Funny how the broken dreams still had the power to hurt her.

"I did it because you can be more," he said quietly. "You can be the best. Rick will stay with explosives. He'll be a good man to have on a team, but he'll never do the thinking."

"Oh, and I will?"

"Maybe. Go ahead and be mad at me all you want. Just don't forget what you learned. Next time I might not be there to rescue you."

"May I remind *you,* Agent Jones, that I'm the one who saved your sorry hide?"

"I know."

His voice was gentle. Too gentle. She felt her defenses slipping away. She tried to hold on to her anger, but it faded, leaving her vulnerable.

She didn't hear him move, but she sensed him come up behind her. She stiffened.

"You have to deal with it," he said softly. "Now. Or it'll eat you up inside."

She closed her eyes. "I'm not going to think about it."

"That's what the psychiatrist told me you'd said."

"So much for confidential patient information."

"You aren't a patient. You were being debriefed. Dammit, Jamie, you killed one man and watched another die. You have to talk about it."

She would have been fine if he hadn't called her Jamie. "You never said my name before," she whispered.

"Sorry. Sanders."

"No, 'Jamie' is fine. I— Do we have to talk about it?"

"Yes."

She swallowed. She didn't want to even *think* about it.

The horror was too great. Seventy-two hours later, she could still see the man falling to the ground. She could still feel the recoil of the pistol and the way her stomach had clenched and rebelled. She could see Havers's body lying there.

When she'd spoken with the agency psychiatrist, she'd answered questions about the mission and her part in it. When the elderly man had tried to bring up the killing, Jamie hadn't wanted to talk about it. She still didn't.

"It wasn't what you thought," Zach said, still standing behind her. "You imagined killing someone, but it was different."

"Yes," she whispered.

She'd slammed the door shut on those thoughts, but his words opened it a crack. The first flicker of feeling swept through her, and she shuddered.

"You're surprised because the killing is easy. It's the forgetting that's so hard."

She turned to face him. He was close enough to touch. Large and looming, but he didn't frighten her. Not anymore. "How do you know?"

"I've been there, Jamie. I want to tell you it gets easier. In a way, it does. But just when you think you won't have to pay a price again, a death will hit you hard. Then you deal with it all over again."

She had thought of him as uncaring, mean-spirited, even cruel. But at this moment, he was the kindest man she'd ever known.

"I can't close my eyes," she said. "I don't see him falling anymore. But I can't sleep. I'm afraid I'll dream. I'm not sorry he's dead. I just didn't think—"

Zach reached up and stroked her face. His fingers brushed away tears. She touched her other cheek, shocked she was crying.

She spun away. "I'm sorry. I never cry." She blinked hard, but the tears continued to fall.

"It's okay."

"No, it's not. I'm stronger than this." She tried to control her breathing. It didn't help. A sob caught her off guard. She clutched the window frame.

"You don't have to be tough all the time," he said.

"Yeah, I do. I can't—" Oh, God, she couldn't break down in front of Zach. "Please leave," she murmured.

Instead of leaving, he put his hands on her shoulders. She tried to shrug him off, but he ignored her efforts. He turned her and gathered her close, pulling her into his embrace.

She resisted, hating her weakness, hating herself for wanting to give in and borrow his strength.

"Hush, Jamie," he said softly. "It's okay. I won't tell anyone."

He knew her better than she knew herself. A sob overtook her, and she sagged against him. His arms came around her. He held her tightly, as if he feared she might be torn away from him. She cried until she was drained and empty.

Gradually she became aware of his body close to hers. Somehow during her outburst, he'd moved them both to the sofa. He was sitting in the corner with her curled up next to him. His arms held her close. She could hear the steady sound of his heart and feel the rise and fall of his chest. He smelled masculine and tempting. Very tempting.

The first trickle of desire was easily explained away. The second was more difficult. Then the trickle turned into a flood and she had to stiffen to keep from reaching out to him. Without thinking, without wanting to, she raised her head to look at him.

His dark eyes brightened with a fire she'd never seen before. A muscle twitched in his cheek.

"Dammit, Jamie, don't look at me like that."

"Like what?"

"As if I'm some kind of hero. You were right when you said I was a bastard."

"I don't understand."

"Yeah, you do. You don't want this."

She wasn't sure what the "this" was, but she was pretty sure she did want it. She'd never felt this way before. Guys had always been friends and amusing companions. She had more in common with them than with women. But she'd never felt the need to—

Slowly, cautiously, knowing he might turn on her at any moment, she raised her hand toward his face. Using just the tips of her fingers, she touched his jaw. It was midafternoon. She could feel the heat of him, and the prickling of stubble.

He grabbed her hand. This time his grip punished. He squeezed her fingers until she thought her bones might crack. But instead of pushing her away, he brought her palm to his mouth and kissed her sensitive skin.

She felt the fire all the way down to her toes. Her breath caught in her throat. Her breasts, which had never been more than a nuisance before, swelled and she began to sense the possibilities. Between her thighs, a different kind of heat formed and grew, leaving her feeling both bold and weak.

Zach bit the soft skin of her palm, then used his tongue to soothe the wound. He released her, then leaned back against the sofa and closed his eyes.

"The first damn day," he muttered. "I spend six months avoiding this, and the first day you aren't my responsibility, I blow it." He swore again.

Blow it? Avoiding it? She stared at him. "You've wanted to have sex with me for six months?"

He grabbed her hand again, but this time he brought it to his crotch. She felt the long, hard desire there. Of course, she knew the mechanics of what went on. She'd seen naked men before. In high school, she'd had to walk through the boys' locker room to get to the weights, and the teenagers often flashed her. But she'd never been impressed or interested. Until now.

Everything clicked into place. They'd both wanted the same thing and they'd both done their best to avoid it.

Zach started to stand up. Without thinking, Jamie shifted until she straddled him. She pressed against him to hold him in place. "Don't go," she said. "Please. I—"

She never got to say what she wanted. Just as well, since she wasn't really sure.

Zach stopped her words with his mouth. He pressed his lips against hers, taking everything she offered and giving back more. When his tongue stroked against her tingling skin, she parted for him. She clung to his shoulders, her legs clamped around his thighs. Her world spun.

Nothing had prepared her for this. His hands were everywhere. Her back, her rear, her stomach, her breasts.

Her breasts. She sucked in a breath as he cupped her curves, then teased the taut peaks. She broke their kiss and arched back to give him more room. Every part of her body cried out for him. When he tugged her to the big bed in the center of the room, she went eagerly.

He made love as he lived—hard, on the edge, with an attention to details that left her weak. He removed her clothes, then traced every inch of her. As his mouth sought, then found, her sensitized nipples, his fingers performed magic between her thighs. She hadn't known it could be like this.

She hadn't known his chest would be so broad, or his muscles so supple. They moved and tightened in response to her tentative touch. He moaned low in his throat when she nibbled on his shoulder and tasted his salty skin. He caught his breath as he entered her tight, virgin body.

Later, when he'd shown her what all the fuss was about, when she'd stopped shaking and panting and the room was finally still, he braced his head on his hand and stared at her.

"You didn't tell me," he said.

She did her best to look innocent of the charge. "Tell you what?"

"That you were a virgin."

"I—" She smiled uncomfortably and tried not to notice that they were both naked and the sheet and blankets were tangled around their feet. There hadn't been any physical proof. Her active life-style had taken care of that years ago. "How did you know?"

His smile was rueful. "You were too surprised by everything."

"Oh." She felt herself blushing and she looked away. "I'm sorry if it was horrible."

"It wasn't."

He placed his hand on her bare belly and stroked her skin. From there he moved up to her breasts. He cupped first one, then the other. Within seconds she was trembling and ready. He leaned close and took her nipple in his mouth. He licked the tight point, teasing her to mindlessness. Then he drew his hand down between her damp curls.

"If we make love again, you'll be sore," he said.

She parted her legs. "I'll be okay."

He smiled. A real smile. One that took her breath away. She realized she knew almost nothing about this man's life. Not the details, anyway. But she knew *him*. She knew his soul. Surely that was more important.

She touched his short dark hair. "Maybe I won't hurt so bad if I'm on top," she said.

He laughed and hauled her close. As they touched from shoulder to shin, as his erection pressed into her belly, she felt a sense of homecoming. As if this was where she'd always belonged.

"How come you're still a virgin?" he asked.

"I was a jock in high school and college. Most men don't find that very sexy. I never got asked out, never went to my prom."

He kissed her forehead. "I apologize for the stupidity of my gender."

"It's okay."

"I have a cabin in Colorado. It's not much, but it's private and the view is spectacular. We could spend the week there."

For the second time that day, she fought tears. This time she won. She smiled and nodded. "Let's go."

Just before dawn of the last day, she woke up alone. Jamie stretched, then reached for Zach, but he wasn't there. She sat up. The back of her neck prickled uncomfortably, and she sensed something bad was coming. She even knew what it was.

A week ago, if someone had told her it was possible to memorize every inch of a person, to bring him to exquisite pleasure with her hands, mouth and body and still not know him, she would have thought that person was crazy. Now she understood the truth.

She and Zach had spent the past week together. She knew everything about his body and nothing about his mind. He silenced her questions with kisses. They ate together, read together, made love together and yet they were strangers.

She stood up and grabbed a flannel shirt from the bedpost. After slipping it on, she pulled on thick socks, then made her way into the living room. Embers from the fire cast little more than shadows, but she was familiar enough with the room to find her way in the dark. She was well trained enough to hear his breathing in the silence as he sat on the sofa.

She glanced at the window and saw the first hint of light. She wanted to get this over with before the sun came up. She didn't want him to be able to watch her face. He read her too easily.

"We leave today," she said. "So just go ahead and say it, Zach. It's over, isn't it?"

"It's not that simple," he said, his voice low and quiet in the darkness. "You have to choose."

She hadn't expected that. She crossed to the small dining set in front of the kitchen and pulled out a chair. The smooth wood was cold on her bare bottom. She shivered. "Between you and my job?"

"No, between your job and the real world. I made my decision a long time ago. I chose this world. I'll never go back."

She'd known from the beginning it wasn't going to work. She'd known when he didn't let her inside, when he didn't share his heart, that this was just about sex. Maybe he picked a woman for every week off. Maybe she was the seventeenth one he'd brought to his cabin, just another notch on the bedpost.

"The job isn't like selling insurance," he said. "You can't walk away from what you do. If you stay with the agency, you give it everything you have and there's nothing left. You don't get to be like everyone else. You live in the shadows, Jamie. You forget what it's like to be in the light. You have the chance to be the best. You'll pay a price for that. I want you to know—"

Her temper flared, and she cut him off. "What a terrific speech, Zach. How many times have you used it before? Shadows and light. Very evocative. But I'm not like your other bimbos. I'm not going to cry and I'm not going to beg. Save the rest of it for someone else. If you want me out of here, I'm gone."

She rose to her feet. Before she could cross to the bedroom, he stood up and grabbed her forearm. She noticed he was careful to avoid the still-healing burns at her wrist. Damn him.

"This isn't about me, Sanders," he said. "It's about you. You're going to have to be faster, stronger and better. After a while, there isn't anything left. I'm talking about an empty life. No family, no home—nothing normal."

His words washed over her. She ignored them, ignored everything but the pain. She jerked free.

"You're saying this because I'm a woman, right?" She shook her head. "You're a hypocrite, Zach. I don't see you having this conversation with Rick or anyone else."

"Maybe they don't have as much to lose."

"Forget it. You're asking me to give up everything I've ever worked for. Leave me alone," she said. "I'm out of here." She went into the bedroom and slammed the door. Ten minutes later, she was packed and heading out the door.

There was only one Jeep, but she didn't care. She would leave it in town and pay someone to drive it back to him.

He made no move to stop her. She spared him one last glance as she started the engine. He stood in the doorway, wearing nothing but jeans. He was the most beautiful man she'd ever seen, and the most dangerous. As usual, she didn't know what he was thinking and she told herself she didn't care.

She put the Jeep into gear and started down the mountain. The beauty that had enticed her the first few days no longer impressed her. She wouldn't be able to look at a mountain without thinking about Zach.

As the sun crept over the eastern horizon, she told herself at least she hadn't cried. She would put this incident behind her and pretend it never happened. Then the lie got caught in her throat, and she had to fight back a sob. Who was she trying to kid? Zach had been right—she took things too personally. She wanted to tell herself that in a few days she wouldn't even remember him, but she had a bad feeling she was never going to forget.

Chapter 4

The Present

Jamie raised the binoculars to her eyes and stared at the compound. The spring desert sun beat down on her. She'd never seen Zach Jones again. She'd heard about him, had even followed his career, without letting anyone know her interest.

Despite her accusations, she'd found out that he didn't take women to his cabin. In fact, no one else knew the small wooden house even existed. Except maybe Winston Danville. Their boss knew everything.

"I owe you this for making me the best, Zach," she said. "Then we're even and I'm out of this business."

She checked her watch. Three minutes.

In three minutes they would find out if their plan was going to work. She pushed away the tiniest flicker of fear. She'd always figured she was going to die on a mission. Why not this one?

"Party time," she said.

She pressed her head into the crook of her arm and began to count. When she reached a hundred and eighty seconds, the ground started to shake.

The explosion was deafening. Even though Jamie was over a hundred yards from the compound and the ammunition depot was on the far side of that, she experienced a few seconds of not being able to hear anything. Dust and bits of debris pelted her like hail. The air was smoky, the smell acrid. Even as her mind registered all these impressions, her thoughts were overwhelmed by one piece of good news. At least there hadn't been any surprises. Just a good, old-fashioned explosion.

She reached for her binoculars and quickly scanned the area. Dozens of men ran toward the inferno. No one headed her way. She shrugged into her backpack, then rose to a crouch and moved toward the compound.

The clock in her head told her about five seconds had passed since the ground had started shaking. Time was not her friend. In less than ten or fifteen minutes, the terrorists would stop chasing each other around and organize. Her window to find Zach and get out was seven minutes, tops. She would waste two of those just getting to the building where he was being held. She shook her head to clear any last cobwebs from the explosion. Her ears stopped ringing, and she could hear the sound of her own breathing.

Then her mind kicked into high gear. She needed all her mental energy to stay alert. Bits of metal and wood continued to fall from the sky. In the distance, a cloud of black smoke reached toward the heavens. Burning fuel. She inhaled, then coughed. The chemical smell grew as she got closer to the main compound.

The south and a bit of the east wall had been destroyed three weeks ago when Zach had been captured. The depot explosion had taken out most of the west wall. A large fire truck rolled out of a garage and headed toward the smoking fire. Jamie paused at the last shallow indentation before the compound itself and looked around.

Only a handful of men remained. Their uniforms weren't much different from her own. In the confusion, she might just pass for another soldier. She tucked her long braid down the back of her shirt and pulled her cap low. After scanning the area one more time, she pulled out her nine-millimeter Smith & Wesson automatic and ran.

When she reached what was left of the east wall, she flattened against it. A minute forty-five seconds had elapsed. Her eyes burned from the drifting smoke. Sharp bits of wood dug into her back. She ignored it all and pictured the compound diagram. Prisoners were kept in the third building over. If it was still standing. If he was still there.

Adrenaline coursed through her, and her heart pounded, but her head was clear. Zach had made her the best. This situation wasn't unfamiliar. She'd performed this particular exercise many times before. The only difference was, now it was personal. Pray that one change in circumstance didn't get them both killed.

She pushed off the fence and ran into the compound. A few soldiers milled around. One she passed looked dazed. When he glanced up, his eyes widened. The edge of her left hand connected with the back of his neck, and he went down.

A jeep raced past her. The officer in the front passenger seat screamed orders. She ignored him and jogged toward the only low, one-story building. The structure next to it had collapsed in on itself, but this one was fine. She pulled open the wooden doors.

Empty interrogation rooms lined both walls. Beyond them were small offices, also empty. The floor was concrete, stained with blood and cracked. The air smelled of fear and suffering, and of the dead. Jamie held her pistol ready and jogged toward the back, where the prisoners would be kept.

The compound was an outpost, its purpose to guard the depot and distribute munitions. There should only be a half-dozen prisoners. The first two cells were empty. The barred opening in the third door showed three starved men huddled together in the far corner. She ignored them and kept moving.

Three minutes twenty-five seconds.

The last door on the right was the one. She felt it in her gut as she approached. She glanced through the barred opening. One man lay on the dirty straw. He was turned away from her, but she would have known him anywhere.

"Zach," she said softly. He didn't stir.

She glanced at the thick, ancient lock, then the sturdy wooden door. Despite how easy they made it look in the movies, in real life it was time consuming to shoot open a door. But she didn't have a key and there wasn't time to find one. She kicked the door once in frustration, then prepared to fire on the lock.

She didn't have to. As her foot connected with the wood, the door swung open. She immediately crouched down and moved away from the opening, prepared to shoot whoever was hiding inside.

No one appeared. She held her gun in front of her as she entered the cell. When she cleared the door, she jumped back and aimed her gun. But there was no enemy.

Zach stirred slightly. She heard the unmistakable clink of metal on metal. The unlocked door suddenly made sense. They didn't need to lock him inside. He wasn't going anywhere; they had him chained.

She was at his side in less than a heartbeat. His clothing hung in tatters, and there were bruises everywhere. She didn't want to think about that. She had to concentrate on getting him out of there. She touched his shoulder, and he moaned.

"It's all right," she murmured. "You'll be fine."

She lowered her backpack onto the dirty straw and flipped open the flap. Her supplies were packed in the order she would need them. Her clippers were on top. As she reached for them, Zach rolled onto his back. Her body stiffened.

She knew about torture. She'd been beaten herself, threatened with death, shot, stabbed. She'd seen prisoners with broken legs and missing limbs. In her head, she'd known what he would look like when she found him. She'd promised herself she would ignore his condition long enough to make their escape. Seeing him now, that emotional distance wasn't possible. Every fiber of her being rebelled against the truth.

Blood matted his dark hair and stained his face. His mouth was swollen, his lips cracked. He wore a black T-shirt over army-issue trousers. His arms were purple and red with welts and bruises. His skin had been split in dozens of places, and most of those were infected. His trousers were rags. She could see more bruises and open wounds on his legs. Some looked as if they'd been made that morning. He was painfully thin and dehydrated. She touched his forehead. Fever, too.

Next to him was a small bowl of grayish gruel and a cup of water. Neither had been touched.

Four minutes thirty-five seconds.

Time was running out. But instead of moving him, she brushed her fingers against his cheek. "Oh, Zach, I'm so sorry."

The feelings returned. They sucked her under like a riptide, threatening to drag her out to open sea. She remembered what it had been like to see him that first day of training. Tall, strong and powerful. He'd held the keys to what she most wanted in the world—a job with the agency. How she'd tried so hard to impress him and how discouraged she'd been when he never seemed to notice. She'd fought against her crush and the odds to be a success. In the end, she'd made it because he'd pushed her so hard.

She remembered their week together, the joy she'd found in his arms, then the pain of realizing he didn't want her. She remembered how long it had taken to forget him and the endless nights when she wondered if she ever really would.

It had been seven years. Why hadn't she been able to let him go?

Five minutes.

She shook her head to clear it and ignored the lingering memories. No time for them now. She pulled a penlight out of a slender pocket on her thigh and checked his eyes. His pupils responded to light. Thank God. From another pocket, she removed a syringe filled with morphine.

"This is going to be a long, painful trip," she said as she gave him the shot. He didn't stir. Next she used the clippers to cut the chains. She didn't worry about the collar around his neck. They could get that off on the plane.

She grabbed both of his arms and pulled him into a sitting position. He was limp, which would make it harder. She took a drink from her canteen, then slipped on her backpack.

"Let's go." She bent forward and drew him up, tugging until she could settle her shoulder against his midsection.

"Please don't have any internal injuries," she murmured, then grunted as she took his weight and started to stand.

She cursed several times as she got her balance. Zach had probably lost thirty pounds, which meant he still outweighed her by twenty. She wrapped her left arm around the back of his thighs, holding him securely. She pulled the nine-millimeter pistol out of her waistband and clutched it in her right hand.

"Show time," she said, and headed for the door.

They made it to the main entrance before she saw someone. A middle-aged man, probably a captain, stepped into the building. When he saw her with Zach, he shouted something. She kept walking toward him. He reached for the gun at his side. She pulled the trigger of hers first.

He slumped to the concrete floor. Jamie was out of the building before the sound of the shot stopped echoing.

Six minutes thirty seconds.

Zach's deadweight drained her energy. She dismissed the pain ripping through her shoulder and down her back. Her thighs felt as if they were moving through quicksand. She glanced around the open compound, but no one was there. The captain might have been the only one left behind.

She hurried back the way she'd come, clearing the fence without incident. Then there was nothing between her and the jeep but two miles of desert. Two miles with Zach's dead weight to drag her down.

"Damn you," she said, more to distract herself than because he was listening. Between his condition and the painkiller she'd given him, he would probably be out until they landed in the States. "All those times you told me I wouldn't be enough. All those days you tormented me about my lack of strength. Well, look at me now. I'm strong enough to save your sorry hide."

Sweat poured down her face, chest and back. Her heart pounded. His arms hung loose, his hands gently bumping against her rear. She settled into a medium-paced walk. Her instinct was to run from the compound, but she couldn't, not with his extra weight. As it was, she wasn't sure she was going to make it back to the jeep. Of course, she didn't have a choice. She would find the strength from somewhere. Once she nearly lost her footing in the loose earth, but she staggered a couple of steps, then kept going.

She used the sun to gauge her position. When she figured she'd gone about a half mile, she pulled out her compass and double-checked her direction. Right on target.

Memories from the past returned. She didn't bother fighting them. What was the point? She remembered everything about their time together, then she cursed him for what he'd done to her. Harsh laughter cut through the silence of the open desert.

"What did you do to me, Zach? Nothing I didn't want. You made me the best. If you hadn't done such a fine job, I wouldn't be here rescuing you today." Her left arm and shoulder were on fire with pain, but she kept walking.

"You told me I would have to work harder and smarter. I did. I beat them at their own game. I'm stronger and better, and you're not even awake to see it."

She sucked in a breath. She felt as if she'd come off a ten-mile run. The temperature had been pleasant on the walk to the compound. Now the air was hot. She paused long enough to drink again from her canteen, then started walking again.

"Even the fact that you dumped me made me a better agent," she said, her breath coming in pants. "After that I decided I would never need anyone's approval again. Do you know how many times you've saved my life? Not just when we were on assignment together. But since then. A dozen, maybe two. I could hear your voice in my head telling me what to do. All that training. And if that didn't help, I would ask myself, 'What would Zach do?' Then I did it. So I guess I'm grateful. But I still hate you."

There were other emotions, but she refused to deal with them now, just as she refused to think about why, after seven years, she still hadn't been able to forget.

"Look at me," she said. "I'm a perfectly trained agent.

A killing machine. The dead don't keep me up anymore. What does that say about me? I want out, Zach. But I don't know what I'll do when I leave the agency. Isn't that funny? I have everything I thought I wanted, and I hate what it's done to me. But I can't say you didn't warn me."

Her thighs trembled with each step. She had less than a half mile to go, but she was starting to worry that she wasn't going to make it. Zach was a hundred and fifty-five pounds of deadweight. She stumbled and went down to her knees. Every breath was agony. She waited until the pain in her chest and legs subsided, then forced herself back on her feet and kept walking.

"I don't know how to be a normal person anymore. I don't know what it means to be a woman."

Zach groaned. She wiped the sweat from her eyes and kept going. Ten minutes later, she heard the sound of a boot against gravel. She pulled out her pistol and spun in that direction.

Rick jogged toward her. He was covered with dust and soot, but he was grinning. "You made faster time than I thought," he said when he was in earshot.

"Why aren't you back at the jeep?"

"I was heading back to help you. It's two miles, Jamie. Did you really expect to carry him all that way yourself?"

"If I had to." But she didn't complain when he took Zach from her.

Rick grunted under the weight. She stretched her muscles, then walked beside him. She grabbed one of Zach's arms and felt for his pulse. Faint.

"We might be losing him," she said, fighting the panic that blossomed inside.

"We're almost there," Rick grunted. His face flushed under the soot.

"Hang on," Jamie said. "Dammit, Zach, don't you dare die on me now."

* * *

Zach felt something prick his arm. The tiny point of pain was so small compared to what he'd endured, he almost laughed. Almost. He didn't because he doubted he had the strength left. The last beating had been the worst. They were going to kill him soon. He was counting the hours.

"Get that IV hooked up, nurse," someone said heatedly.

Zach fought to remain conscious. Nurse? He tried to move, but his arms and legs felt sluggish. Only then did he recognize the pleasant blurring feeling. Someone had pumped him full of painkillers. The roaring in his ears became the discernible rumble of a plane taking off. He'd been rescued.

Gentle hands probed at his body. Clothing was cut away. Something damp brushed against the open wounds. He barely felt any pain, just vague discomfort.

"Is he going to be all right?" a female voice asked.

Zach stiffened. He knew that voice, knew the woman. Then he dismissed the recognition. It couldn't be her. The beatings might have stopped, but he'd found a new way to torture himself. Just as he'd been doing for years.

Without wanting to, he opened his eyes. At first he had trouble focusing. He could see the ceiling of the plane and a uniformed doctor examining his legs.

"He's awake," an unfamiliar voice said. "Zach, can you hear me?"

But he didn't want to talk to the nurse. His head turned to his right. He blinked to bring her into focus. At first he wasn't sure. Had his tormentors found a unique way to break him?

Familiar but different. Same high cheekbones, same wide mouth. She looked thinner, honed. Almond-shaped eyes stared at him. Concern darkened the hazel irises to a muted blue. She raised her hand and touched his cheek.

So gently. He didn't want her to stop. He opened his mouth to tell her that, then pressed his lips together. He didn't have the right. He'd never had the right where she was concerned.

The doctor said something. Jamie turned toward him, and a long, thick braid fell over her shoulder. The soft end brushed against the back of his hand.

She stepped away, or so he thought. Then he realized the blurring was deepening and the walls of the plane were fading. His last conscious thought was that he was pleased she'd grown her hair back.

Jamie brushed her bangs off her forehead, then let them flutter back into place. Winston stared at the letter, read it once quickly, then motioned for her to take a seat. She did so reluctantly.

She'd never considered herself a coward, but right now she wanted to bolt from the room.

Winston looked up at her. His pale eyes gave nothing away. "You're sure about this?" he asked.

She nodded. "I want to quit the agency."

"Just like that."

"You know I've been thinking about it for a while."

He dropped the letter on the desk. "Jamie, you're the best female operative this agency has ever had. You're number three in the overall ranking. You don't get that high up in the standings without a hell of a lot of hard work. Now you're telling me you want to walk away from it?"

If she was number three, who were two and one? She had a feeling Zach took first place. He'd always been excellent. Funny, seven years ago Zach had warned her what would happen if she stayed with the agency. Now she faced that reality.

"I'm not sure I can explain it to you," she said.

"Try."

She leaned back in the chair and rested her hands on her lap. Once the mission ended, she'd changed back into jeans and a sweatshirt. Nothing stylish, despite being in the nation's capital.

"I know eight different ways to kill a man. I shot one rescuing Zach."

"I know. I read it in the debriefing report."

"Did it mean anything?" she asked.

"What? That soldier's death?"

She nodded.

"No. Why should it?"

"My point exactly." She stared at him. "I killed someone. I took a life. Not my first, but certainly my last. I didn't care when I shot him. I still don't. But I can't keep doing this. I can't continue to be a mindless killing machine. I've got to find out what it's like to be a normal person. I want to know how it feels to wake up in the same bed every day. To have a routine. I'm a woman with all the working parts of every other female walking this planet, but I've ignored that side of myself for years. I want something different. I want to find balance. I don't know if I can, but I have to try."

"There's nothing I can say to change your mind?" he asked. "You're not angling for a big raise?"

For the first time since finding Zach, she smiled. "It's not my style."

"You're right, it's not." Winston picked up his pen and tapped it on the desk. "What will you do now?"

"Go home. Recover. Think."

"You're willing to walk away from everything you've trained for? You worked harder than any other operative, Jamie. This agency has meant a lot to you."

"I know." She drew in a deep breath. "I've thought about this on and off for a couple of years. I have to do whatever it takes to find my way back. I don't want to end up chained in a foreign prison like Zach."

"Zach lived."

"You didn't see him there, Winston. I did. That's no life. It's just surviving. What price did he pay for that?"

Winston glanced toward the window. Silence filled the room.

"That's what it comes down to," she said. "No one knows the price. And I'm not willing to pay it anymore."

Chapter 5

Zach listened to the steady drip-drip of the IV and tried not to think about anything but getting well. Even though he knew it was going to hurt, he shifted uncomfortably on the hospital bed. He'd spent three days drifting in and out of consciousness. Three days of people hovering over him, giving him injections, examining him—three days of slipping back into a drug-aided sleep.

He knew it was three days because the nurse had told him when she'd brought his lunch. He was still on a "clear" diet, which meant broth, a flavored gelatin and tea. Although he longed for real food, just getting the broth down was hard enough. He was going to have to wait a couple of days for steak.

"You're awake."

He turned toward the sound of the voice and saw Winston walk into the room. As always, his boss was impeccably dressed, from his lightly starched oxford shirt down to his shined wing tips.

Winston grinned as he moved closer. "You look pretty

bad, Jones. But at least you're alive. We weren't sure there for a while." He patted Zach's shoulder. "Welcome home."

Zach raised the bed so he was sitting up. "Thanks. It's good to be back. How's it going?" he asked, and was surprised when his voice came out scratchy.

"That's my question." Winston pulled up the cloth straight-back chair in the corner of the private room, then settled next to Zach. "I spoke to your doctor. She said you'll live."

"Comforting thought. Did she also say how long I'd be stuck here?"

Winston shook his head. "You've been awake, what—" he glanced at his watch "—maybe an hour, and you're already trying to get out of the hospital? Slow down, Zach. You're fighting several bad infections, not to mention healing from some nasty bruises that might go down to the bones. You're suffering from dehydration, exposure and a whole list of other things I can't even pronounce. According to the good doctor, you're going to be in here at least three weeks."

Zach grunted. Figures. He hated hospitals. With the danger inherent in his line of work, he'd spent more time than he would like to think in them, too.

"She says your recovery time at home is going to be three to five months. You're going to have to take it easy. I know you're not very good at that, but you're going to have to make an effort. I need my best agent back at a hundred percent. So don't even think about cutting your recovery time short."

"She's overestimating the time," Zach said. "Don't worry. I'll be fit and back before you know it."

"Have you thought about what you're going to do when you leave the hospital? Do you want me to look into private nurses?"

Zach grimaced. "No, thanks. I'll be fine."

The last thing he needed was a stranger hanging around, fussing over him. He had a lot of places he could go, although at the moment he could only think of one.

The cabin.

It was isolated. He could retreat to his cave and lick his wounds. With enough supplies, he wouldn't even have to go to town. It made perfect sense. After all, no one even knew about the place. Except Jamie.

He closed his eyes and fought back a groan. But this one didn't come from pain. It came from deep inside, from the place where the ghosts lived.

The cabin had once been his favorite retreat. He'd always looked forward to going back. Until seven years ago when he'd brought an innocent young woman there and she'd changed everything. Now he couldn't spend more than a couple of days at the cabin without remembering her, them and the time they'd spent together. Then he started to want her, ache for her, until want and ache gradually turned to need. Then he had to leave.

Could he risk the cabin for several weeks? Did he have a choice? Maybe this time it would be easier to forget her. Hell, who was he trying to kid? He hadn't been able to forget her in all this time. He wondered if he ever would.

He glanced over and saw Winston watching him. "It won't take me five months," Zach said at last. "Once I'm out of the hospital, we're talking two at most."

"But the doctor said—"

Zach cut him off. "I've been injured before, Winston. I know what to expect from my body. She's used to civilians. I know how to train and I know how to rest. Trust me."

Winston frowned, but didn't disagree. "Tell me when you're feeling up to an official debriefing. We have reports from all the men who survived, so your information can wait. I was thinking about a day or two before you're released from the hospital."

"Fine. I don't have a whole lot to tell you. I spent most of my days unconscious." He thought for a moment, remembering the pain of the last beating. He'd been ready to go then, willing his spirit to give up on his battered body. "How'd you get me out?"

"It wasn't easy." Winston leaned forward in his seat. Pale blue eyes brightened. "I sent in a team right away. Half of them couldn't get close, and the other half didn't make it back."

Zach closed his eyes and swore under his breath. He didn't need any more souls on his already heavy conscience. "Who?" he asked quietly.

"No one you know."

"Liar."

"Calling your boss names isn't a great way to get a raise." Winston's light tone belied the seriousness of their conversation.

"I don't recall asking for one." Zach forced himself to push the disturbing thoughts away. He would deal with them later, when he was alone. "So how'd you get me out?"

"A couple of operatives came to me with a rather unique plan."

Before he could continue, there was a knock at the door.

"Come," Winston called.

Zach was expecting a nurse or maybe his doctor. Perhaps even one of the guys he knew from the agency. He was almost right. The person stepping through the door was a fellow employee, but it wasn't one of the guys. After seven long years, Jamie Sanders stepped back into his life.

Her hair was long again, more than halfway down her back. The sight of the dark blond strands caused a memory to nibble at the edge of his mind, but he couldn't place it. He brushed his fingers against the back of his hand, as if something there tickled.

She was lean, leaner than she'd been in training. High cheekbones defined her features. Her mouth was full, her eyes almond-shaped. She wore a black T-shirt with the long sleeves pulled up to her elbows. Through the thin material, he could see the definition of her muscles. He'd heard about her victory on the obstacle course. Seeing her now, he knew the talk hadn't been exaggerated.

She walked into the room. Worn jeans hugged slender thighs and narrow hips. She moved with the grace of a panther. He returned his attention to her face. There was a time he'd known everything she was thinking. While she'd been his student in training, he'd been aware of her mixed feelings. Sometimes her hazel eyes would darken to green with resentment at the way he pushed her. Other times, when he'd turned quickly and caught her staring at him, those same irises had shifted to blue and deepened with interest and affection. He'd been battling his own attraction. He'd wanted her from the first moment he'd seen her, and their six months together in training had done nothing to change that.

As her instructor, he'd had a responsibility to keep his personal feelings to himself and he had. He'd been tough, just as he was with all the recruits. He'd ridden Jamie extra-hard. Because he was hard on all his recruits and because he saw in her the potential to be the best.

She'd done them both proud. She was an excellent agent. A lean, strong, thinking, killing machine. She was everything he'd known she could be.

''Here she is now,'' Winston said, rising to his feet and crossing the floor. He wrapped his arm around Jamie's shoulders. ''Here's the agent responsible for your rescue.''

The simple sentence caught Zach unaware. Jamie? Why the hell had she risked her life for him?

It was like taking a sucker punch to the belly. All his air rushed out. Every part of his body ached. He stared uncomprehending.

She met his gaze. Her body wasn't all that had changed in the past seven years. She'd learned to hide what she was thinking. He knew what she'd become. While he was proud of her, he knew the price she'd paid. What had she lost along the way?

Without wanting to, he remembered being with her, holding her, being inside her. Making love to her. Fighting all the emotions that invoked because he knew the risk of feeling anything. He'd let her go because it was the kindest act he could offer. He'd let her go because he'd cared about her.

Looking at her now, he knew he'd made the right decision, but he wasn't sure she had.

Pleasure and pain mingled in his gut. Pleasure at seeing her again, at being close to her...and pain, for all the same reasons.

But she wasn't the only experienced agent in the room. He molded his features into a neutral expression and raised his eyebrows. "A couple of operatives? Wasn't that risky?"

Jamie shrugged. The movement freed her of Winston's arm, and she stepped away. "The other team had failed. We figured we'd travel better light."

"We?"

"Rick Estes and me."

Zach remembered Rick. He'd worked with him several times. He was a good man. "What was the plan?"

Winston stepped close to the hospital bed and grinned. "They blew up the munitions depot next to the compound. While everyone was distracted, Jamie carried you out."

In one moment, he realized two things—the vision of

her standing over him in the plane hadn't been an illusion, and the fact that she'd risked her life for him.

He glared at Winston. "You approved this plan? What the hell were you thinking about? Last I heard, no one was sure exactly what was stored there."

Jamie squeezed the jacket she held in her hands. "There was a calculated risk. We were willing to take it."

He didn't want to think about what could have happened to her, but he couldn't think about anything else.

"If it wasn't for the two of them, you'd be dead right now." Winston sounded cheerful about the fact.

Zach ignored him and focused on Jamie. "Why'd you do it?"

Once again, she met his gaze easily. She'd changed so much, yet he would have recognized her in the dark. He could inhale the scent of her body. He wanted to touch her and find out if her skin still felt the same, if she would respond as quickly as she had before. But he didn't dare let her know what he was thinking. Seven years ago, he'd been too dangerous to her well-being. Nothing had changed.

"I owed you," she said quietly. "I always pay my debts."

Two simple sentences. Amazing that they could cause as much pain as they did. Foolishly he wanted her to say more. He wanted her to confess she hadn't been able to forget him. He wanted her to be as torn up about this meeting as he was.

No such luck.

"You've got what you wanted," he said. "You're a damn good agent. Congratulations."

"Funny you should say that," Winston said.

Jamie shot him a look and shook her head.

Winston's pale eyebrows arched. He nodded, then continued. "She'll probably move up to your place on the list, while you're in here."

"You'll be the best, then. You earned it," Zach told her. He'd warned her, and she hadn't listened. There was nothing he could do about it now except try to forget.

Winston said something, but Zach didn't hear the words. Exhaustion descended, and the drugs kicked in. He just wanted to sleep.

Jamie moved to his side and touched his hand. "Are you all right?" Concern straightened her mouth. One strand of her dark blond hair brushed against his wrist.

He hated that she'd been able to read him almost as much as he hated still feeling connected to her. Dear God, why hadn't he been able to forget?

"Get out," he ordered with as much force as he could muster.

Her body stiffened, then she slowly withdrew her hand.

"Zach," Winston said, walking toward him.

Zach speared him with a glance, then returned his attention to Jamie. "You've done your good deed," he said. "You've proven what a great operative you are. Great. Congratulations. Now get the hell out of my life."

Jamie picked up her leather bag and handed the cab-driver his fare plus the tip. Airport crowds moved around her. Normally, being with too many people made her nervous. Just one more legacy from her training. Today she ignored the businessmen, the woman traveling with a toddler and an infant. She ignored the families on vacation and the automatic announcement about the area in front of the terminal being for unloading passengers only. She was going home.

Usually that excited her. Home meant long days resting, building up reserves to face the next mission. But this time home meant something else. Facing the past, which was always kind of scary, and facing the future, which terrified her. How was she supposed to know what to do with the rest of her life? How would she know which was the right decision? What if she chose poorly? The thought of spending the next couple of months in her solitary apartment in San Francisco trying to figure everything out was more than she could bear.

She turned toward the terminal and stepped inside. The television screens showed departures. She stared at the flight numbers and destinations. The letters and numbers blurred.

She wasn't crying; she just couldn't see for a minute. How was she supposed to make a fresh start when she couldn't let go of the past? How was she supposed to get over a man who still had the power to rip her to shreds?

She drew in a deep breath, but it didn't help. Her stomach churned, and her skin felt as if it had been scrubbed with sandpaper. There wasn't a part of her that hadn't been affected by Zach's words.

Get the hell out of my life.

As long as she lived, she would never forget the impact of hearing them, of seeing the disdain in his eyes. He hadn't been happy to see her. He'd hated her touching him. Why had she bothered?

As she stared at the television screens, she reminded herself that she'd accomplished all she'd set out to do. Zach was alive and the debt was paid. Surely that was enough.

But it wasn't. She'd foolishly hoped for more. Some kind of miracle, maybe. Or just the tiniest hint that seven years ago she'd meant something to him. That he hadn't gone back to his life so easily that time. That maybe, just maybe, he'd thought about her and regretted losing her.

Foolish fantasies, she told herself. She should know better.

She walked toward the airline counter. There was a

long line. She got in place and set her leather bag on the ground. As usual, she traveled light.

She should just let go of the past. But it had been seven years, and she hadn't been able to get him out of her mind. There had been something about him, a link she couldn't shake. Maybe she was an idiot for not letting it go.

Forget the maybe—she *was* an idiot.

When she reached the counter, she smiled at the attendant. "I don't have a reservation but I'd like to buy a ticket."

"Where to?" the young woman asked.

Jamie paused. San Francisco. Home. She opened her mouth. "Denver," she said, then swore silently. Denver was a couple of hours from the cabin. Zach's cabin. She would be crazy to go there. He'd made it clear he wasn't interested in her or being with her. What was she thinking?

"We have a flight leaving in about forty minutes," the clerk said. "There are a few seats available. First-class or coach?"

"First-class," Jamie said, and pulled out a credit card. The agency paid her well, and she didn't have many needs. After the morning she'd been through and what she was about to face, she deserved a little self-indulgence.

Ticket in hand, she went through security, then headed for the gate. By the time she arrived, they were beginning to board. Jamie stowed her small bag in the overhead compartment, then found her seat. She settled into the wide, leather-covered cushions and leaned against the window.

She was making a huge mistake. Zach was going to stay with the agency until he died. She had decided to get out. They had nothing in common. He'd lost his humanity years before, and she wanted to find hers again. He had nothing to offer her, so why was she going to the one place where she knew he would show up?

"You're a fool," she murmured, then refused the wine the flight attendant offered. She just wanted to sleep. At least there she could escape the confusion of her life.

Jamie parked the rented Bronco in front of the cabin and stepped out into the crisp spring afternoon. She could feel the difference in the air from being at a higher elevation. But instead of feeling winded, she felt invigorated.

She turned in a circle, taking in the tall trees and deep blue sky. Last time she'd been at the cabin, it had been fall.

Everything had been readying for winter. Leaves had littered the ground with a blanket of brown and gray. Now the trees budded. Brilliant green leaves shimmered in the sunlight. Birds chirped. New life struggled to come forth.

Snow covered the ground, but the guy at the rental-car agency had said they were close to done with snowstorms for the season. Jamie continued to turn, stopping only when she faced the cabin.

The small house looked exactly as she remembered. Compact, well made, welcoming. Even after all this time. She smiled slightly and hoped Zach would be as friendly when he arrived. The doctor had said he would be in the hospital three weeks. Jamie doubted he would stay that long. Zach didn't like being confined. She figured she had at least a week to prepare herself for his arrival. A week to decide what she was going to say when he asked what the hell she was doing here. Not that she hadn't asked herself the same question a hundred times already.

"What *are* you doing here?" she said aloud as she moved to the rear of the Bronco and opened the back. She didn't have an answer yet.

She grabbed a couple of grocery bags and headed toward the front door. There was a small knot in the door frame, just below waist level. She pressed it twice, and it popped open, exposing a compartment just large enough for a key.

After unlocking the door, she stepped inside. The cabin was cold and musty from being closed up. She wondered how long it had been since Zach had visited the place. She would like to think that her presence that week had somehow affected him so he found it difficult to return here, but she would also like to think a lot of other things that weren't necessarily true.

In the living room, an overstuffed sofa sat in front of a fireplace. End tables stood on either side, stacked high with books. Zach liked to read when he was at the cabin. A table and four chairs filled the far end of the room, next to a doorway that led to the kitchen.

The place had been built in the forties, and Zach had never bothered remodeling. Jamie actually liked the old-fashioned stove unit and creamy tile. The refrigerator was new since her last visit. She put her groceries on the counter and checked out the bedrooms. The first one was the largest. It shared the fireplace, and the heat, with the living room. Jamie glanced around, pretending not to notice she was avoiding looking at the bed. But she couldn't stare at a dresser lamp forever. Instead, she allowed her gaze to rest on the king-size mattress she and Zach had shared.

She leaned against the door frame and closed her eyes. Was it possible that time they'd spent together had meant nothing to him? Could they really not have connected emotionally? She didn't want to believe that. He had to have felt something. At least that was her hope.

He wasn't the only man in her life. There had been others. Once she'd discovered the pleasures available to her, she'd stopped saying no when someone who interested her asked. But it wasn't the same, and eventually she'd given up trying to duplicate the experience of one magical week. None of the other men had made her feel what he did.

Zach was the last person she'd felt close to—heart and soul close to. He was the only person she'd cared about outside of her family. Maybe it wasn't logical, but she couldn't help thinking if he'd shown her the way in, he could also show her the way out. He was her only hope of returning to the ordinary world.

She left the large bedroom and checked out the smaller one next door. There was a single bed, a three-drawer dresser and a small, gas, room heater. Perfect.

After bringing in the rest of the groceries, Jamie put the food away, then made herself some coffee. While she heated water for instant, she picked up a woman's magazine that she'd bought at the grocery store. She flipped through the glossy pages, staring at the ads. The models were so perfect and feminine. She studied their luminous skin, then touched her cheek. Seven years of living in the shadows hadn't left her a whole lot of time for skin care.

The articles made her uneasy. "Six Ways to Be a Better Lover"; "Fruit Acids—Are You Getting Hooked?"; "Shape Up for Summer Diet and Exercise Plan"; "Lose Ten Pounds by Memorial Day."

After being a jock through high school and college, then joining the agency, she'd never really had the time or inclination to do the female thing. She put down the magazine and picked up the cosmetics she'd bought. There'd been so many colors and types. She didn't know if she'd purchased the right things.

Jamie stared at the jars and tubes, then dropped them back in the plastic bag. She couldn't deal with them right now. She also didn't want to think about the clothes she'd bought. Feminine things. A skirt and blouse. Something millions of women wore every day. She couldn't remember the last time she'd put on anything but pants.

But she was going to learn. After seven years of living

for her job, she wanted to know how the rest of the world survived. She wanted to be normal. The only problem was, she might be too late.

The water began to boil. She poured the steamy liquid into a cup, then stirred in the instant coffee. She drank it black because it was easier. Somehow making fresh coffee for just one person seemed foolish.

She walked out to the front porch and sat on the old swing. She remembered nights spent in Zach's arms on this swing. She closed her eyes and let the memories come. When they flooded her being, she absorbed the pain. There was nothing to do but remember and wait for him to arrive. The waiting was going to be easy. Waiting was what she did best.

Chapter 6

The morning of her tenth day at the cabin dawned crisp and clear. Jamie pulled the blanket tighter around her shoulders as she sat on the porch swing and watched the sky lighten from light gray to pale blue.

It had been another sleepless night. One more occupational hazard. Assignments usually required her to be up and moving after midnight. While the rest of the world slowed down, those in the shadows came to life. Unfortunately years of living on a different schedule had played havoc with her body clock.

She tried to get to sleep at a reasonable hour, only to wake up sometime after midnight to face the ghosts of the past. She would spend the lonely hours before dawn pacing or thinking or trying not to think, then she catnapped in the late morning or early afternoon.

But this morning she didn't feel like returning to bed. The skin on the back of her neck prickled. As Zach had instructed after that first assignment in the Central American jungle, she'd learned to pay attention to her premonitions. She knew something was going to happen today. What she didn't know was if that something was going to be good or bad.

She rose to her feet and walked inside. After picking up the few items she'd left scattered around the living room, she made her bed, showered and put on clean jeans and a sweatshirt. For the first time since she'd arrived ten days before, she used the coffee maker instead of settling for instant. Then she checked supplies. With two people eating, they had enough to last about four weeks. They would be fine, even if the man at the car-rental agency had been wrong and there was a late-season snowstorm.

When everything was prepared, Jamie took a mug of freshly brewed coffee onto the porch. She curled up in a corner of the swing, facing the two-mile-long driveway that led to the main highway and settled in to wait.

She knew how to slow her breathing and still the pounding of her heart. She knew how to flex and stretch her muscles so they wouldn't cramp. She could hide in brush for ten hours, then be up and running without even a twitch to slow her down. She knew how to stay alert for days.

She sat in the morning sunshine for nearly two hours. Her coffee was long gone, but she didn't bother with a second cup. Instead, she watched and listened. Then she heard it. The slow whine of a truck climbing the steep driveway. The engine strained against the incline, the vehicle bounced through potholes and over rocks and still it moved closer. Despite her calming breaths and relaxation techniques, her body tensed.

Zach had come home.

Jamie uncurled herself from her position and walked to the edge of the porch. Even as she told herself everything was going to be fine, her heart pounded in her chest. She could feel her palms sweating. She would rather face an army of enemy soldiers than explain to Zach why she was here, but it was already too late for retreat. The truck slowly came into view.

She stared straight ahead. The sunlight reflected off the windshield, so she couldn't see who was inside. Then the truck moved into shadow. The driver was unfamiliar—Zach must have hired him in town. She turned her attention to the passenger, who had already seen her. Their gazes locked. Nothing registered on his face, not surprise, not anger, certainly not a welcoming smile.

She hid her apprehension behind a mask of her own. As the driver stopped the truck, Jamie stepped off the porch. The older man, maybe in his midfifties, got out and retrieved two duffel bags from the truck bed, then tossed them on the ground.

"Morning," he said, and gave her a quick nod.

"Good morning." Jamie smiled.

Her smile faded as Zach stepped out of the cab. He moved slowly, like an old man. The thick down jacket couldn't conceal his thinness or the way he had to hang on to the truck door to keep his balance. He reached back inside, fumbled with something, then seemed to steady. Jamie's breath caught in her throat when she realized he was using a cane.

It made sense. His bruises went down to the bone. He was still recovering. But seeing such a proud man broken in body, if not in spirit, tore her heart out. She wanted to go to him and hold him close. She wanted to comfort him and promise she would make it all right. But she did none of those things. Zach was like a wounded wild animal. He would lash out at anyone who tried to get too close. Especially her.

"You all right?" the driver asked.

Zach took a lurching step and nodded. "Thanks, Charlie."

"No problem."

The older man got back into his truck and started the

engine. Seconds later he'd turned around and headed for the highway. When the sound of the engine had faded, she and Zach were alone.

He took another step, then cursed when his left leg buckled. Before she could move toward him, he found his balance and straightened. Then he glared at her. "Why aren't you on assignment?"

"I quit the agency."

She studied his dark eyes and grim mouth. He didn't even flicker a lash. She might as well have told him it was clear and sunny today.

"What the hell are you doing here?" he asked, his tone surly.

They were standing maybe fifteen feet apart. Birds chirped in the trees. The sun beat down. Yet nothing about this moment was real to her. Why was she here? Hadn't she been asking herself the same question for the past ten days? She still didn't have a great answer.

She was here because she wanted to find balance. She wanted to know if the past was real. Why had Zach been the only man to make her feel those things? She wanted to know if he'd been right when he'd told her there was no going back. There was a way in; there had to be a way out. Zach had taught her everything else; surely he could teach her that.

But he wouldn't understand any of those statements, so in the end she settled for another kind of truth. An easy truth. "I wanted to make sure you were going to be all right. I didn't risk my life in the desert to save your sorry butt just to have you collapse and die up here."

He stared at her. "You expect me to believe that?" he asked.

"I can't help what you believe. I'm surprised they let you out of the hospital so soon."

"They didn't have a choice."

She could imagine that scene. No doubt the doctor had

thrown her hands in the air and told Zach if he wanted to kill himself, she couldn't stop him.

"You always had more guts than sense when it came to taking care of yourself," she said, and walked toward him. As she reached for his duffel bags, his neutral expression turned to a glare.

"I don't need your help. I don't know what you're doing here, Jamie, but whatever it is, I don't want any part of it."

His words stung. She looked from him to his bags, nodded once, then returned to the porch. If he wanted to do it himself, let him. He took one tentative step, then another. After a minute or so, he was moving at a speed close to a slow walk. It was painful to watch him. As she turned away to go inside, she heard a thunk, followed by a low curse. She spun back.

He'd slipped on a patch of wet ground. Zach sprawled on his belly in the dirt. She moved toward him. He pushed up into a sitting position.

"I told you to get the hell out of my life," he growled. "You were supposed to be a quick study, but you're having trouble understanding me. I don't want you here."

Dark hair hung nearly to his eyes. Lines of pain bracketed his mouth. Yet he would rather die of exposure than let her help him. All the old feelings of inadequacy returned.

She glanced at her rented four-wheel-drive vehicle. It would be easy enough to grab her stuff and leave. Her apartment was waiting in San Francisco.

"I don't need this," she muttered, and walked inside.

She headed for her bedroom, then paused halfway across the living room. No. She'd come here for a purpose. Zach was trying to scare her off because...well, she wasn't sure why. Seven years ago, he'd been the one to dump her. If anyone had a right to be angry, she did. What was he so furious about?

Now it was her turn to swear. He needed her. Physically he couldn't take care of himself. And like it or not, she needed him.

Jamie paced inside for nearly thirty minutes. She glanced out the window, but Zach hadn't moved. Finally she couldn't stand it anymore. She went out and walked toward him.

"Dammit, woman, can't you understand what I'm saying? I don't want you here. I don't want your help."

"Uh-huh." She picked up the duffel bags and carried them inside.

When she returned for him, he really started in on her. An assortment of curses in an assortment of languages. She ignored them all and reached for his arms. Before she could get hold of him, he switched to Turkish and accused her of being the result of a union between a goatherder and his favorite charge.

Jamie stared at him for a second, then started to laugh. "A goatherder?" she asked. "Is that as original as you can get?"

He stared up at her. Something flickered in his dark eyes. A glint of humor and maybe something close to respect. She didn't analyze it. Instead, she took courage where she could find it and figured she would wing it the rest of the time.

"I don't know a lot of Turkish," he said. "So it was either the goatherder or a snake charmer."

She shuddered. "I still hate snakes."

"I know."

They both smiled, and the tension between them lessened. With a flash of insight, she realized this was what had been missing in her life. Pleasant human contact. Zach hadn't had enough, either, she knew. The job might have its humorous moments, but for the most part it was intense and grim. Even their week together hadn't allowed them to laugh. There had been too much passion.

That was the change she wanted to make. More laughter, like normal people had in their lives.

She stepped behind him and helped him to his feet. She was shocked at how much more weight he'd lost.

"Dammit, Zach, you haven't been eating. How can you expect to get well?"

"You ever eat when you're in the hospital?"

She thought about her brief stays for various injuries. "Not really."

"I feel the same way about their food."

It was their first civil verbal exchange in seven years. She told herself not to read too much into it, but she couldn't help feeling relieved. Zach could make her stay pleasant or he could turn it into several weeks of hell. She hoped he chose the former.

She bent down and grabbed the cane, then looped his right arm over her shoulders and wrapped her left around his waist. Moving in slow, steady steps, she helped him into the cabin.

Once there, she moved him toward the large bedroom. She'd already pulled down the covers.

Zach sat heavily on the mattress and glared at her. "I want you out of here."

So much for civil exchanges. Guess he wanted to make her as miserable as possible. Two could play that game. After all, she'd had a great teacher. "Yeah, right. You're in no condition to take care of yourself."

"I don't need you or anyone."

"Probably not, but you're stuck with me." She knelt on the floor and pulled off his boots.

"You're just like every other woman. Butting in where you're not wanted."

She ignored the sting his words produced. How ironic that he thought she was just like other women. She *wasn't* like them, but she was doing her best to learn what they already knew. She wanted to understand what it was like to feel pretty, or take pride in preparing a meal, or keeping a house. Maybe she would get brave enough to consider having a child.

She shook her head. A child wasn't likely. She wouldn't trust herself to have one on her own. What did she know about being maternal? And no man had ever wanted her enough to commit.

She set the boots in the closet, then turned back to Zach. He was staring at her. She wished she could think of something witty to say, but her mind was blank. She could only stare at his handsome face and wish things had been different. If only he'd welcomed her back into his life. They could have healed together, him on the outside, her on the inside. Instead, they were to be adversaries.

She was about to concede defeat when something flickered to life in his eyes. Just as it had outside. She wasn't sure if it was longing, or maybe pain. A need for connection. He blinked, and the emotions were gone. But she'd seen them.

"Sorry, Zach, you can complain all you want, but I'm staying." She moved toward the door and paused there. "You should be grateful I'm willing to look after you. No one else wants to, and you would never have made it on your own."

"I like being alone. I'm perfectly capable of surviving without help."

He might like being alone, but she'd grown tired of the solitude. "You can whine all you want," she said. "But I'm not going anywhere."

"Then I'll take your car and leave myself."

She smiled. "No problem. First you have to find the strength to get to my car. I don't suppose that's going to happen today."

He curled his hands into fists. ''Dammit, Jamie, I won't put up with this.''

''What are you going to do about it? Try to beat me at arm wrestling? Face it, Zach, you don't have a choice. You need watching, and I'm the only one here. It doesn't have to be awful, you know. We could try to be friends.'' When he didn't answer, she shrugged. ''Suit yourself. I'm going to make you some lunch. Don't go anywhere.''

Unintelligible curses followed her out of the room. Oddly his temper lightened her spirits. If he had the energy to resent her, he had the energy to heal.

Once in the kitchen, she opened a can of soup and poured it into a pot. After putting the butane flame on low, she grabbed a crescent wrench from the toolbox by the back door. Then she pulled a large green trash bag out of the box in the pantry and headed outside.

Ten minutes later, she wrapped the Bronco battery in plastic and set it into a shallow hole in the ground. She covered it up, then smoothed leaves in place. When she stepped back to survey her handiwork, she was pleased. No one would know that she'd buried something here. She glanced at the vehicle as she walked back to the house. Zach might want to leave, but he wasn't going anywhere without her knowing about it first.

On her way to the kitchen, she poked her head into his bedroom. He'd collapsed on the bed and was sound asleep. Even resting, the lines of pain still bracketed his mouth. He shouldn't have been traveling, but he was a stubborn man. Fortunately for both of them, she was just as stubborn. She paused long enough to pull the blankets over him and smooth the hair off his forehead. Then she went into the kitchen and turned off the soup.

Zach opened his eyes and tried to peer into the darkness. He couldn't figure out where he was. For one horrifying heartbeat, he thought he might be back in his cell and the events of the past couple of weeks had just been a soul-destroying dream.

He sucked in a breath, held it, then relaxed. He inhaled again, smelling the mustiness of the room and the biting scent of trees beyond the walls. He knew this place. The cabin. Another breath brought an elusive scent... something he couldn't quite place, something—

Jamie.

Memories crashed in on him like a collapsing building. He ducked to avoid them, but there was no escape. He remembered it all. The rescue, his time in the hospital, Jamie coming to visit him and him throwing her out. The argument he'd had with the doctor when he'd wanted to check out early. The difficulty traveling to the cabin. His relief at finding Jamie waiting for him. His *anger* at finding her waiting for him.

"You are one confused son of a bitch," he muttered to himself, and slowly sat up. He immediately felt better. He was weak, but healing. Pain throbbed from every inch of his body.

He had pills in his bags. Where the hell were his bags?

He reached for the lamp on the nightstand. He might like isolation, but he didn't want to be without electricity. The lamp clicked on, filling the room with soft light.

The first thing he noticed was the blanket draped neatly over him. He didn't remember falling asleep and he was reasonably sure he hadn't taken the time to cover himself. Which meant Jamie had done it. What had she thought while she watched him sleep? She probably hated him, which wasn't a bad thing. She should hate him. Lord knew, he hated himself.

He allowed himself to experience very few emotions these days, but self-loathing was one of them. He'd lost any of the positive ones years ago.

He threw back the blankets and got to his feet. His cane

rested against the nightstand, but he ignored it. He wanted to make it on his own.

By using the wall for support and balance, he slowly walked into the kitchen. A pot sat on the stove. When he lifted the lid, he could smell the soup. Some freshly baked rolls sat on the counter next to his neatly lined-up pills and a glass of water. His zipped duffel bags were on the kitchen table.

Jamie had obviously gone through his stuff. The idea should have annoyed him, but he didn't mind. Which meant he was in more trouble than he'd first suspected.

His stomach growled. For the first time since the rescue, he was hungry. He ate standing up, leaning against the counter and not bothering to reheat the soup. He finished the whole pot and two rolls, then downed his pills. He wouldn't mind a drink, but figured he was in no condition to wrestle with a hangover. Not to mention the problem of combining alcohol with prescription medication. Better to face the world sober, he decided.

He glanced at the clock on the stove. Nearly one. He'd been asleep for fourteen hours. No wonder he felt better. He probably should head back to bed, but he couldn't. Not now. Not at night.

Without considering the consequences of his action, he made his way through the front door and onto the porch.

He knew instantly Jamie was already out there. He almost apologized for invading her space, then reminded himself that it was his cabin.

The night was still, the sky clear and dark. The stars seemed low enough to touch. It took a couple of minutes for his eyes to adjust, then he saw Jamie sitting in a corner of the swing.

"It's near freezing," she said by way of greeting. "Did you bring a blanket?"

"No." He inhaled the frigid air and felt invigorated.

"Sit down. I'll get it."

She stood up and walked past him. He used the front wall of the house for support and limped to the chair sitting at right angles to the swing. By the time she returned, his teeth were chattering.

She'd brought a blanket and a quilt. She dropped both over his shoulders, then returned to the swing.

They sat in silence for several minutes. Zach enjoyed his first night outside since he'd been captured. For a while, he hadn't thought he would see a starry night again.

This last capture hadn't been the first time he'd been taken prisoner. He'd been beaten, shot, stabbed and otherwise abused. But this time had been the worst. They'd come after him with chains, which was new, but he didn't think that was the reason he was having trouble shaking the experience. Some of it was that he was getting tired of the game.

"Better than the cell," Jamie said.

He didn't answer. He didn't have to. She could read his mind, and he could read hers. She knew exactly what had happened to him back there. She knew about the pain, the nightmares, the memories.

The silence grew companionable. His breath came out in clouds, and he tried to blow smoke rings. Around them night creatures rustled and called out. He glanced at Jamie, studying her silhouette. In the darkness, he couldn't make out individual features. She could have been seventy or seventeen. She was, in fact, thirty.

She turned her head away, and he saw the movement of her hair. She wore it loose tonight. Moonlight caught the waves left after the braid had been loosened. He wanted to touch her hair. What would it feel like against his skin? All those years ago, he'd hated making her cut it, but he hadn't had a choice. His job had been to teach her all she needed to know in order to stay alive. Thank God it had been enough.

"How long since you've been able to sleep through the night?" he asked.

She laughed. The sound, so light and pleasing in the stillness, cut through him like a knife. It caught the edges of old soul wounds and ripped them open, leaving him to gasp at the pain. This ache couldn't be helped by his pills or even by liquor. God knew, he'd tried the latter enough.

For that moment, before she answered the question, he longed to tell her the truth. That he'd never meant for it to end the way it had. That he'd never meant to hurt her. Their week together had been a miracle for him, something he'd never thought he would experience. But he couldn't promise anything else. He didn't know how and even if he did, he didn't have the right. So he'd stolen that week, thinking she wouldn't really miss it. Surely he could be forgiven that one selfish act? But he hadn't been. Because he'd hurt her badly, then he'd had to let her go.

"I slept at night for the first year," she said. "Then I'd get some time off and I couldn't sleep much past one or two. I'd be up until dawn. I thought there was something wrong with me, until I asked around and found out everyone had the same problem. Winston told me it would get better. Eventually I'll learn to rest like normal people. Eventually I'll recover."

"Is that what you want?"

"I'd like to learn how to forget."

"Good luck." He'd never been able to forget any of it.

"Other people forget."

"Not agents."

"Are you telling me you don't know one operative who left the agency and made a normal life for him or herself?"

Zach shrugged. "A few have, but not if they've been in it for a while."

"Define a while."

"Five or ten years."

"Gee, that's comforting," she said sarcastically. "Thanks."

"I'm just telling you what I've seen."

"Or what you've wanted to see. I believe there's a difference."

She'd always been quick. "Maybe," he conceded.

He leaned back in the wooden chair. The blankets had kept him warm for a while, but now the cold seeped through. He could feel his muscles start to contract, then the shaking began.

He hated weakness. He wanted to get back to work. Being here only gave him too much time to think. That was dangerous. If he thought too much, he might start to feel. Then where would he be?

"It's a beautiful night," Jamie said, staring up at the stars.

His irritation at his vulnerability turned to anger, and he lashed out at the only person available.

"Why are you here?" he asked. "I want the truth, not some do-gooder bull neither of us believes."

"The truth? Are you sure?" She didn't wait for an answer. "All right. I'm here because seven years ago you told me I had to choose between a normal life and my job. I chose my job. I don't regret those years. I'm proud of what I've done. I'm also ready to make a change. I want to be normal. I want to find my way back."

Anger bubbled to the surface. "There isn't a way back," he said. "There never has been and there never will be. You can't escape. The job is as much a part of you as your scars and your inability to sleep at night. I warned you, but you didn't want to listen. You had to have it your way and now you're paying the price. Don't come crying to me expecting comfort or solutions. I don't have either to give."

Jamie had straightened in her seat and stared at him.

He didn't need a light to know that she was startled by his outburst. He told himself to stop, but he couldn't. He had to say it all. He had to hurt her because if he didn't, she might learn the truth.

"If you came back here looking to relive our time together, forget it. I'm not interested in giving any more lessons to rookies."

She didn't move. His words lingered in the silence. God, he wanted to call them back, but he didn't.

Finally she stood up and headed for the front door. "I'm not fooled. You've got to be wounded pretty badly to be lashing out at me like that. My question must have hit pretty close to home." She fumbled with the door. "How long have you wanted out, Zach?"

Chapter 7

Zach didn't speak to her for three days. He and Jamie moved through the house like sharks, circling around each other, silently staking out territory. Neither dominated. It was an uneasy truce at best.

"Not very mature," she muttered to herself on the morning of the fourth day as she filled the sink with soapy water so she could wash the breakfast dishes. But she wasn't sure if she was talking about herself or Zach.

She wondered how long they could coexist without having a conversation, then decided she didn't care how long it went on. Her head told her Zach had been caught off guard by her questions. The way he'd lashed out had proved that. Her heart didn't care. No words were preferable to the ones he'd thrown in her face three nights ago.

I'm not interested in giving any more lessons to rookies. The sentence still had the power to hurt her. Just thinking about it made her shudder and want to fold her arms protectively across her chest.

Is that all it had been to him? Love lessons? Not even that, she reminded herself. More like sex lessons. Detailed instructions on the pleasures available to the human female—a hands-on workshop given by a master at the art of seduction.

She shook her head. That wasn't fair. Zach had never tried to seduce her. If anything, he'd gone out of his way to treat her like one of the guys. Not by a single breath had he given away the fact that he'd been interested in her. If he had been interested. Maybe he'd kept her around for that week because it was convenient. He could have a lover without having to work to get one.

"Stop it," she told herself aloud. She would make herself crazy if she kept this up. She didn't know all the facts. As she had no plans to ask Zach to explain his motivation and feelings seven years ago, she wasn't likely to ever really know what he'd been thinking. Maybe he had just been using her.

But even as the thought formed, she pushed it away. That wasn't the Zach she knew. And if the rumors at the agency were to be believed, he rarely got involved with women and never made it personal. She knew she was the only one he'd brought up to the cabin. Her presence that week hadn't been about convenience. It couldn't be. Convenient was an anonymous hotel in a big city, not a private cabin used as a retreat from the world.

He'd tried to hurt her because she'd hurt him. She'd probed a raw wound.

She picked up the bowls and plates and plunged them into the hot, soapy water. As she did, Zach's bedroom door opened, and he limped out.

He'd given up his cane the second day. She didn't turn around to look at him, but she could hear his unsteady steps. He might not be speaking to her, but he was eating everything she put in front of him. Usually he washed up the dishes while she went outside after they ate. While he wasn't sleeping much at night, he more than made up for it during the day, so he was going to regain his strength fairly quickly. That was probably his plan.

It would be easier to strangle her with his bare hands if he was physically fit.

Her mouth pulled up in a smile that quickly faded when she heard the jingle of keys. She glanced up and saw Zach heading to the back door with the Bronco keys in his hand.

He wasn't going anywhere. She knew that. Yet the fact that he wanted to try to leave cut her to her heart. She sucked in a deep breath and felt the pain clear down to her gut. Damn him for being so difficult, and damn herself for caring about him.

She looked out the window. Zach was still too thin. His jeans hung loose around his narrow hips. He walked slowly, but more confidently than he had the day before. His broad shoulders still stretched out the flannel shirt he wore. She'd always thought he was a beautiful man, if men could be called that. His darkness, the way he held himself aloof from the rest of the world, only added to his charm as far as she was concerned.

He slid onto the driver's seat. After a few moments of silence, he popped the hood, then limped to the front of the vehicle. She knew the exact second he saw the battery was missing. He turned toward the house and glared at her through the window. She met his gaze without flinching.

"Did you hide the battery?" he asked when he entered the kitchen and slammed the keys down on the counter.

"Yes. The first day."

"Where is it?"

Dark brown eyes deepened with anger. It was like teasing a tiger. Her momentary feeling of self-satisfaction could easily be followed by a quick slash of killer claws.

She grabbed the pot she'd used to cook oatmeal and

dropped it into the sink. For a full minute, the only sound was the slosh of water as she scrubbed the pot clean.

"What do you want from me?" he asked at last.

"Surprisingly, nothing," she said, staring at the bubbles and avoiding his gaze. After all, she lied. There were so many things she wanted from him, she couldn't begin to list them all. But this wasn't the time to discuss them. Neither of them was prepared to be honest.

"I take that back," she continued. "I do want one thing. I want you to get well and I'm going to stay here and make sure that happens."

"Why?"

She shrugged. "Call it something to fill my time until I figure out what I want to do with my life."

"Domesticity doesn't suit you."

Another barb hit its mark. She accepted the sting but refused to flinch. "You're welcome to take over the cooking anytime you want."

"I don't know what kind of game you're playing." He exhaled. "Dammit, Jamie, at least have the guts to look at me while we're talking."

She stiffened slightly, then carefully rinsed her hands and dried them on a towel. Only then did she turn toward him and raise her head.

The overhead light reflected off his shiny dark hair. He stood with his hands on his hips, his feet spread. Despite the fact that they were in a cabin in the middle of woods that had probably never seen conflict, he was a warrior. Brave, strong, sure.

Something deep inside her resonated with his presence. It had been so long. She should have gotten over him, or at least found an antidote to his lethal charm. She hadn't. She was just as smitten as she'd been the first day of class. Damn him. Damn them both.

"I'm leaving," he said.

"It's a long walk to town."

"Where's the battery?"

"I'm not going to tell you," she said. "I'm not going to let you run off and die somewhere."

He swore. "What will it take to get rid of you?"

He was determined to make her pay, she thought sadly. "Get well, Zach," she said. "When you can run to the bottom of the driveway and back up, I'll know you're a hundred percent and I'll be gone. Not before."

She held her breath, waiting for him to insist she tell him why she was *really* doing this. Surely he could guess the truth. But instead of saying anything, he moved toward the back door.

"You'll never find it," she called after him.

"I'm not going to look for the battery. I'm going to run to the highway and get you the hell out of my life."

The door slammed shut behind him.

Jamie returned to the sink and quickly finished the dishes. She figured Zach would make it maybe a quarter of a mile before collapsing. She wanted to go after him and make sure he was okay, but she didn't. When the kitchen was clean, she put on her own running shoes and headed out.

The morning air was crisp. On the radio last night, they'd mentioned a late cold front could be moving in at the beginning of next week, but for now it was a perfect mountain spring day.

Overhead the sun rose in a brilliant blue sky. Every morning more and more trees exploded with leaves. Delicate flowers poked their heads out of the soggy ground. The air was heady enough to leave her giddy.

She started out slowly, walking for the first couple of minutes, then breaking into a slow jog, heading away from the driveway so she wouldn't run into Zach. The sound of her steps and her breathing was her only accompaniment on her run. When she ran at home, she usually used a radio and headphones, but up here she savored the silence.

She'd been at the cabin over two weeks and she could see why Zach kept it. There was something cleansing and healing about the location. Maybe it was ancient sacred ground. Or a secret spot for lovers.

She quickly pushed away that last thought. Under present circumstances, being Zach's lover was impossible. He wasn't going to ask, and she wasn't going to offer. Even if he did ask—

She broke into a run and headed up an incline between a row of trees. She wasn't sure what she would do if he asked. She liked to think she would be strong and say no, but it was unlikely.

Her breathing deepened as she broke out into a sweat. Her heart picked up its rhythm. She could feel the energy filling her. Up here, among the trees and the clear sky, all things were possible. If she could feel one with nature, surely she could find a way to be one with herself. She could remember what it felt to be human, and to be a woman.

Easier said than done, she thought. Although she had all the working parts, she wasn't sure what to do with them. She couldn't imagine herself hosting teas for the Junior League. She didn't even know what the Junior League was or why it existed in the first place. But there had to be some kind of middle ground between a clichéd female existence and what she'd become.

Another half hour of running didn't bring her closer to an answer. She turned around and headed back to the house, slowing to a jog. When she spotted a tree with a thick branch about a foot above her head, she stopped and jumped up to grab it.

When her grip was secure, she started doing pull-ups. She worked slowly, thoughtfully, exercising her muscles, keeping them strong.

Her body was still as she slowly raised and lowered herself, her feet together, her legs straight. "Not the most feminine exercise," Jamie said as perspiration dampened her back and face. But she couldn't imagine not being strong. Strength was a part of her now. Her strength made her feel safe.

"Thirty-eight, thirty-nine, forty." She released the tree branch and jumped to the ground. Once there, she shook out her arms and continued walking toward the cabin.

Was she hiding behind her need to be strong? Did she use that part of herself to keep people away, emotionally, as well as physically?

She didn't want to think about that. As she tried to ignore the thought, she reminded herself she'd quit the agency so she would have time to answer all those questions. She wasn't here just to help Zach, but also to explore and discover. To find balance. She was going to have to stare down the scary questions and figure out the answers.

When she got back to the cabin, Zach wasn't there. She wondered how far he'd gone and if he'd hurt himself. She checked the clock. If he wasn't back in an hour, she was going after him.

Forty-eight minutes later, he came into view. He was covered in sweat and barely able to walk. She moved out to the porch and waited for him to approach. Although her nerves were stretched tight, she struck a casual pose and tried to act unconcerned.

When he reached the three stairs leading up to the house, he raised his head and looked her straight in the eye. "I made it to the road," he said. "It's time for you to go."

She'd expected a lot of lines, but not that one. Without meaning to, she burst out laughing.

Zach surprised her by turning his lips up in a grudging smile. "I didn't think you'd buy it."

She was too stunned by the way the smile had affected her to bother responding to his words. The tingling started at her toes and worked its way up. Her breathing increased, as it had while she'd been running, but this time it wasn't from physical exertion. Looked as though he still got to her. A dangerous concept.

He sank down on the steps. "I barely made it past the bend." He pointed to the curve in the driveway. "Then I puked my guts out and just about collapsed. I had to rest all this time just to make it back."

So he still needed her. The thought should have pleased her, but it didn't. She knew the truth. He might not make it down to the highway today, or tomorrow, but he would keep trying. And one day he would make it. Then it would be time for her to go.

Zach stepped into the cabin. He preferred spending time outdoors, but an unexpected cold front had arrived and the snow had driven him inside.

He was restless. A good sign. It meant he was healing. He'd been running a little every day for nearly a week. His strength was returning, although it would be another six or eight weeks before he was back to a hundred percent.

As he walked into the kitchen, he saw Jamie had made a fresh pot of coffee. He glanced toward the bedrooms. Her door was closed. They both tried to sleep in the afternoon because neither of them slept at night. As she'd said, insomnia was a hazard of the job.

He poured himself some coffee, then headed for the bathroom. He needed a hot shower to get the chill out of his bones. Before he opened the door, he moved close to Jamie's room. He imagined her sleeping there and hated himself for the pleasure the image brought. He didn't want to be connected to her. He couldn't allow himself to feel anything. The price was too high.

The only way to endure the horrors of the world was to let go of them. Early in his career, he'd wrestled with injustice and hatred. He'd seen the suffering and not known how to ease it. Gradually he'd learned not to feel any of it. Once he let the feelings disappear, he could do his job. After all these years, it was all he knew.

If he allowed himself one strong emotion, if he cracked the door a little, everything would rush out and overwhelm him. He had a bad feeling Jamie was hoping for a miracle, but she wasn't going to get one from him.

She wanted to know if he was looking for a way out. He shook his head. He couldn't leave. This was all he knew.

Still carrying his coffee, he pushed open the bathroom door. Jamie wasn't in her bedroom sleeping. She was in the bathroom, wearing nothing but a towel.

He stopped suddenly. Hot coffee sloshed over his hand, but he didn't feel the burning. He stared at her, realized she was practically naked and started to back up.

"Sorry," he mumbled.

The bathroom was small, with a single sink in a narrow vanity. The metal-mirrored medicine chest was about twenty-five years old. The only indulgence was the claw-footed tub that ran the length of the room. When he'd first bought the cabin, he'd put in a shower head over the tub.

"It's all right," she said, and smiled up at him. "I'm just finishing up."

The room was steamy, the mirror fogged. He didn't notice any of that. Instead, he stared at the woman in front of him.

She'd piled her long hair on top of her head. A few strands escaped and clung to her damp shoulders. Dark smudges under her eyes told him of her battles with restlessness and changed her hazel eyes to green.

Her face was a perfect oval, with high cheekbones and a wide mouth. She never wore makeup and rarely needed it. Now her skin was flushed and luminous. His gaze moved down her body. He could see the lean lines of her muscles. She was strong but not bulky. She amazed him.

She'd become a hell of a woman. He almost told her, too. But at the last minute, he held the words inside. Why would his opinion matter to her? She knew what she'd accomplished.

"Just let me get my things," she said, and reached for a pile of clothing. "I know I used all the hot water, but I soaked in the tub for nearly forty minutes, so it should be heated again."

She moved with the easy grace of a wild creature. He wanted to tug on the corner of the towel tucked near her arm and let it fall to the floor. He wanted to go to her and hold her. He wanted to taste her and make love to her over and over, as they had seven years ago.

He wanted to tell her he'd never forgotten her. That she was the closest he'd ever come to loving someone.

Instead, he watched as she collected her belongings and slipped past him. One hand clutched her clothes; the other tugged a clip from her hair. The long, shimmering strands tumbled down her back. His body clenched reflexively as desire poured through him.

Then she was gone. He closed the door and set the coffee mug on the vanity. When he moved to the tub, he stared at the few bubbles still twinkling against the white porcelain.

How she tempted him with her soft smiles and gentle ways. But he would never act on his desires. It was too risky. Her smiles brought him more joy than he'd ever felt. They also brought him more pain than the beatings ever had. She was here now, but eventually she would find what she'd come looking for and she would leave. Then what? He could heal from the beatings, but the wounds Jamie inflicted would be with him always.

Chapter 8

Jamie woke as she did each night. After listening to the silence for a few minutes, she rolled over and glanced at the clock. Nearly two. It had been over three weeks since she'd quit the agency, but she still couldn't sleep through the night. She wondered if she ever would.

After staring at the ceiling for nearly a half hour, she gave up trying to pretend she could relax. She rose, collected jeans, socks and a thick sweater, then put them on. She walked silently to her bedroom door and listened. Nothing. She hadn't heard Zach's door open or him moving about the cabin, but she knew he was awake and outside. She sensed it.

Sometimes she felt as if they'd been fused together in some mysterious way, joined on a cellular level. She couldn't stop thinking about him. The past and present blurred in her mind until she forgot what was from today and what remained of their long-ago week together. She wondered about his hopes and dreams, his plans for the future, as if his goals had something to do with hers. She sensed when he was pushing himself too hard, when he was in pain, when he was tired. She had no feeling that their bond was of another world, just that the connection was earth-shatteringly strong.

Yesterday he'd walked into the bathroom before she'd had a chance to dress after bathing. She'd been wearing a towel, and he'd certainly seen her in less. So she hadn't been embarrassed. If anything, the intimacy had pleased her. She'd wanted him to want her at least as much as she wanted him. But their connection wasn't perfect, and she couldn't always read his mind. At that moment, his dark eyes had remained impenetrable barriers, protecting both his thoughts and his soul. She'd been left to wonder...and to want.

Slowly she eased her door open and stepped into the living room. A single light shone from the kitchen—the one over the stove. By mutual consent, they left it on all night. The scent of coffee drifted to her. In the kitchen, she found a fresh pot, minus one cup. She poured herself some, then picked up a blanket from the back of the sofa and headed for the front door.

Once there, she paused. She wanted to go outside. Being in the cold night air would soothe her restless spirit, but there was danger in the darkness. Zach.

The last time they'd shared the porch had been the first week he'd arrived. It had started out well enough, then had ended with him saying he wasn't interested in giving lessons to rookies.

His words still had the power to wound. Even knowing what he was trying to do—that he wanted to hurt her enough to drive her away—hadn't been protection against the pain. She knew their time together had been more than that. If he'd only been interested in bedding a virgin, he wouldn't have invited her to his cabin. Her mind was sure, but her heart still questioned. Had she really been the only one to feel anything? Had she been the only one to fall in love?

She opened the front door. Chilly air swept around her. She paused, waiting for her eyes to become adjusted.

"You coming out or are you just going to stand there?" Zach asked.

Instead of answering, she stepped onto the porch and closed the door behind her.

He sat in the chair next to the swing. A thick quilt covered him. He was slouched down with his head resting against the wooden slats as he stared at the sky.

"I kept telling myself one day I would learn the names of the constellations," he said, his voice low and quiet. "All those nights I spent staring up, never sure what I was staring at. I can find the Big and Little Dippers. But that's about it. You know any of the stars?"

Jamie slipped onto the swing and drew her blanket around her. She took a sip of coffee. "Just the ones you named. And the Southern Cross when I'm in the Southern Hemisphere. Oh, there's the North Star."

"Yeah, I can find that one, too."

Silence settled around them, but it wasn't an awkward pause. It was the comfortable quiet of two people who don't always have to talk. Tension eased in her body, and she found herself relaxing. They were going to be all right, at least for tonight.

Gradually the noises of the night creatures returned. The air was scented with spring. Flowers, trees, grass. Her breath came out in puffy clouds of steam.

"My father would like it here," Jamie said. "At least I think he would. He always talked about the outdoors."

"Where's he now?"

She held her coffee mug in both hands. "He died when I was eight. I don't remember very much about him. My mother remarried a couple of years later, but my stepfather and I were never close."

"Losing your father must have been hard on you."

She glanced at him. He was looking at her. The light was too dim for her to read his expression, but his words were kind. "It was. I adored my dad. I wanted to be just like him. He was a cop."

"Why'd you choose the agency over law enforcement?"

She shrugged. "I respected what he did, but as I grew up, I thought it would be too confining. I wanted to be going and doing, not just writing tickets and filling out forms. I've since realized there's a lot more to being a cop than that, but at eighteen I needed to see the world."

"And you saw it. Was it what you expected?"

"The world?" She shook her head. "Not really. But going on assignment with the agency isn't the same as being a tourist or even living somewhere. Just like cops have a hard time believing the good in people, I have a hard time thinking about the rest of the world as a glamorous, exciting place. It's too easy to remember the bad stuff."

"Weren't there good things, too?" he asked.

"Sure. Lots of them. I guess I have to remind myself to remember them, too. What about you? How did you end up as a spy? Or is that something you don't like to talk about?"

He returned his attention to the sky. "I can talk about it, although it's not a very interesting story. I was a street kid. I started getting in trouble when I was about eight. By the time I was twelve, I'd already stolen a car. I spent high school in a juvenile facility. When I turned eighteen, they sealed my records. I'd been around long enough to realize I'd been given a second chance, so I took it. I went into the military to save money for college. I never got that far. The agency recruited me before I was discharged."

Jamie stared at him. He'd just told her more about himself in less than a minute than everything she'd learned in the past seven years. Just like that. Personal information. She wasn't sure what stunned her more. The story of his life or the fact that he'd shared it with her.

"So you're a bad kid who turned out good," she said.

"Let's just say I saw the error of my ways."

His story didn't surprise her. Most good field agents came from troubled backgrounds. Normal people usually didn't choose to put their futures on hold so they could run around the world risking their lives.

"What about your parents?" she asked. "Are they dead?"

"Not to the best of my knowledge."

"Are you still in touch with them?"

He laughed, but the sound wasn't humorous. "I haven't seen them since I was fourteen. My dad was a small-time criminal. He fancied himself on the fringes of the Mafia, but he was just a joke. The old lady—" He paused. "She wasn't much into children."

He spoke the words matter-of-factly. As if they had no personal meaning. As if they had never had the power to hurt him. She'd grown up in unhappy circumstances, but at least her mother had continued to acknowledge her existence. It sounded as if he'd been abandoned.

"Once you went into the juvenile facility, your parents never came to visit you?" she asked.

"I preferred it that way."

He said the words with the confidence of an adult, but as the connection between them strengthened, she felt the pain of the fourteen-year-old boy he'd been. She wasn't surprised that he'd lived his early years outside of the law. The fact that he'd chosen to take a chance when one was offered was a testament to the kind of man he'd become. He was strong, capable. *He* didn't need anyone. But the boy inside still did.

She wondered what it must have been like, growing up

in his world. Hers had been lonely, but she'd never had to be afraid. Zach had been locked up for four long years. How had he spent Christmas? His birthday? She knew instinctively that no one had remembered. No one had sent a card or visited. No one had ever cared.

"Do you ever see your mom?" he asked.

"Not really. I call her a couple of times a year. She's still married to my stepfather and, well, we still don't get along."

She didn't want to think about the hideous things the man had said to her. All these years later, the memories of his verbal abuse still had the power to make her feel small and vulnerable.

Zach was at her side in an instant. He took the mug from her fingers and set it on the ground, then he grabbed her arms and shook her slightly.

"What did that bastard do to you?" he asked, his voice low and furious. "Did he hurt you?"

She stared at him. She could make out the shape of his face and the fury in his eyes. "What are you talking about?"

"Did he touch you?"

She realized what he was asking. Color heated her cheeks. She shook her head. "No."

"Jamie!"

"Zach, I swear, he never touched me. He didn't hurt me that way. He was smarter than that."

"Then what?"

"I—" She didn't really want to tell him. The memories were too humiliating. Zach's anger didn't give her a choice. "He was very nice to me in front of my mother, but as soon as she left the room, he turned on me. He said mean things to me." She sucked in a breath. "We moved to Phoenix when I was eleven. I came home from school one day in tears. I couldn't make any friends and I felt so alone. For some reason, he was home instead of my mother. He got me to tell him what was wrong, then he started laughing. He told me that I was too ugly and stupid to have friends. No one would ever like me. He said my mother didn't even like me, but she pretended because she was supposed to."

"And you believed him." It wasn't a question.

She nodded. "I was a kid. I didn't know what else to believe. I'd never had a lot of friends. I was pretty much a loner. I stopped trying to fit in."

His hands slipped down her arms to her hands. He squeezed her fingers. "So you became a spy."

Surprisingly talking about the memories wasn't as painful as she'd expected. For some reason, the telling was easier. Maybe it was the dark night. Maybe it was the fact that a lot of time had passed and she was her own person now. Maybe it was Zach.

"Actually I became a runner. When the kids teased me, I ran away. I just kept running. I started to like it, and by high school I was a track star."

"A jock," he said, brushing his thumbs against the backs of her hands. Shivers raced up her arms. She wanted to cuddle close to him, but she didn't dare. The moment was special enough. She couldn't risk rejection.

"Absolutely. I was the girl who was good at all the sports. I was better than a lot of guys, too. You can imagine how popular *that* made me. It was the same in college. For a long time, I couldn't figure out what was wrong. I was growing up, but I didn't have many friends. I thought the world was weird, but then one day I figured out it was me. I was hiding behind the sports, keeping to myself rather than risking relationships with other people. Despite this aura of confidence, I'm basically shy. I decided to start taking risks. Talking to students in my classes, that kind of thing."

"Did it work?"

"Sort of. I was never popular. I never got asked out, but I had more friends."

"You have friends now," he stated.

"I know. I've learned a lot." She smiled. "Do you know there was a time I'd actually thought about going into the FBI?"

"Why didn't you? You could have traveled."

"I suppose. But I wanted more autonomy. That's what the agency offered." But sometimes she wondered. If she could turn back time, if she could do it all again, would she do things the same? She wasn't so sure.

He released her hands and straightened on the swing. They were close enough that their body heat combined, making her warm. She ignored the tingling in her fingers and the blood settling low in her belly. At least he didn't move back to the chair.

"Why'd you come after me?" he asked.

"I told you. I pay my debts."

"Is that what you told Winston?"

"Sure."

"And he believed you?"

She shrugged. "Why wouldn't he? It's the truth." She struggled to keep her tone light.

"We both know better than that, Jamie. What's the real reason?"

"Does it matter? Isn't it enough that you're alive?"

He didn't answer. She bit down on her lower lip and considered her options. She could change the subject, she could lie or she could tell the truth. Somehow the latter seemed easiest.

"I couldn't bear to think of you dying there," she said softly. "The feeling in my gut told me you were still alive, but Winston wasn't going to send in another team. I didn't have a choice."

"Thank you for saving me." He gave her a quick smile. "Alive *is* better than dead."

"You're welcome." His proximity and their conversation gave her courage. "Do you have any regrets?" she asked. "About the agency, I mean."

"Sure. Doesn't everybody?"

She wanted to ask what his were, but courage deserted her as quickly as it had come. Was she one of them? Did he regret their time together? She would have sold her soul to know he regretted letting her go, but that would have required a miracle and she didn't think she was due for one.

You're a fool, she told herself. At least that hadn't changed. She'd always been a fool where he was concerned. Seven years ago, she'd handed over her heart, only to have it returned broken and bleeding. Now she was still throwing herself at him, only this time the reasons weren't as clear.

"What are your regrets, Jamie? Not just about the job, but about anything."

She pulled her knees up to her chest. Her blanket slipped down. Before she could reach for it, Zach tucked it around her. The unexpected gesture made her want to have him hold her forever. Instead, she thought about what he'd asked.

"I'm sorry I didn't try harder to fit in when I was younger. School would have been a lot more fun."

"Do you regret the job?"

"Why would you ask that?"

"Because you left."

She thought about the question. "I don't regret all I accomplished. I have the satisfaction of knowing I made a direct difference in people's lives. What I did mattered."

"You did good work."

She turned toward him. "How would you know?"

"I make it a habit to keep up with all my students."

Bitter disappointment coated her tongue. She didn't

want to be one of his students. She wanted to be special. Different. Important.

Wishes...they were such a waste of time. If wishes were horses, then beggars would ride.

The night closed around them. Jamie looked up at the stars twinkling from the heavens. "I didn't think it would cost this much," she whispered. "I didn't know that the darkness would get inside of me and eat me alive."

"I tried to warn you."

"A lot of good that does me now."

"Jamie, I—"

She cut him off with a wave of her hand. "Don't bother explaining, Zach. You're right. You did try to warn me. I still remember what you said. That this wasn't going to be a nine-to-five job. It wasn't selling insurance or working in an office. That once I crossed the line, I could never find my way back. I suppose I should have listened."

But she couldn't have. Not then. At that moment, seven years ago, all she'd been able to focus on was that Zach didn't want her. The pain had filled her until nothing else was real. She'd carried the hurt for years. In some ways, it was still with her. The job had been the only constant she could cling to. She would never have wanted to hear the agency might not be the right place for her. After Zach rejected her, she had something to prove.

"I didn't believe you," she said at last.

"And now?"

"Now I know you were right. Satisfied?"

"No. Despite what you think about me, I didn't want to be right. I wanted you to make it work. No one else had, but I thought you might have a chance."

It took her a couple of minutes to figure out the burning in her eyes wasn't from exhaustion but from tears. Dammit, she refused to cry.

"Sorry to let you down," she said lightly as she blinked

away the moisture. "I guess I can't be your best student after all."

She wondered if he heard the bitterness behind her attempt at humor. If he did, he didn't mention it.

"I can't help you find your way back," he said quietly. "I don't know that there is a way. I'm sorry. I wish it could be different." He leaned forward and rested his elbows on his knees. "I'm proud of what you've accomplished. I knew you could be the best. I knew the price you would pay and I tried to warn you, but I think I always knew you weren't going to listen. Whatever else happened between us, I always respected you."

She didn't know what to say. It was the first time he'd referred to their time together without being cutting or sarcastic. Intense longing filled her. She wanted to wrap her arms around him and hold him close until they both forgot everything but being together. She wanted to be near him, naked, touching, loving. She remembered what it had been like to make love with him. He'd been so considerate, teaching her everything she would ever need to know.

But she didn't reach out to him. Instead, she cringed as she recalled her innocent enthusiasm and how eager she'd been to learn. What had he thought of her then? She'd held nothing back, not physically or emotionally. She'd exposed her very soul to this man, and he'd chosen to walk away.

She'd learned her lesson. She would never risk that much again.

"By the end of the first week of class, I knew you were special," he said. "You had so much potential. That's why I rode you so hard. And you didn't let me down. But as graduation got closer, I wasn't so sure. You would be a damn fine agent. But at what price? We all pay it. There's no getting away from it. The danger, the life-style, it requires everything. When the assignment is over and we go home, there's nothing left inside. When the war is over, the warrior is simply unnecessary."

"But is the war ever over?"

"It is for you," he said. "You chose to walk away. What are you going to do?"

He had her there. She'd quit, but she didn't have a plan for her life.

"I don't know. There are so many options. Sometimes I'm immobilized by my choices."

"Your price is higher because you're a woman," he said.

She swore loudly.

He turned his head toward her. "You know it's true, Jamie. You're what, thirty?"

She nodded.

"Can you honestly tell me you've never regretted not having a child?"

"It's not too late," she reminded him. "I've got lots of childbearing years left. What about you? Don't you regret never having a family?"

He faced front. "Sometimes. The difference is you still believe it's possible, and I know it never was. At least not for me. Therefore, you've lost more."

His logic made sense in a twisted sort of way. "You continue to surprise me, Zach. Just when I think you're an insensitive clod, you go and say something insightful."

"Hey, I'm full of surprises."

He was. This conversation was a surprise. She supposed it was the night that allowed them to talk so freely. Over the years, shadows had become their home. Darkness a friend. Something about the light made them feel exposed. Here the shadows made it safe.

"Surprise me again," she said. "Tell me when you're going to get out."

He stood up and walked to the edge of the porch. It was only three feet away, but she felt as if he'd moved to another country. Their connection severed instantly, and the cold seeped into her bones.

He pulled the quilt over his shoulders and braced his hands on the railing. "I won't be. This is all I know."

She dropped her head to her knees. The hell of it was, he was telling the truth. He didn't know any other world. Her heart ached for him.

"I'm not sure you have a choice," she said. "How many more times can you go through what you just endured? How many more times can you face death and walk away?"

"I can't answer that. Maybe death is the only way out."

"Don't say that. Of course there's another way."

"When you find it, let me know."

She glared at his back. "I hate it when you're cynical. I refuse to believe this is all there is. We are intelligent creatures. We make choices. If we choose to let go of the past, then the future opens up to us."

"Keep saying it long enough and you'll start to believe it."

She stood up and crossed the porch. "There has to be more."

"Why?"

"Because—" She bit her lower lip. She didn't have an answer.

He shook his head. "Just because you want it to be true, doesn't make it so. There doesn't have to be more. There doesn't have to be anything. Sometimes this is all there is."

"Other people have lives. Normal lives. I've seen them. They feel things and survive being ordinary. Are you saying that's not available to us?"

"Those ordinary people you so admire couldn't do what we do."

She leaned against the railing. "Probably not."

"Have you considered that there might be two different kinds of people? Those of us who live on the fringes, and everyone else? We aren't the same for a reason. We can't pretend to be what we're not."

"I refuse to believe that."

He shrugged. "Whatever gets you through the night."

She turned away from the forest beyond them and stared back at the house. Zach couldn't be right. There were always choices. She'd chosen to enter the agency and she'd chosen to walk away. Two distinct choices that would affect her in radically different ways. Surely that changed everything. She was determined to get in touch with parts of herself she'd ignored, to find some kind of balance. Of course it wasn't going to be easy. Change never was. But it would be worth it in the end.

"I wonder how many people stay in because it's easier than getting out," she said. "After all, leaving means facing the demons."

"There are no demons."

"Aren't there? What about the ghosts of the dead? What about the ugly memories, the pain, the suffering? Aren't those demons?"

"They only exist if you believe in them. That's what gives them power."

She wished that were true. She knew it wasn't. "How do you keep them quiet?"

"I don't listen to them. You feel too much, Jamie."

"And you don't feel enough."

She rubbed her arms and pulled the blanket closer. Was this why Zach stayed in? Because he couldn't face the demons of the past? Not feeling. That would do it. That would keep the memories at bay. But at what cost? How much of himself was tied up in keeping that door firmly closed?

"Everyone has demons," she said. "Our work feeds them and helps them grow."

He didn't answer.

She glanced at him. He'd straightened and leaned against the post by the stairs. He was stronger than he'd been just a few days ago. Soon he would make the run to the bottom of the driveway, and she would leave. To go where? That empty apartment that only served to emphasize her aloneness? Why wasn't there a "normal" school where she could train to be ordinary? And, dammit, why wasn't Zach willing to help her?

"What are you hiding from?" she asked.

He turned toward her. Even in the darkness, she felt the force of his glare. She had to consciously keep herself from flinching.

He turned on his heel and walked inside.

Jamie sucked in a breath. Obviously that question had struck close to home. Maybe she should ask it of herself. What was she hiding from?

Life, maybe? The past, or was it the future? Neither, she decided. She wasn't hiding. She was doing her best to step into the sunlight.

But could she find a place to belong? Could she figure out what she wanted most of all?

A small animal rustled in the darkness. The cold stung her skin. She could feel her heart pounding as if she'd just run five miles. Realization dawned and with it a unique, intense pain.

She reached up and touched her cheek. Stunned, she brought her fingers to her lips and felt the moisture there. She was crying.

And then she knew. The truth was so obvious, she wondered why it had taken this long for her to figure it out. She hadn't rescued Zach because she owed him and she hadn't come to the cabin to have him help her find her way back. She'd come here because after seven years, she'd never been able to forget him. She'd never let go. She'd come here because she still loved him.

She'd never stopped loving him.

Chapter 9

Zach jogged around the bend in the driveway and headed for the house. At the last minute, he made a sharp right and moved into the forest. For the first time, he'd run over a mile and he didn't feel as if he was going to collapse and die. He wanted to take advantage of his newfound strength and find that damn battery. He had to get out of here.

He and Jamie had been living together for nearly five weeks. Five weeks of bumping into her on the curves, of sharing domestic chores, of being in the same small, confining cabin. Even when he worked on it, he couldn't go more than a few hours without catching sight of her. Even when he didn't want to, he found himself watching her, studying the graceful movements of her body and the lean strength that was as much a part of her as her heartbeat. Even when he tried not to, he found himself inhaling the scent of her skin and wanting her.

That was the worst of it. Wanting her. Day after day, night after night. He would lie awake feeling the heat in his groin and know he could never have her. He would wake up in an agonizing state of arousal, having dreamed about their week together. Cold showers weren't working anymore. Nothing helped. He had to get away from her.

When he reached the woods, he slowed. He'd already searched the house and hadn't found the battery. Which meant she'd stowed it somewhere in the woods. If she'd been any other female, he could have limited the search area to how far she would be able to carry the battery. Because he was dealing with Jamie, that information wasn't going to help him. She could have carried it for miles.

But she wouldn't have, he reminded himself. She would want it relatively close by in case of a medical emergency. After all, he'd been in pretty bad shape when he'd arrived.

He stood with his back to the Bronco and surveyed the foliage in front of him. New, bright leaves covered the tree branches. The temperature still dipped toward freezing at night, but the days were warming up. Spring had arrived.

Zach started his search in a small diamond pattern, expanding it every time he returned to the vicinity of the Bronco. He had to find the battery and he had to leave. If for no other reason than that Jamie was dangerous. Last week she'd talked about demons. He'd understood all too well.

He thought of his enemies as ghosts. Ghosts of the past. Of things done, or undone. Souls of the dead who still cried out. Feelings. He was a damn good agent because nothing got to him. Long ago he'd learned to ignore the slightest hint of emotion. He'd blocked it all away, hiding it behind a thick, locked door in his mind. If he occasionally had to stand vigil at night, using all his considerable strength to lean against that door and keep it closed, it was a small price to pay for sanity.

He didn't really have a choice in the matter. If he let

the door open, even just a crack, if he let out one sliver of emotion, everything would burst free, burying him alive. He would never survive.

He'd seen it happen to other agents, good agents. They went along fine, then something got to them. A child's death, a wife's betrayal. They got lost in the pain and never found their way out. Some retired to live quiet lives of suffering. Others made stupid mistakes and got killed. Others took the quick way out and killed themselves.

Many rookies had a hard time learning the principle of shutting down emotionally. For Zach, the process had already been second nature. He'd learned it on the streets when he'd been a kid. His time in the juvenile facility had simply reinforced the lesson. Feel nothing. Protect your back. Survive at all costs.

But with Jamie around, he was doing more than surviving. He was living. Every day she forced him to face the world, when all he really wanted to do was hide. She made him stand in the light, damn her. She made him talk—worse, she made him laugh. With her he couldn't pretend to be half-dead. And most frightening of all, she made him desire her. That desire left him vulnerable.

It wasn't just the physical ache of wanting a woman. That he could handle. When he was between assignments, he often found someone uncomplicated with whom he could spend some time. As long as the woman provided decent sex and didn't ask a lot of questions, he was willing to get involved for a week or even a month. Then he returned to his world, and she was forgotten.

He'd never forgotten Jamie. Even after all this time, he recalled being with her. If he were a different kind of man, he might be willing to admit he'd missed her. But he wasn't...and he hadn't.

But the desire was unfamiliar. As unfamiliar as her need to find answers to her questions. She wanted a way out. He only wanted to go in deeper. She wanted answers;

he didn't want to hear the questions. He wished her luck on her journey. She was going to need it. No one he'd ever known had found his or her way back. Zach had given up looking a long time ago. Soon she would figure that out and leave him to his shadows.

That realization should have made him feel better. But what if she didn't go? So far, she showed no signs of moving on. He often thought about that. When the pain of his injuries and lack of sleep brought him to his knees, he wondered why Jamie was here. With him. She couldn't think that he would be the one—

He shook his head. "Yeah, right," he muttered as he kicked at the loose earth around the base of a small bush. "As if you're anyone's idea of a prize." She wouldn't want a life with him. She probably wanted to marry a banker or an accountant.

Somebody *normal.* Frustration pushed him on. Tall pine trees reached for the sky. He ignored the beauty, the sweet smell of spring, and stared intently at the ground. After nearly an hour of searching, he found it.

The ground looked undisturbed, but there was a small notch in the base of a mid-sized pine tree. He squatted and ran his finger along the length of the notch. It was new. A clean cut, made by a knife.

"Gotcha," he murmured, and began scraping the leaves to one side.

Five minutes later, he pulled the battery out of the loose earth. She'd wrapped it in a trash bag. "You always did good work, Jamie. I'm glad to see that hasn't changed."

He rose to his feet and headed for the Bronco. Halfway there he paused, then slowly came to a stop.

Of course he wanted to leave. What else mattered? Yet even as the thoughts formed, another voice whispered that he really wasn't ready to go. He should be but he wasn't. They had unfinished business together. And if he drove away now, he knew he would never see her again. The thought was more than he could stand.

Without wanting to, and all the while calling himself ten different kinds of fool, he headed back into the woods and buried the battery. He didn't bother concealing the hiding place.

As he stomped on the soft ground, his temper flared. What the hell was he thinking? Why was she tying him up in knots? Why was he letting her?

He stalked to the cabin, then angrily stepped inside.

Jamie's bedroom door closed as he entered the living room. "You were gone a long time. Are you all right?" she called through the door.

He swore loudly. He was acting like a damn idiot, and it was all her fault. "Leave me alone. I'm fine. I don't need you baby sitting me."

He slammed the front door. The loud crash made him feel both better and childish. All right, so it was wrong to yell at her. But if he started yelling at himself, the white-coat crew would be after him with a net.

He paced the living room, walking the length of the room twice, balled his fists and glared at Jamie's door. He was ready for a fight. At least arguing with her would burn off some energy. The great thing about Jamie was that she could give back tenfold what she took. He could always count on her to not take any garbage from him.

"What are you doing in there?" he asked abruptly.

Something crashed to the floor, followed by an odd sound.

Had it been any other female but her, he would have thought it was a stifled sob.

"Nothing," she said quickly, her voice muffled through the door. "I'll be right out."

He moved toward her room, temper forgotten. "Jamie, what's wrong?"

"Nothing, I said. Just go make coffee or something. I'm fine."

An unfamiliar urgency welled up inside of him. "Jamie, what are you doing?"

"Leave me alone."

Her words were thick with tears. He didn't have to see her face to know; he could feel it in his gut.

Knowing she was going to have his head for this, he placed his hand on the doorknob and turned it quickly. Then he opened the door and stepped into the room.

His practiced gaze took in the closed window, the narrow bed, the shopping bags scattered on the blanket. The thunk he'd heard earlier had probably come from the small cosmetics bottle resting on the carpet by her bare feet. Once he'd cataloged the room and eliminated it as the source of her distress, he turned his attention to her.

She stood in front of the mirror on the wall. Her long hair was loosely pinned on top of her head, as it had been the day he'd accidentally caught her leaving her bath. His fingers itched to pull the pins free and watch the long strands tumble to her waist.

His gaze lowered and he frowned. Instead of a sweatshirt and jeans, she wore a frilly blouse. The pale peach fabric sucked the color from her face, leaving her looking drawn. The oversize, puffy sleeves dwarfed her slender frame. A full skirt hung loosely from her waist to about midcalf. She looked awkward, like a child playing dress-up.

She made a harsh sound in the back of her throat. He looked at her face in the mirror. Makeup stained her cheeks, smearing on her skin like a melting mask. Lipstick darkened her lips until they stood out like bruises against her pale skin.

"Go ahead and laugh," she said, then turned away from her reflection. "Lord knows, I would if I were you. Pretty pitiful, don't you think?"

"What are you doing?"

She sniffed. "Isn't it obvious? Trying to wear makeup. 'Trying' being the operative word. Or maybe 'trying and failing' would be more descriptive. I look ridiculous." She picked up a washcloth and brushed it across her mouth. The lipstick stained the white cloth like blood.

She was a sleek cat dressing like a china doll. He was about to tell her when the light from the window illuminated the side of her face and he saw the one thing he'd never imagined coming from her. A tear.

His chest tightened, and his heart squeezed painfully. He couldn't bear to see her suffer. Not this woman. Never Jamie.

She was all things to him. Despite what he'd done to her, despite how he'd treated her, she'd survived. She was fearless and strong. For reasons he could never understand, she'd chosen to save his life. When he would have died, she'd stepped in to save him. She'd been at risk on the assignment, yet she'd come for him. He didn't know why and he was afraid to ask her reasons. There was a part of him that didn't want to hear the confession.

What she'd done for him only made watching her pain worse. Not because he owed her, although he'd incurred a debt he could never repay. But because he knew her strength and how deep a wound would run before she would give in to tears.

He took a step toward her. But she either didn't see his approach or didn't care. She spun, presenting him with her back, then sank gracefully to the floor.

"It's all a mistake," she said, picking up the makeup bottle. "I'm not sure who I was trying to kid. I can't be like everyone else. I don't have a clue about how to be a woman. Look at me." She tugged at the gaping neckline of the blouse. "I can't even dress myself. I don't know what to buy." She tossed the bottle on the bed. "I sure don't know anything about makeup. I'm missing the female gene or something. Now, if some fashion types needed a sharpshooter—then I'd have it made."

"Jamie—"

She shook her head. "You can't teach me this one, Zach. I have to find it inside myself and I don't know if I can. I've read articles about female bonding. Bonding! I don't know how to bond. I'm not even sure what it is. I don't have friends I call on the phone. I don't go to lunch with anyone. I've never even dated. I can kill a man with my bare hands, but I don't know how to buy a skirt and blouse that don't look stupid on me." Her voice cracked. She cleared her throat. "I thought I could find the answers. I thought I could retrain myself—like going backward in time. I just didn't know my clock had stopped. I've failed, Zach. For the first time in years, I've failed."

He was at her side in an instant. "You haven't failed," he said, crouching down beside her. His hands hovered over her shoulders. He wanted to touch her but didn't know if he dared. He had no rights here. He'd thrown them away years ago.

"It's sure not success," she muttered.

Despite his misgivings, her pain spurred him to action. He couldn't let her go on suffering like this. "It's not about clothes," he said. "It doesn't matter what you wear, Jamie. You're still a woman."

"You're not exactly the picture of mental health yourself," she said, then sniffed. "Forgive me if I don't get all enthused about your opinions on my femininity."

He grabbed her arm and tugged. As he rose, he pulled her to her feet. "I may not be Joe Normal, but I am a man. There's not a doubt in my mind that you're female down to your soul."

His dark eyes blazed with a light that should have blinded her. Instead, Jamie found herself wanting to move closer and bask in the glow. Worse, she wanted to believe him. When the temptation grew too strong, she forced herself to remember what she'd looked like when she'd glanced in the mirror. The shock had left her breathless.

She hadn't expected to be instantly beautiful, although that would have been a nice fantasy. But she also hadn't thought she would look so incredibly stupid. Who would have thought it would be so hard to look like a girl?

"You don't have to be kind," she said, and tried to move away.

But he didn't let her go. He held on to her right arm, just above the wrist. His grip wasn't enough to bruise, but she knew she wasn't going to get away until he chose to let her go.

"I'm not being kind. I'm telling the truth. You're a beautiful woman."

Humiliation stung in her throat and behind her eyes. She blinked to hold back the tears. "Yeah, right." She started to twist her arm, not caring if it hurt. She had to get away before she did something stupid, like cry.

"Dammit, Jamie, what can I say to convince you?"

"Nothing."

"I guess you're right about that."

He slipped his hand down until it covered hers, brought her palm to his belly and slid it lower. He moved so quickly, she didn't have time to figure out what was going on until she felt the soft fabric of his sweatpants and the hard ridge of his maleness underneath. Her breath caught. Slowly she raised her gaze to his.

"That's right," he said, his voice a low grumble. "You're woman enough to turn me on. You've always had that power."

The fire brightened in his eyes. She could feel the heat. Some of it came from him, but most of it flared to life inside her body. Blood flowed rapidly, causing her breasts to swell and her thighs to ache. She swayed slightly.

She remembered the last time she'd touched him intimately. Seven years ago. He'd broken her heart. If they were intimate again, she wouldn't get off so lightly. This time she *would* be destroyed.

"Jamie," he whispered, and drew his hands up to her shoulders. She placed her fingers on his narrow waist.

The price didn't matter. She hadn't been able to resist him then and she still couldn't resist him. It wasn't even about the desire she felt boiling inside of her. The need to be with him came from a much more dangerous source.

Love. She loved him. And in loving him, she could deny him nothing. It didn't matter that this was just temporary, or that it would mean the world to her and little more than relief to him. For this hour, this afternoon, these few days, however long it lasted, she needed to be with him. Really with him.

He lowered his head. The slow, deliberate movement warned her of his intentions. If she'd planned to run, now was the time. But she didn't. Instead, she lifted her head toward his.

Their mouths touched. She'd relived their kisses a thousand times before. She knew what he would feel like, even after all this time. But he surprised her. Instead of overwhelming her with hard, hot desire, he kissed her gently. His lips barely brushed against hers. A sweet, almost reverent touch. As if they were innocent and this was the first time for both of them. As if the moment were meant to last a lifetime.

Her eyes drifted closed. She didn't want to see anything; she just wanted to feel. His body was close to hers. They shared heat. Her heart rate increased—or was it his? It didn't matter. Soon they would be one, with a shared experience to keep them connected always. His mouth clung to hers, lightly, like the brush of a feather. He exhaled her name and cupped her face as if afraid she would move away.

She wanted to tell him she would stay for as long as

he wanted her, but she didn't have the power of speech. All she could do was feel his mouth on hers and know that she'd finally found what she was looking for. All the time she'd spent searching and the answer was right in front of her. Zach was her solution. She should have known.

He didn't try to deepen the kiss. Instead, he kept brushing back and forth, so soft, so tender. As her body trembled, she clung to him. He was the strong and solid part of her world. The long fingers holding her face slipped against her skin in the lightest caress. As if she were fragile. As if she mattered.

He tilted her head toward him and kissed her forehead, then her nose and her cheeks. He returned his attention to her mouth and stroked his tongue against her bottom lip. Sensation shot through her, like lightning across a summer night sky. It burned through to the bottoms of her feet and the bottom of her heart.

She opened for him. Instead of slipping inside, he nibbled on her lips, teasing her, making her want him more. When she couldn't stand it another minute, she pushed her tongue forward until she reached his mouth. He parted and she slipped inside.

He tasted of passionate madness, of promise. He tasted as tempting as she remembered. They touched, tip to tip. They circled together. When she retreated, he followed her.

It was a kiss of reunited lovers. Her body recalled the ecstasy he'd brought her before and began to ache in anticipation. Memories returned, as tangled as the sheets on their bed so many years ago. Past and present merged, making her willing to brave the certain heartache that would follow.

His tongue explored her mouth, discovering points of pleasure. She sighed and returned the heated caresses.

He slipped his hands into her hair and tugged on the

pins holding it in place. She felt it tumble over her shoulders. He buried his fingers in the long strands.

"I'm glad you grew your hair," he whispered against her mouth.

"I thought you'd hate it."

"Why?"

They were standing pressed against each other. Her breasts flattened against his chest; their thighs brushed. His hands were in her hair; hers clutched at his waist. How could they be this intimate and still have a rational conversation? She was having trouble coming up with complete sentences, although he seemed to be doing fine.

She felt a flush stain her cheeks, but she tried to ignore it. "You're the one who wanted me to cut it in the first place."

"For safety reasons," he said. "You grew it back when you were an experienced agent."

She risked glancing up at him. A faint smile tugged at the corners of his mouth. "As simple as that?" she asked.

"You make things too complicated."

He bent down and kissed her neck. The moist heat of his mouth made her knees buckle. She clung to him. He moved lower, nibbling at the curve of her shoulders, then lower still, licking a line down to the V of her blouse.

Her breasts swelled in anticipation. She wanted him to touch her there. He seemed content to taste her exposed flesh.

When he returned his attention to her neck, she arched her head back, accepting his homage.

She drew her hands up his chest. His sweatshirt was old and faded. Through it she could feel the contours of his chest. He was thinner than he'd been seven years before, but she could still feel the strength of him, the ripple of his muscles under her touch. She moved slowly, massaging first up, then down, trying to lure him into a sensual trap.

He raised his head and stared at her. The fire burned out of control. "Tell me you've missed me, missed this," he coaxed.

She raised herself on tiptoes, then leaned close and pressed her mouth against his throat. She could feel the rapid thundering of his heart and the prickling stubble under his chin.

"You know I have."

He groaned when she sucked on his hot skin. "Yeah, me too."

It was as close to a confession of affection as she was likely to get. She raised her hands and wrapped her arms around his neck, pulling him down so she could kiss him. His mouth angled on hers. This time he took her as she remembered. Hard, hot and deep. Sexual desire exploded between them, loosening her fragile grip on sanity. She needed him; she wanted him. At last he was here.

He raised his head and stared at her. "What are you thinking?"

"About how much I want you."

"I've got you beat on that one." He touched her lips, then swiped his thumb across her mouth. She bit the sensitive pad.

His pupils dilated.

"Damn you," he murmured, but it was a benediction, not a curse.

He reached behind him and pulled her arms free from around his neck, then he knelt in front of her. Large hands cupped her slender hips. He buried his face into the fabric of her skirt.

"Don't doubt, Jamie. Anything but that," he said, then reached for the zipper on her skirt. As he pulled down the metal fastening, the material slipped over her hips and sank to the floor. "You're beautifully feminine. Soft and yielding—like silk."

Her panties were cotton, high cut on the thighs, but

more sensible than seductive. Zach didn't seem to mind. He pressed his mouth against her flat stomach. She had to clutch his shoulders to keep her balance. His hair tickled the back of her hands. The dark, silky strands invited a caress. Even as her legs were trembling, she risked falling and freed one hand to stroke his head.

His breath was hot through the thin cotton. One of his arms wrapped around her thighs, and one hand traveled the length of her legs as if rediscovering something once familiar. He found a scar about the size of a half dollar.

"This is new," he said.

"Bullet wound."

"I thought I taught you to be more careful than that."

"You did. I was just— Ah!"

His mouth closed over her most feminine place. Through the fabric of her panties, he bit down gently, raising her level of arousal to an unbearable pitch. He worked his teeth back and forth, grating deliciously, forcing her to focus all her attention on staying upright.

"Zach, I can't stand much more of this."

He stopped, and she had to hold back a whimper.

He stood up, then reached for the first button on her shirt. His large fingers worked quickly, as if a woman's clothing wasn't a mystery to him. It probably wasn't, but she didn't want to think about that. And when he pulled off her shirt and stared at her breasts, she found she didn't really care.

Her bra was as sensible as her panties. White cotton, underwire. Her breasts were average. Nice, but not her best feature. She wasn't sure she had a best feature. Zach apparently didn't agree.

He touched her gently, through her bra, cupping her breasts as if they were magical and precious. Lean fingers supported the curves while his thumb moved back and forth over her already erect nipples. The pleasure was too exquisite to be borne.

He dropped his hands to her behind and drew her hard against him. His arousal pressed into her belly. She ground her hips, trying to get closer still. They were both breathing heavily.

"Zach, please," she murmured.

"Yes," he said, his voice hoarse. "But not here."

He cupped her behind. She gave a little jump and wrapped her legs around his hips. In his weakened condition, she was probably too heavy for him, but he didn't seem to notice. He wrapped his arms around her waist and held on tight. She clutched his neck.

Their mouths met in a kiss that drove the air from their lungs and filled every cell with the need to make love. She was shaking and ready to be with him, under him. She needed his body to join with hers. She needed him to be a part of her.

He moved slowly into the larger bedroom, then settled on the edge of the king-size mattress. She spread her legs so she straddled him. Their gazes locked. She brought her fingers up to touch his face. Stubble rasped against her skin. Her mouth parted, and she traced the outline of his lips. A shudder ripped through him.

Every part of their joining felt right. This was where she belonged. With Zach.

Always with Zach.

Chapter 10

Jamie dropped her hands to Zach's shoulders, then tugged on his sweatshirt. "Let's see what you've got, sailor."

"You've seen it before."

"I know. That's why I want to see it again."

He grinned briefly, then pulled the sweatshirt over his head and tossed it on the floor. He stretched back on the bed, placing his hands on her hips and adjusting her so the apex of her thighs covered him. She shifted, teasing them both with a shimmer of pleasure, then turned her attention to his chest.

He was as beautiful as she remembered. Thinner, but still strong. She leaned over him and placed her hands on his shoulders. His skin was naturally darker than hers, a dusky color that tanned instantly. A pattern of hair, wide at the top, then narrowing to his waistband, emphasized the rippling outline of his muscles.

She traced a line down the center of his chest, then paused. Something wasn't right. Something had changed from the last time she'd seen him undressed. It took her a moment to figure it out, and when she did, once again she had to fight back the tears.

Dark smudges coiled across his chest and belly like snakes on the move. She touched one and frowned. What on earth had caused this?

He placed his hand over hers and squeezed her fingers. "The bruises," he said simply.

Realization dawned. The bruises from the chains went so deep, it had taken weeks for them to fade. Even now they weren't completely gone. She leaned forward and pressed her mouth against a mark just below his left nipple. His skin was hot and sweet. She found another bruise and kissed it, then another, as if her touch were enough to erase the hurt he'd endured.

He reached for her, slipping his fingers through her hair and bringing her face to his. Their lips brushed together. She opened for him, and he ravished her, plunging in as if he'd been lost a lifetime and she was his only way back. The intimate caress shot need and desire through her body. She clung to him to keep her sanity.

Strong arms encircled her shoulders. He shifted, and she rolled onto her back. They sprawled width-wise across the bed. One of his thighs nestled intimately between her legs, and a hand lay on her belly between her panties and her bra. His mouth continued to tease her. She inhaled the scent of him, savored the taste. She didn't want this moment to stop, even though she knew the truth.

There was a better-than-even chance Zach was doing this because he felt sorry for her. She'd claimed not to know how to be female, so he was fixing the problem the only way he knew how. By proving she was a desirable woman. The sweet gesture made her love him more. Perhaps she should question his motivation, but for now it was enough to be in his arms again.

He slipped one hand under her back and unfastened her

bra. She pulled the undergarment down her arms and let it fall off the side of the bed. He gazed at her breasts for a few seconds, then lowered his head and took a nipple in his mouth.

Jamie forgot to worry about why Zach was doing this. She forgot to think, even to breathe. She could only feel.

He drew the tight point in deeper. The moist heat and the flicking of his tongue made her want to scream. She writhed against him, rotating her hips, clutching at his arms. Pleasure raced through her, ricocheting down to her thighs, to her feet and hands, making every part of her tingle.

He reached up and cupped her other breast, holding it delicately, tracing the soft skin. Long fingers stroked the underside, then moved to the taut peak and rubbed it between his thumb and forefinger.

The combination of sensations was more than she could stand. She was forced to gasp for air. Every part of her was on fire. She couldn't imagine wanting him to ever stop. Better for them to stay this way always—she would die in ultimate pleasure.

A soft giggle escaped her lips.

He raised his head. "And here I thought I was doing it right." His eyes were dark with passion, his mouth moist from their kisses.

She brushed the backs of her fingers against the side of his face. "I was thinking that I don't want you to stop, ever. In a hundred years, they'll find our bones on this bed. Whatever will the archaeologists think?"

"That it's not a bad way to go. If they find your picture, they'll be jealous as hell."

Her throat closed with emotion. Just when she least expected it, he said the perfect thing. She tried to give him a smile, but her lips trembled too much. He kissed her briefly, then returned his attention to her breasts, shifting slightly so he could switch sides. Heat began to spiral inside her. If only they could spend the rest of their lives like this. No questions or decisions, only bringing each other pleasure.

He suckled on her breast until everything else was forgotten, then he moved lower, nibbling a damp path to her belly button. Once there, he pushed down her panties and drew them off her legs.

He knelt between her thighs and stared at her body. "You're incredible." He ran his palms up her thighs, kneading the muscles there. "Did you really carry me the two miles to the jeep?"

"No. I carried you a mile and a half. Rick met me and carried you the rest of the way."

"I was deadweight and I outweighed you by about twenty pounds."

She shrugged, feeling a little self-conscious. "There really wasn't any alternative. I figured if I tried to steal one of their jeeps, they would notice. If it makes you feel any better, I cursed you the whole way."

"I'll just bet you did. What did you say?"

It was hard to concentrate on his words when his hands continued to move up and down her legs. On the upstroke, his thumbs swept tantalizingly close to the place that would bring her pleasure. She wanted to part her thighs and beg him to take her. But she was enjoying their conversation too much.

Their lovemaking was different this time. More relaxed and playful. Was it age that had mellowed them, or the familiarity of the rite? She decided it didn't matter. This was the Zach she loved, and she wanted to spend as much time with him as possible.

"I reminded you that if you'd had your way, I wouldn't have ever been in the agency and then no one would have come after you to save your sorry hide," she said.

His hands stilled. His fingers rested on her knees.

"You're right. And then when I saw you for the first time, I didn't even have the courtesy to thank you, did I?"

She shook her head. "You told me to get the hell out of your hospital room."

His mouth twisted down. "Sometimes I can be a jerk."

"Tell me about it."

"Thank you for believing that I was still alive and for coming back to get me."

At that moment, with her lying naked to his gaze and their bodies about to join in the most intimate way possible, she wanted to tell him that she loved him.

She didn't.

Regardless of their physical intimacy, he wouldn't want to be burdened with the workings of her heart. Instead, she chose a safer route.

"Thank you for not dying."

"My pleasure."

He lowered himself onto the bed. She spread her legs and closed her eyes in anticipation. Gently he touched a single finger to her most secret place, dipping it into the waiting heat, circling, then moving higher to that tiny point of ecstasy.

Her reaction was instantaneous and electric. Intense pleasure swept through her. Her hips tilted toward him, she drew her knees up, her fingers clutched at the comforter. She rocked her head from side to side and begged him not to stop.

"Not so fast," he murmured. "I want to take my time."

"I'll die."

He chuckled. She felt his warm breath fan her thighs. He shifted, reached for her and parted the protective folds, exposing her to his gaze. She didn't care. The sensation he brought was so intense, he could do anything he wanted. She would never complain, never protest, never—

He touched her with his tongue. She half rose into a sitting position, then sank back on the bed and groaned. He tasted her, licking her gently, as if rediscovering a favorite treat. She breathed his name.

He touched her again, flicking against her over and over in a rhythm designed to make her his slave. She still remembered the first time Zach had touched her that way. She'd been shocked at the intimacy and uncomfortable with the concept. Until he'd actually brought her to release that way. The experience had been so intense, she'd been afraid she would faint, or scream, or both.

Now she sank into the sensual sensations, giving up control and free will to his mastery.

Muscles tensed in anticipation of her release. His tongue continued to move lightly, quickly, taking her past reason. One finger slipped inside of her. He circled around the sensitive opening, those movements a delicious counterpoint to what he was doing with his tongue.

She tried to open her eyes but couldn't. She tried to speak his name, but her body failed her. Every cell focused on the unbearable sensation. Tension built. Her muscles clenched tightly; her breathing came in short gasps. She could see the release. Behind closed lids, the colors of the world appeared to her. So close, so close.

He stopped moving. For a second, her body hung suspended, then gently sank back to earth. Muscles relaxed, breathing slowed. The momentum was lost, control taken from her.

She laughed, the sound husky. "You're determined to make me suffer, aren't you?"

"Just playing."

She knew about his games. They left her weak and satisfied to her bones. She willed herself to ease into nothingness and let him have his way.

At first she barely felt his tongue on her. The light touch was more of a whisper than actual contact. She forced herself to stay calm, to ignore the insistent need to rush forward toward her climax. As his movements quickened, she consciously held back, letting him pull her along rather than pushing to the finish.

In less than a minute, he had her quivering on the brink again. The finger circling her plunged inside, mimicking the act of love. She arched against him. Once again he stopped, but this time just for a heartbeat. She hung, suspended over a bottomless pit. He stroked her once with his tongue, then drew her into his mouth.

She exploded into a thousand perfect pieces. Satisfaction filled every pore. Wave after wave surged through her until she thought she might never stop experiencing the joy of being with him again.

Slowly she returned to awareness. Zach's head lay on her thigh. His finger continued to slip in and out of her, making her shudder with lingering delight.

She touched his hair, letting the silky strands tease her fingertips. "Thank you," she murmured.

"My pleasure."

"Not exactly."

He glanced at her. Fire still burned in his dark irises. "Yeah, it was." He pressed a kiss on her flat stomach, then sat up.

She shifted on the bed to give him more room. He stood up and pulled off his sweatpants and briefs. His maleness was hard and ready. She stared at him, feeling the desire build again. She wanted him inside of her.

But instead of joining her, he bent over the nightstand and started to dig through the top drawer.

"What are you looking for?" she asked.

"What do you think? I hope I didn't throw them out."

Protection. She'd forgotten.

He pulled out a box that looked vaguely familiar. "How old are those?" she asked.

He frowned. "Old. They're from the last time you and

I..." His voice trailed off, and he looked uncomfortable, as if he'd confessed something he'd meant to keep to himself.

Jamie sat up and reached for his arm. She tugged him down on the bed and kissed him. Her heart swelled with gladness. He hadn't had anyone at the cabin since her. Oh, he'd been with other women, but none of that mattered. He hadn't brought one *here.* This was their refuge. She hadn't been wrong to keep believing in him.

She broke the kiss. "Don't go anywhere," she said, and slipped off the bed.

She walked to her room and rooted around in her suitcase. The condoms were in the corner. When she returned with them, Zach raised his eyebrows.

"You always did plan ahead."

Color heated her cheeks. "These weren't for you," she said as she handed him the box.

"Then for who?"

"No one. Rick gave them to me as a going-away present. They were meant as a joke."

He opened the box and pulled out one of the flat packages. "I always liked Rick's sense of humor." He tugged on her hand, then pulled her down next to him. "Where were we?"

He kissed her thoroughly, cupped her breasts in his hands and teased the nipples into hard peaks. When desire filled her again, he put on his protection and knelt between her thighs.

He didn't enter her right away. Instead, he brushed the hair from her face and stared at her. "Don't doubt yourself," he said. "You're the most amazing woman I've ever met. The outside trappings don't matter. It's what's here." He touched her head. "And here." He placed his hand above her left breast. "And here." He pushed into her.

She wanted to reply, but for a moment, all she could

do was feel him slowly moving inside of her. It had been a long time, and her body was tight. He groaned low in his throat. She raised her hips, urging him forward, and he slid home.

Once there, he braced his weight on his elbows and kissed her. "No more worry about not being a woman, okay?"

She slipped her arms around to his back and stroked his skin. She could feel his muscles rippling under her questing fingers. "I'm not just a woman. I'm a warrior."

He flexed inside of her. "Don't say that," he gasped as he withdrew and plunged in again.

"Why?"

The muscles in his neck and face tightened. "Because we're making love and I'm inside of you. This isn't the time to tell me I'm doing it with a warrior."

She laughed.

He moaned. "That feels great. Laugh again."

She giggled. "I can't laugh on command."

He continued to move in and out of her. "Sure you can. These two guys walk into a bar."

She touched his face, and he glanced down at her. "What?"

"I don't remember laughing before. Thank you."

He smiled and said again, "My pleasure."

"I think the pleasure is mutual."

"Yeah?"

"It would be if you'd stop talking."

"When'd you get to be so bossy?"

"Zach!"

"Okay, I'll be quiet."

He was as good as his word. He sank into her again and withdrew. Over and over until her body began to collect itself for another release. She tried to watch his face, wanting to see when he was near his climax, but she couldn't concentrate on anything but the feelings between her thighs. He filled her completely and left her no option but to follow him into an ecstasy that left them clinging together in an aftermath of fire.

Zach woke sometime after midnight. He felt rested and figured he'd probably been asleep for nearly seven hours. A two-mile jog and hot sex were a powerful combination.

He shifted so he could face Jamie. Moonlight streamed in through the window above the bed; otherwise, the room was dark. Her blond hair spread over the pillow. He touched one strand, rubbing it between his fingers—silk, so damn soft, just like her skin.

He could make out her high cheekbone and the shape of her mouth. The rest of her features were lost in shadow. But he knew everything about her. The muscles defining her arms, the sweep of her ribs and narrow waist, the jut of her hipbones, the power of her legs. She'd changed a lot in the past seven years, yet he could still recognize her in the dark.

He inhaled, smelling the combined scent of their bodies and the musky fragrance of sex. Just thinking about what they'd done made him want her again. Desire stirred between his legs. It would be easy to part her thighs and enter her again. She wouldn't protest.

But he didn't. He would rather watch her sleep, at least for now.

He slowed his breathing so she couldn't know he was awake. But Jamie was one of the best field agents. She sensed his attention and opened her eyes. A smile hovered uncertainly at the corner of her mouth, as if she wasn't sure what her reception would be.

Unfamiliar feelings threatened. He wanted to tell her it was going to be all right. Yet he knew that wasn't true. Whatever Jamie had come looking for, he wasn't the person to provide it. If he kept up the emotional facade of being available for her, he was bound to hurt her. Logically he should tell her that right now. But he couldn't. He needed this, too.

He picked up her hand and kissed her palm. Her breath caught, then she smiled.

He'd seen her smile dozens of times, maybe hundreds. This one caught him like a sucker punch to the stomach. Pain flared, and with it, vulnerability.

"How long have we been asleep?" she asked.

"Too long. I'm starved."

"Me, too."

He got out of bed and pulled on a pair of jeans. She stood up, then glanced around for clothes. Hers were in the other room. He thought about the skirt and blouse she'd had on. They'd been all wrong for her. Acting on impulse, he opened the wardrobe and snagged one of his cotton long-sleeved shirts. He tossed it to her.

When she caught it, she glanced at him. "An interesting kind of bathrobe."

"Humor me. I want to look at your legs."

It was too dark for him to see what she was thinking, but he hoped she blushed.

Together they walked into the kitchen, flipping on lights as they went. The clock on the wall showed the time to be nearly one-thirty—their usual hour for restlessness. But instead of escaping to the porch or wanting to be alone, Zach was content to spend time with Jamie.

While he started coffee, she opened the refrigerator. "We've got some defrosted steaks, potatoes, vegetables."

"Too heavy," he said.

"How about eggs and toast?"

"Perfect."

He clicked on the coffeepot, then reached for the carton of eggs.

"I'll cook," she said. "You go sit down. This kitchen is too small for both of us."

He allowed her to push him into a chair at the small

dinette. Watching her work was hardly a hardship. The tails of his shirt fell to midthigh on her, but the sides exposed her legs nearly to her hips. She moved with the easy grace of a dancer; her breasts swayed against the cotton shirt.

Passing time had left her more comfortable with her body. He remembered the first time she'd cooked for him in his kitchen. She'd been wearing a nightshirt and nothing else. She'd spent the whole time tugging at the short hem.

So much had changed, yet one thing remained the same—the heat they generated in bed.

"Scrambled okay?" she asked as she pulled eggs out of the refrigerator.

"Great."

She cracked several into a bowl, then whipped them with a fork. Her movements were smooth and practiced.

"Do you cook much?" he asked.

"Almost never. It's impossible on assignment, and when I'm home, it doesn't seem worth it to cook for just me."

An uncomfortable thought occurred to him. "There's no one else?"

She looked up. Her hazel eyes were almost gray in the bright light. "A man? As in a relationship?"

He nodded.

"Zach, I wouldn't be here with you if I was involved with someone else."

"I know, but what about before? It's been a long time since you and I..." He trailed off, not sure what to say about them.

She poured the egg mixture into the frying pan, then put toast into the toaster. He stood up and headed for the refrigerator. While she cooked, he set the table, adding butter and jam, coffee cups and plates.

"There have been one or two interested parties," she

admitted. "But no one I wanted to spend the rest of my life with. What about you?"

"I prefer to travel light."

He watched her and wondered if he believed what she was saying. In seven long years, she hadn't once fallen in love? It would be easy enough to ask the question—assuming he wanted the answer. He didn't. The fact that he didn't want to know about the men in her past annoyed him.

The toast popped. He stuck in two more slices of bread and set the brown ones on a plate. Jamie finished the eggs and served them. They sat down together.

They'd eaten at the small table before. They were both tall, and their legs brushed. Before, he'd tried not to notice. Now he relished it. After all, they'd just made love. He'd tasted every part of her body and listened to her quiet cries of passion. They'd become intimate again, and it scared the hell out of him.

They didn't talk while they ate. When he'd finished his eggs and was buttering his third piece of toast, he glanced at her. She sat angled toward him, one knee pulled up to her chest. She'd rolled the sleeves of his shirt up to her wrists. The extra fabric made her look fine boned and petite. He knew she was strong, but at that moment it didn't seem possible that she'd really carried him through the desert.

"You risked your life going on a rescue mission without knowing for certain I was alive?"

She looked up at him. Her eyes widened. "I just had a feeling."

"You risked everything for a feeling?"

"Gee, now you sound like Winston. I can't explain it better than that. I wish I could. Remember that time, right after graduation, when we were in the jungle together?"

He nodded. He'd requested her on her first assignment because he'd known what her weakness was. He'd planned to force her to face it. Instead, the lesson had backfired. Not only had Jamie been captured, but she'd nearly been killed. If anything had happened to her, he didn't know how he would have survived.

"I had a feeling that night before the ambush," she continued. "When I finally mentioned it, you told me to pay attention to those feelings. You said they'd keep me alive. You were right. I've always listened to them. It's weird. Sometimes I just know things." She ducked her head. "I knew the day you were coming to the cabin. I can't explain why, I just had a feeling."

"Why didn't you just convince Winston of your feeling and let him send in a team? Why just you and Rick?"

"A team had already failed. Our plan was simple."

"You both could have been killed."

She shrugged. "It was a risk we were willing to take."

He slapped his palm on the table. "Why?"

"I owed you, Zach. You saved my life."

"Bull. You paid that debt when you shot the guard in the jungle. Quit jerking me around and tell me the truth."

Her only response to his harsh words was to smile faintly. He had to admire her guts. No one got the better of her.

"The truth is you saved my life a hundred times," she said at last. "In every difficult situation, in every rough spot, I remembered what you'd taught me. You kept me alive. That's why I came for you."

He studied her face, but she was too good for him to know if she was lying. He knew there had to be more, but what? Then he decided he didn't want to know. Better if all Jamie felt was gratitude. That he could handle. Anything else, anything emotional, would be deadly for both of them. He wouldn't risk feeling. Not ever.

She stood up and carried their plates to the sink. "You should be grateful," she said. "Who else cares as much about you?"

"You're right," he said.

She picked up a towel and wiped her hands, then turned toward him. "Now it's my turn to ask questions. Why didn't you make me leave?"

He didn't want to answer that. He wasn't sure himself and he wasn't about to try to figure it out. Danger signs flashed in his head every time he thought about Jamie.

He looked at her bare feet, then raised his gaze higher to her legs, then her face. "Take off the shirt," he said.

"What?"

"You heard me."

He stood up and unbuttoned his jeans. When he pushed them off, her gaze locked on his arousal, now free, and her eyes widened.

"Zach?"

"What are you afraid of?"

Her shoulders straightened. "Nothing."

She unfastened the buttons, then shrugged out of the shirt. It fell silently to the floor. She walked closer, until she was in front of him. He sat in the chair, spread his legs, and she moved close enough to touch.

He brushed his hands against her hips, her waist, her breasts, then lower, slipping one finger between her thighs. She was already hot and wet. He found her center and circled around it. A ripple sped through her. She grabbed his shoulder for balance.

When he raised his gaze to her face, he found her watching him. Every flicker of pleasure registered on her face. As he brought her closer, her breathing increased, but she didn't close her eyes. It was as if she dared him to watch her climax.

He moved faster, driven by the need to see her shatter at his touch. With his free hand, he reached up and teased her hard nipples. A flush spread from her chest to her neck. Her mouth parted to draw in more air. Her whole body quivered.

She forced her eyes to stay open through the moment of fulfillment. He could see her effort. Spasms drew her mouth straight and tightened her legs around his hand. She gasped for air. He felt as if he'd seen down to her soul. The intimacy shocked him.

Before he could withdraw both physically and emotionally, she pushed his legs together, then straddled him. It happened so fast, as he entered her, he could feel the lingering aftershocks of her release. Then it was too late to think about escaping.

She touched him nowhere but between his legs. Her body rose and lowered with amazing control. He felt himself being milked to the point of no return.

Her gaze met his. While she had been brave, he was not. He closed his eyes, unwilling to let her see the horror he kept locked inside. Then he brought his mouth to hers and kissed her. With a clench of her powerful muscles, she brought him to the edge and forced him over the side.

Jamie opened her eyes and blinked. Something was wrong, but it took her a second to figure out what it was. She glanced around Zach's bedroom, then realized it was light. Sunshine streamed in through the window. Morning had come, and she'd slept through most of the night.

She sat up and rubbed her face. She was alone. The thought didn't terrify her. Not after yesterday and last night. Her fearlessness wasn't just because of the amazing sex, although that had been enough to heal whatever might have ailed her. It was the connection. She and Zach had bonded on a primitive and lasting level.

She flopped back in bed and grinned. Parts of her ached that hadn't ached in years. She felt alive and happy and hopeful. There were still lots of things for them to work out. Differences to overcome. Zach had his demons to fight. But this morning, for the first time, she could believe in the promise of being happy.

She stood up and stretched. Her body was stiff from the unaccustomed activity. She needed a good run to loosen her up. That's probably what Zach was doing.

She walked into her room and pulled on sweats. After washing her face and brushing her teeth, she headed into the kitchen. It was empty, but he'd made coffee before leaving. She smiled at his thoughtfulness. If she hadn't already fallen for the man, she would have done it right then.

She poured herself a cup, then walked to the front window. She couldn't see him, just the tall pine trees and the blue sky. She sipped and let the contentment slip over her.

She'd fallen asleep in his arms. They'd talked of silly things until exhaustion had stolen their words. She recalled him rolling over and pulling her closer. As if he'd needed her next to him. As if...

She set the coffee down and frowned. Even as she fought them, the doubts returned. Had Zach gone running because he needed to be alone? Did he regret their intimacy? They'd started making love because he'd felt sorry for her. Maybe he'd just been without for a long time, and that's why he'd—

"Stop it," she said aloud. "Don't do this to yourself. Have a little faith in you and Zach. He's not like that."

The words made her feel a little better. She headed for the front door and pulled it open. As she stepped out on the porch, she heard an unfamiliar sound. She froze in midstep and turned to her left.

The Bronco stood where she'd parked it. The hood was up, and Zach climbed into the driver's side. He turned the key, and the engine sprang to life.

Her knees buckled. She had to grab the railing to keep from going down. He'd found the battery. He was leaving her.

It wasn't fair, she screamed silently. Not now, not after

they'd just found each other. It wasn't right. She deserved her chance.

She didn't mean to make a sound, but she must have. Zach looked up and saw her. She didn't dare think about what he must be reading on her face. The pain at having everything within her grasp and having it ripped away.

He got out of the vehicle and slowly walked toward her. Sunlight glinted off his dark hair. She swallowed hard and forced herself to straighten. He might be able to rip her heart out, but she would never let him know how much it hurt. It looked as if pride was all she was going to have left.

"How'd you sleep?" he asked when he reached the porch stairs.

She glanced down at him and willed herself to be strong. "Great, and you?"

"Not bad, considering." He looked at the truck. "I found the battery."

"I guessed that."

He shoved his hands into his jeans pockets. "I was thinking. Denver's not that far away. You want to go into the city, maybe stay for a couple of nights? Eat out, take in a movie?"

She didn't get it at first. She was so prepared to hear that he'd made up his mind to leave that the change in direction caught her unaware. She blinked and let everything sink in. Denver? Go to a restaurant?

The silence stretched between them. Something very like apprehension flickered in his eyes. If she didn't know better, she would swear he was nervous.

"Really?" she asked, not daring to believe he wasn't going to leave her.

"Yeah. It would be fun."

She launched herself off the porch. He caught her hard

against him and hauled her close. She wrapped her arms around his shoulders and her thighs around his hips.

"Is that a yes?" he asked, then laughed.

She kissed him. "What do you think?"

Chapter 11

They left the cabin before ten in the morning and arrived in Denver shortly after stopping for lunch at an inn with a beautiful view of the mountains. They picked a downtown hotel for their stay. Jamie followed Zach into the exclusive establishment, where he asked for a suite. Minutes later they were shown to the spacious lodgings and left alone.

Jamie prowled the luxurious space. The single-bedroom suite was larger than her apartment in San Francisco. "And decorated better," she murmured with appreciation as she studied the sitting room.

It had been done in antiques. A sideboard held a crystal decanter set. An elegant armoire housed both a television and a VCR. There was a small wet bar tucked discreetly in the corner, fully stocked, of course.

The bedroom was just as impressive. Pale blue dominated. A silky spread covered the king-size mattress tucked into a sleigh bed. In the bathroom was a Jacuzzi tub big enough for two, a separate stall shower, two vanities and a phone.

She picked up the receiver and listened. Sure enough, there was a dial tone.

"Just in case you get a hot tip on the stock market," Zach said, coming up behind her and wrapping his arms around her body. "You wouldn't want to waste a moment."

She glanced up at him in the mirror and smiled. "My broker does complain about how difficult it is to track me down sometimes."

"I'll bet."

His energy from the previous night seemed to have faded. Dark smudges stained the skin under his eyes, and his mouth looked drawn. He shifted his weight slightly and winced.

Jamie turned toward him. "What's wrong?"

"Just all the activity catching up with me. Don't worry about it."

She placed her hands on her hips. "I asked you to let me help with the driving, but no. You had to do it all yourself. Typical macho posturing. May I remind you I'm strong enough to save your life by carrying you across the desert, so maybe you should listen to me."

He bent down and kissed the tip of her nose. "No."

"Zach!"

"All right. What do you want to say?"

"That we should try sleeping this afternoon. We're not likely to sleep well tonight."

His eyebrows rose. She fought embarrassment. "I really mean sleep. Not that. We're both going to wake up at two in the morning. There'll be plenty of time to do the wild thing then."

"The wild thing?"

She ignored him and pushed at the center of his back. He allowed her to guide him toward the bed. Once there, he peeled back the covers, then stripped down to briefs before crawling between the sheets.

"Aren't you joining me?" he asked.

"Not yet. I slept a lot last night. I'll be in shortly."

"What if I get lonely?"

She bent over and kissed him briefly. "I can see you're exhausted, so while that invitation is intriguing, we both know it's just cheap talk."

He stifled a yawn. "I think I liked you better back when you were a rookie and still in awe of me."

"I was never in awe of you."

He pulled up the covers. "Sure, you were. You used to stare at my butt during class."

She fought against embarrassment. Was he guessing or had he really noticed? She made a guess of her own. "And you couldn't keep your attention off of mine when we were working out together."

He closed his eyes and grinned. "You're right."

She laughed softly. "Go to sleep."

She left the bedroom and closed the door behind her. So he had been looking. The thought pleased her. Sure, it had been a long time ago, and sure, he'd broken her heart. But it was nice to know the attraction had been mutual.

Once in the parlor, she opened the small refrigerator, poured herself a soda and settled on a sofa in front of one of the wide windows. From here she could see tall buildings and a bit of the city beyond. After weeks of being at the cabin, all this life was shocking to her. It was always like that coming off an assignment. The volume of humanity startled her. There had been times she'd felt like the only living person in the world. Then she returned to a civilization that seemed like an anthill of activity. Everyone had a place to go but her. Alone by herself or alone in a crowd, it still came down to lonely.

She stared out the window and fought a feeling of uneasiness. She knew why she was unsettled, but she didn't want to think about it. No one liked dealing with a personal weakness. But she didn't have a choice.

When she'd seen Zach working on the truck this morning, why had she instantly assumed he was leaving her? Was her assumption of the worst about her, or about him? She'd been in relationships before. She'd met men she'd cared about. No one had touched her the way Zach had, but a few could have stolen her heart...if she'd let them.

Was that the difference? Usually she was pretty rational in her relationships. She had a good time, laughed, shared stories, went out. Some of the men had even been lovers. She'd been responsive and had enjoyed the experience. But never had she felt out of control. Her emotions were kept carefully in check. When she found herself drifting toward getting serious, she'd stopped long enough to consider her options and what she really wanted to do.

She'd been logical, knowing that her job didn't allow for long-term commitments. Walking away hadn't always been simple, but she hadn't regretted any of her decisions to do so.

Why was it so different with Zach?

She sipped on her soda, then leaned back on the sofa. What was it about the man that got to her? She hadn't been logical this morning. She hadn't considered her options. She'd reacted, assuming he was leaving her. The pain had taken her breath away. Why did he have that kind of power over her?

She closed her eyes and fought against the truth. The battle didn't last very long, and in the end, the truth won. Zach could destroy her with a word because she loved him with all her heart. With those other men, she'd held back pieces of herself. If the relationship didn't work out, she could walk away whole. With Zach that wasn't possible. She loved him fully, with every fiber. If he rejected her, then each cell in her body would bear its share of the pain.

It was more than just loving him. She'd committed to him with her very soul. That left her vulnerable and made it difficult to be logical. She wanted to be with him, no matter what. Even if it meant more pain later.

She wondered if he understood the power he had over her, then figured he probably didn't. The Zach she knew didn't deal with intangibles like love and commitment. Which was, she acknowledged, a terrifying thought.

Neither of them had ever been in a long-term relationship.

Neither of them had been married or even engaged. Neither of them had ever been normal, by the world's definition of the word. She was willing to try, but she didn't know what he wanted. For now it was enough to go on with things the way they were. This once, she was willing to risk her heart for a chance at something she'd never dared to dream about. This kind of love was worth the potential heartache.

In her heart, she wanted to believe it was going to work out. That by being together, she could convince Zach to join her on her journey to find her way to a regular life. She didn't think he could survive going back to the field. He'd used up most of his luck. Next time she wouldn't be around to rescue him. Next time he might die. And if not next time, then soon. If he stayed, it was inevitable.

Would he be willing to leave? Could he walk away? Would he face down the past and everything that went along with it? Would he be willing to feel? To love?

She didn't have any answers. She could only go forward on faith, hoping that her love was enough. At times she believed everything would be fine. How could he turn his back on what they could have together? At other times, she wasn't so sure. After all, he'd already broken her heart once.

She continued to stare out the window at the city. At some point, she must have dozed off, because when she next looked out, lights had come on in the offices across the street.

The sitting room was dark. She stood up, straightened and stretched, easing the kinks in her muscles. Her soda was warm and flat. The grandfather clock by the front door chimed the hour.

The floor lamps came on with the touch of a button on the wall. She walked over to the antique desk in the corner and found the room-service menu, then she headed for the bedroom.

The large room was dark. Drapes had been pulled across the windows. She couldn't tell if Zach was asleep or awake. She hesitated, then figured it was important for him to eat.

"Zach," she said softly from her place by the door. "It's seven. Are you hungry?"

He reached for the lamp on the nightstand, turning it on, then sat up. Dark hair tumbled onto his forehead. He hadn't shaved that morning, and stubble shadowed his jaw. He was a dangerous man, every inch a predator. She thrilled at his male beauty and wanted nothing more than to go to him and make love. But there was something odd about his expression, something that made her stay by the safety of the door.

"I was awake," he said.

"Did you sleep?"

"For a few hours."

"Good." She studied his face. "What's wrong?"

His mouth twisted down. "You stood by the door and called my name. Why didn't you come to the bed and shake my shoulder to wake me up?"

She laughed. "Because I'm a damn good agent and I don't want you ripping off my head. I mean that literally."

She'd learned early on that most agents were like tigers—dangerous awake, deadly asleep. She'd forgotten the rule once on assignment and had touched a sleeping agent's arm. In less time than it took to draw a breath, he'd had her pinned beneath him, a knife blade at her throat. It had been her first year out of training. She'd never made the mistake again.

She hugged the menu close to her chest. Zach didn't join in her laughter. His mouth twisted down.

"You don't seem satisfied with the answer," she said.

He waved his hand. "It's not that. You're right. You are a good agent. What does it say about us that we are reduced to just rooting?"

"It means we stay alive."

His gaze met hers. "I'm glad you're getting out, Jamie. You deserve more than what this job has to offer."

She didn't like hearing him say that. "It's not so hard. You could come with me. If we stayed in bed and made love all the time, we wouldn't have to worry about getting enough exercise." She forced herself to sound teasing and playful when in fact she was deadly serious.

He shook his head. "It's too late for me. Hell, it was probably too late when I first signed up."

"That's not true. Why would you believe that?"

He shrugged but didn't answer.

She knew he'd been through a lot more than she had. His childhood, growing up with parents who weren't interested in him, serving four years in a juvenile facility, plus time in the military. Then fourteen years with the agency on some difficult assignments, including his last one. How many times had he faced death and walked away?

"Was it worth it?" she asked, not really expecting an answer. "Was the job worth your life?"

"The job is my life. I never thought I had a choice. And now I don't know any different. I've been out too long. Tucked too much inside. Even if I could find my way back, I'm not sure I'd do it. What's the point?''

"How about something less dangerous? Surely that's worth a little effort?''

"You're talking about being normal. For me normal has always been a bizarre concept.''

He was hiding from the truth, she thought with a flash of insight. It wasn't that leaving the agency didn't appeal to him; it was that he believed the price would be too high to get out. He had too much locked away. The thought of letting it out must be terrifying.

In the past, he'd hinted that feeling meant destruction. Was that true or just an excuse?

She thought about pushing the point, but Zach was stubborn enough to choose not to cooperate if he thought that best.

"We could go out to dinner if you want,'' she said, changing the subject. "But it seems like a hassle to me. Why don't we just order in?''

"Sounds great.''

She walked to the bed and handed him the menu. While he studied it, she wondered if she was really capable of saving Zach. After all, she hadn't saved herself yet.

"I can't believe you ordered that,'' Zach said, pointing at Jamie's dinner.

She looked up and grinned. Since they'd made love the previous night, she hadn't tied her hair back in a braid. It hung loose around her shoulders. In her sweatshirt and jeans, with bare feet and no makeup, she looked about as sophisticated as a puppy at a formal dinner.

"Why not? It's everything I've been craving. When I bought food for the cabin, I was more concerned with healthy foods that wouldn't spoil. This is heaven.'' She speared another piece of lettuce from her salad.

She'd ordered two green salads, a fruit salad and french

fries. Zach shuddered at the combination. He, too, had wanted a salad, but just one, and a steak—served rare.

"Speaking of weird," she said. "Why are you eating raw meat?"

"It's not raw."

"Sure, it is. It's probably not even warm." She grimaced. "I suppose I should be grateful it's not goat."

"You don't like goat?"

"Not anymore." She wrinkled her nose. "I was in a little village in the Middle East a few years ago. I stayed with this family, posing as a visiting relative. There were guns being smuggled in and out of the village. Anyway, they didn't really have room for me, so I slept under a lean-to with the goats. There was this one young goat that always curled up next to me. We really got to be friends."

He could imagine the scene. Jamie's blond hair dyed dark brown. Dirt smudging her face. By day she would have fit in with the other women, performing household chores. At night she would have slipped into the village and figured out what was going on. He wished he could have been there to see her.

"You bonded with a goat?" he asked, teasing her.

She laughed. "Sort of. So I found the gunrunners, took care of the problem. The family's oldest son was involved with them. I managed to get him out so he wasn't caught and taken away to prison. They were very grateful." She popped a french fry into her mouth and sighed. "Heaven. That night they prepared a special dinner. Goat, of course. I wasn't too concerned until I went to go to sleep and my friend was missing."

Zach tried to appear sympathetic, but he couldn't help chuckling. "They served you your friend."

"Exactly." She shuddered. "I haven't had goat since."

"Try two weeks in the desert with no supplies. Goat would have looked pretty good."

She reached for her glass. They'd ordered wine with dinner. "Where was that?"

"Africa."

"James Bond makes it look so easy," she said. "Fancy technology, close escapes, great clothes. In the movies, no one mentions how bad you smell after living with livestock or camping in the desert."

"Agreed. But I still like James Bond."

She leaned back in her chair and grinned. "Me, too. Okay—longest assignment and where?"

"Eight months, South America."

She stuck her tongue out. "Mine was a year."

He cut off a piece of steak. "Yeah, but where?"

"Berlin."

"There's a hardship. Living in a house, having access to electricity and stores. Boy, Jamie, what a rough life."

"It was hard," she said, sounding faintly indignant, although it was difficult to take her seriously as she licked the salt from the fries off her fingers. "I had to learn German. I did okay, but my accent was very shaky."

"Strangest escape," he said.

She thought for a second. "Pretending to be a sheepherder in the Ukraine."

"Air balloon from China to India."

"Oh, I guess you win that one."

They continued to play the game, comparing assignments without sharing details. They were both too good to let secrets slip out, even with each other. It was an odd way to pass the evening, but he enjoyed it. He hadn't ever shared much about his work. Jamie was different from any woman he'd ever known.

His experience with the opposite sex was limited to brief encounters. He'd had his share of lovers, although none of them had stayed long enough for him to get used to them. As a rule, he preferred those who didn't demand much. He liked being able to walk away without leaving anything of himself behind. Someone easily bought off with an expensive bauble.

Jamie wasn't like that. She expected more. With her he was often tempted to share all of it, even though he knew the danger. With her he wanted to believe it was possible even though it wasn't.

She looked up at him. "Zach, when did you find the Bronco battery?"

"A couple of days ago."

"Before we—" She cleared her throat.

"Yeah, before." Before they had become lovers. Before she'd tempted him with the silky heat of her body.

"Why didn't you leave?"

He didn't have an honest answer for that. Not one he was willing to share. He hadn't been ready to go. He knew this time when he left her, it was forever. She'd forgiven him once—he wasn't going to get a second chance.

"We had a deal," he said lightly. "I have to be able to run to the highway and back."

She didn't look as if she believed him. For a moment, he thought she might pursue the question, then she let it go.

She'd once asked him if he had regrets. He had one. Her. But he wasn't sure if he regretted having her in his life or having to let her go.

Chapter 12

Jamie jogged in place at the stoplight. It was a perfect spring morning in Denver, the kind of day that made tourists think about permanently moving to a place. A few white, puffy clouds added contrast to the brilliant blue sky. The mountain peaks were still snowcapped, but the city was lush and green with budding trees and new grass.

It was barely after eight in the morning, and her breath formed small clouds as she breathed. Around her, businesspeople in suits hurried to their offices, their expressions intense, their strides inhibited by dress shoes. For once Jamie didn't mind being dressed differently. Although she often thought about trying to look like everyone else, right now she didn't want to be anywhere else. She was happy in shorts and a sweatshirt, no makeup and her long hair tied back in a ponytail. She fit in right where she was—at Zach's side.

"You're breathing pretty hard, Jones," she teased.

He wiped sweat from his brow and grinned. "Don't worry about me, Sanders. I can keep up."

The light turned green, and they started across the street. Jamie set their pace. She kept them at a slow jog, knowing Zach wasn't up to a hundred percent yet. Every step was a fight because she wanted to race around, running hard and fast with the sheer joy of being alive. She'd been happy before; she'd even felt joy. But she'd never experienced this soul-healing sense of being one with the universe, of knowing that it was all going to work out.

She turned and jogged backward. "Thanks for suggesting we come here," she said. "I love this city."

He shrugged. "It's pretty nice. I usually avoid people when I'm at the cabin, but I've never spent more than a couple of weeks there at a time. All that solitude starts to play with my mind."

"So you were suffering from cabin fever, too?"

His gaze met hers. Something wild and passionate surged to life. She felt the heat clear down to her toes.

"Oh, yeah," he said.

She flushed and faced front again, so he wouldn't see. Cabin fever brought on by her presence? She hoped so. She would like to think that she got to him.

After all, he got to her in a big way.

As they dodged pedestrian traffic, she thought about last night. They'd laughed about their time with the agency, something that didn't happen very often. By an unspoken agreement, they'd only shared the funny times. Then they'd returned to bed.

They hadn't made love. Instead, Zach had held her long into the night. He'd stroked her hair and whispered her name in the darkness. In a way, it had been more intimate than any physical joining. She'd known that time was specifically about her, and not because he had an itch that wanted scratching. She'd also liked that he was comfortable enough not to have to perform. She wanted their relationship to be about more than sex. She wanted to get him to see the possibilities.

She glanced ahead at another signal. "Think we can make it before it turns red?" she asked.

"Sure."

"Great." She sprinted to the curb, quickly checked traffic, then darted into the street. When she reached the other side, she was alone. Zach stood on the corner with his hands on his thighs. He was breathing heavily.

After the light turned green again, he started across at a slow jog. "Why don't you go on ahead?" he said when they were together again. "I don't have my speed back."

"I don't mind." She jogged around him once, then slowed her pace to his. "I can think of this as my good deed for the day. Helping the elderly across streets and the like."

He gave her a mock growl. "Thirty-seven isn't elderly. I have the soul of a teenager."

She grinned. "Other parts are pretty young, too."

He raised his eyebrows. They both laughed.

Jamie stayed at his side. Zach was seven years older than her, and he'd been in the agency seven years before she'd joined. That meant fourteen years in the field, altogether. A lifetime. No wonder he didn't do well in the real world. If she could barely remember what it was like to be a regular person, to him it was probably just a half-remembered dream. Could she change that or was she wishing for the moon?

They turned right at the corner and spotted the hotel a few blocks up. By mutual agreement, they slowed to a walk to start their cool down.

"You did great," she said.

"It's getting better." He wiped the sweat from his face. "At least here the terrain is level. At the cabin, I can't get away from uphill running."

"I know. But think of the great workout."

He shook his head. "I prefer this, thanks."

She thought about him running in the woods. Every day

she watched him go away, then come back. She wanted to believe it would always be like that. Sometimes he would have to leave her, but later he would return. Was that possible, or would he one day just keep going? After all, they had a deal.

She shook her head to banish the question. She didn't want to spoil their time together. It was enough that they were here and having fun. She wouldn't deal with the "what ifs" until she had to.

When they reached the front of the hotel, they stretched their aching muscles.

"How do you feel?" Jamie asked.

"Not bad." He tugged on the end of her ponytail. "What do you want to do with the rest of our day?"

Make love. For a second, she wasn't sure if she'd just thought the words or actually said them. Zach continued to look at her inquiringly, so she figured she'd only thought them. Fighting a sudden burst of shyness, she could only duck her head and say, "I'm not familiar with the city. What would you like to do?"

He draped his arm around her shoulders and ushered her into the hotel. "I was thinking about a visit to the zoo. How does that sound?"

"I haven't been to a zoo since I was kid. It sounds great."

Zach stared at the pacing leopard. Unlike some zoos he'd seen in the past, the Denver zoo emphasized natural habitats. The animal had the feel of being in the wild, although it knew it was confined. The illusion of freedom was something Zach understood. In an odd way, he'd come to pay his respects to those most like him—the caged beasts.

"They're so beautiful," Jamie said, leaning against the railing. "Seeing large cats on television is impressive enough, but that doesn't give you any sense of their strength. Even from this distance, I can see his shoulder muscles bunching and releasing with each step. He could rip a person apart with a casual blow."

"Then eat you from the inside out," Zach said.

Jamie glanced at him. "Thanks so much for the share. That's a cheerful thought I want to carry with me."

He tapped the end of her nose. "Don't worry. You wouldn't be his first choice. Meat eaters prefer to dine on plant eaters."

Her dark blond eyebrows drew together. "How'd you know that?"

"I'm a repository for useless bits of trivia."

"All right, answer me this. Are black leopards solid black?"

He turned his attention back to the pacing animal. It moved through the shadows of several rocks. "No. Watch when it comes out into the sun. You'll be able to see that black leopards are spotted like their lighter cousins. They also have the same squared nose and wide head. With that information, we've exhausted everything I know about leopards."

"It's more than me," she said, and leaned against him.

He wrapped his arms around her. She wore an oversize sweater and tight jeans. He rested one hand on her hip and buried the other in her loose hair.

"What do you suppose they think about?" she asked.

"Getting out. But if they've spent their whole lives in a cage, they wouldn't know what to do with their freedom."

Other people liked different animals at the zoo. The birds, or maybe the primates. Not Zach. The cats had always reminded him of himself. He knew exactly how they felt as they paced back and forth. His cage was larger, and he couldn't always see the bars, but it was still there.

He was a prisoner of the life he'd chosen, a prisoner

of his past. He wasn't free to come and go like everyone else.

Jamie placed her hand flat on his chest. Desire flickered through him. He liked being around her. She reminded him he was alive and could still experience physical need.

"There's something familiar about that animal," she said, and frowned. "I just can't quite figure it out." She stared for a couple of seconds, then snapped her fingers. "I know. It's you. You pace the cabin just like that."

"You're right," he said, surprised that she got it. "We're both trapped. I can't come out, neither can he. We'd both be too dangerous to let loose."

Jamie glanced up at him. Her hazel eyes had a greenish tint that made her look faintly exotic. Her mouth twitched, then she started to laugh.

"Gee, Zach, could you be more melodramatic? I mean, I'm sure that line works great on the bimbos you normally go out with, but you're going to have to do better with me. 'We're both too dangerous to let loose,'" she said, mocking him sotto voce. "Get over it. You're a spy, not an assassin. We've both done some dangerous and scary things, but we haven't been brainwashed into behaving like monsters. You make it so complicated."

His first instinct was to get angry with her. It faded in the light of the obvious affection shining from her face. She cared for him. He knew that. He didn't know how much, nor did he want to. For now those feelings were enough to make him smile.

"Okay, maybe I was a little melodramatic," he admitted.

"A little? You're too dangerous to be let loose?" She laughed again and hugged him.

He kissed the top of her head. This was the Jamie he liked best. The one who wasn't afraid of him. "You've always been disrespectful of your elders," he said. "I should have written you up during training."

She pushed away and planted her hands on her hips. "I was the best recruit you ever trained, mister, so don't be telling me I did anything wrong."

Sunlight made her hair gleam. Her skin was clear, slightly tanned and touched with pink. Her mouth parted. She wasn't elegant or sophisticated. He knew she didn't even believe in her own femininity, but in his mind, she was the best thing that had ever happened to him.

"You always were fearless," he said.

"Sometimes that got me into trouble, but most of the time, it saved my butt."

"Mine, too."

Her smile faded. "I couldn't have left you there to die. I would have come after you, no matter what Winston had told me. Even if I'd had to do it on my own."

Her hazel eyes saw too much. Because of their shared life-style, she knew most of what he'd been through and she could accurately guess at the rest. Her knowledge made him want to hide, because there were some things he couldn't bear to think about. It also made him want to trust her more.

"Zach, I—" She paused. An emotion flitted across her face. One that made his chest tighten and his heart thunder. He didn't dare name it. He didn't want to think about what would generate those feelings in her. Yet he couldn't look away.

He didn't want her to care. He couldn't handle that. Caring implied the potential for a relationship. Or was he just fooling himself by thinking they didn't have one already? He didn't know how to play this game, and the rules were unfamiliar to him. The only thing certain was he didn't want Jamie to leave him today. He could bear anything but that, even the knowledge that she would leave him eventually.

Before she could say anything else, a family came around the corner and joined them by the enclosure. Zach glanced at the two parents, the infant in the stroller and the small child bringing up the rear.

The little girl couldn't be much more than four, with short, tousled red hair, freckles and huge blue eyes. She wore a miniature khaki jacket over jeans.

Jamie glanced at the family and smiled. The little girl smiled shyly back, then hurried toward the enclosure.

"Daddy, up," she said, and raised her arms.

Zach watched her in amazement. There was an implicit trust in that statement and gesture, as if her father had always been there to take her where she wanted to go. As if he'd never dropped her or let her down.

Jamie moved close to him and wrapped her arm around his waist. He absorbed her heat, using it to chase away some of the chill from his dark soul.

"Isn't she sweet?" Jamie asked, whispering in his ear. "So small and cute."

He didn't respond, but she didn't seem to notice. All her attention focused on the little girl. Her father raised her so her feet rested on the waist-high railing. She leaned back against him and clapped her hands. There was no fear that she would fall. Her father anchored her with a strong arm around her waist.

"Kitty," the child said.

"Leopard. That's a black leopard." Her father, nearly six feet with a medium build, said patiently.

The girl giggled. "Pretty kitty. Here, kitty. Come play with me."

Jamie's mouth parted as if her breath had caught in her throat. She stared at the child as if she'd never seen one before. Zach saw the longing in her eyes, the hint of pain in the set of her mouth.

He knew what she was thinking. Seven years ago, he'd tried to warn her about all she would give up if she chose the agency as her career. It wasn't just coming home at five every day; it was being like everyone else. There wasn't room for close friends, for relationships, no room for a proper marriage or a close family.

Now she wondered if she'd waited too long. Had she been too damaged by her experiences to let her dreams come true? She was hoping that because he'd been the one to show her the way into that life, he could help her reverse the course. When was she going to figure out that he never wanted to find his way?

Zach saw the exact moment the leopard spotted the child. The animal stopped pacing and froze in place. Golden eyes focused on the chattering little girl. Muscles coiled, whiskers twitched. Her size and quick movement marked her as prey.

He and the cat were too much alike. Killers, honed by instinct and knowledge. Like the leopard, he was deadly. Jamie still had a chance, but it was too late for him. He couldn't risk it.

For a single heartbeat, he allowed himself to think about what it would mean to have a child of his own. Someone who loved him and trusted him because he'd always been there, done the right thing. Then he pushed away the fantasy. He wouldn't always be there and he wouldn't know how to do the right thing. In the end, he would be dangerous for the child. Not because he wanted to, but because one day he wouldn't be able to keep perfect control. One day the demons inside would escape, and everyone around him would be destroyed. He refused to risk hurting anyone he cared about.

Jamie released him and took a step toward the next enclosure. Zach grabbed her hand and followed.

"It's so weird," she said when they were staring at a pair of black bears. "That woman was probably a couple of years younger than me and she's already got two kids. I bet a lot of the girls I went to high school with are married with families."

"If they knew what you had done with your life, they would envy you."

She leaned forward on the railing. "You think so? I'm not so sure. I mean it's hardly glamorous."

"Not James Bond?" he teased.

"Exactly. Sometimes I think about going back and making other choices."

"What would they be?"

She scrunched her nose up as she thought. "Maybe I'd be a barrel racer instead." She laughed. "Or a pilot. I always wanted to learn how to fly. I could have been a scientist."

"I can't see you trapped in some lab all day."

"Me, either. I'm not conventional enough. But sometimes I wonder what it must be like to have regular goals, to live a perfectly ordinary life." She straightened and smiled. "I knew girls who wanted to be cheerleaders or the homecoming queen. I never went to a dance my whole life. I don't even know how to dance."

"It's not so hard."

She looked startled. "You can dance?"

"I get by. An undercover assignment put me in an embassy once. It's a real party circuit. I learned how to dance to protect my cover."

"You mean like the tango?"

"No. I do simple stuff. Waltzes, fox-trot, even a pretty mean Texas two-step."

She laughed. "Every time I think I know everything about you, you surprise me. What other secrets are trapped inside?" She placed her hand against his chest.

He grabbed her fingers and bent down, then kissed her palm. Her smile faded, but a hot light burned in her eyes.

"No more secrets," he said, and knew it was a lie. He had plenty—they both did—but it was easier to pretend there was nothing left to hide.

Jamie turned and leaned her back against his chest. He

wrapped his arms around her waist and held her close. Although he'd had short-term relationships with women before, no one had touched him the way she did. No one made him want more than was safe.

She'd done more than save his life by rescuing him. She'd also come to the cabin to make sure he got better. In return, he wanted to give her something special. Jamie wasn't the kind to appreciate an expensive bauble, so he would have to think of something else. Something that could never fade or be lost. Something precious, like the memory of their time together.

He was getting stronger every day. Eventually he would have to go back. It was, he told himself, a great-sounding concept that had its basis in deceit. He wasn't willing to give Jamie the one thing she wanted—the truth. He wouldn't even give her something real and lasting. Instead, he was going to show her a good time. When had he become a low-life bastard?

She turned her head slightly and nuzzled his neck. The moist heat of her kiss aroused him. Her position left her off balance, but she trusted him to keep her upright. Just like the child with her father. Implicit trust—when the hell had he earned that?

If he was any kind of a man, he would tell her what she wanted to know. He would explore the emotions he'd seen flickering through her eyes. He would risk some feelings of his own. If he was any kind of a man, he would tell her—

Tell her what? He didn't have the answers. Truth was a relative term. The only thing he knew for sure was that when the time came, he was going to let Jamie go. Because it was right for her, because he didn't deserve any better.

Chapter 13

"But why?" Jamie asked, then realized her voice sounded uncomfortably close to a whine. She couldn't help it. She really, really didn't want to do this.

"It will be fun."

She stared at the elegant lettering on the front of the upscale boutique and shook her head. "No, it won't. It's physically impossible to have fun while shopping."

Zach smiled. "And here I thought all females loved to shop."

"I'm not like other females. That's the whole problem. I never learned how. I don't have the shopping gene. I don't know what's in style or what looks good on me. Please don't make me do this."

She stared up at him and begged silently. His eyes darkened with something that looked like compassion. She didn't care if he thought she was crazy or even if he pitied her. At this point, she would take a month in prison rather than face going into the store in front of them. She couldn't do it again. Her last shopping trip, an impulsive stop she'd made on her way from the airport to the cabin, had been a disaster. She'd bought that hideous frilly blouse and full skirt. Just thinking about how awful she'd looked made her shudder. She wanted to burn those clothes and all clothes like them.

She glanced down at her casual attire of jeans, a shirt and a blazer. This was as feminine as she was likely to get.

"I thought you wanted to find balance," Zach reminded her. "Shopping is a part of being normal."

She grimaced. "I thought you were going to say shopping is a part of being female."

"I have a lot of flaws, but sexism isn't one of them."

She drew in a deep breath. "I don't want to."

"I know, but it will be good for you."

He took her arm and started to pull her toward the store. She resisted, wishing they were standing on soft earth instead of a concrete sidewalk so she could really dig her heels in.

"Jamie." He sounded impatient.

"Just tell me why I have to do this."

"Because we're going out to a nice restaurant tonight, and you don't have the right clothes."

She fingered the lapel of her blazer. "I look fine."

"You look great, but you'll look even better with a cocktail dress. If you behave, I'll even give you a surprise later."

That caught her attention. She wondered if this surprise would take place in bed. They hadn't been intimate since arriving in the city. Although her body was still pleasantly sated from their time at the cabin, she wouldn't complain about a repeat performance.

"What's the surprise?" she asked.

"I'll tell you later."

"I want to know now."

He glared at her. "Have you always been this stubborn?"

She nodded once. "It's my best quality."

"Sanders, get your butt in the store. Now!"

There didn't seem to be any way of talking him out of the situation, so she gathered the little dignity she had left, pulled her arm free of his grasp and pushed open the glass door.

The interior was terrifying enough to make her knees quake. Frighteningly elegant furnishings, complete with antiques, subtle lighting and carpet thick enough to hide a cat. The pale walls were a neutral but warm color between white and gray. Racks of clothes stood in small collections. Jamie couldn't tell if they were bunched by size, function or color. In her entire thirty years, she'd never been in a place like this.

There were other women shopping. Well-dressed women in coordinated outfits. Pants with fitted jackets, dresses with stockings and high heels. Well made-up women who wore jewelry and scarves and probably had an entire dresser covered with perfume bottles.

Jamie felt as if she were from another planet. A place where ugly, stupid people hid out until they were forced into landing on earth. She knew the saleswoman and other customers were going to know instantly she was inept. If she was lucky, they would just throw her back into the street and tell her to come back when she knew what she was doing.

"May I help you?"

She spun toward the voice, feeling oddly guilty, as if she'd been caught reading someone else's mail.

"No," she said quickly.

"Yes," Zach said just as fast. He frowned at her, then turned his attention to the clerk. "We're looking for a cocktail dress."

The woman was in her midforties, with perfect, pale

skin and red hair swept back into some kind of twist-bun-looking style. Jamie was sure it had an unpronounceable French name. The clerk glanced between the two of them, but her gaze never dipped below the neck. If she noticed Jamie was dressed worse than the cleaning lady, she didn't let on.

"This way," she said, and turned toward the back of the store.

She was dressed all in black. Slim dress, stockings and midsize pumps. Jamie wondered how she kept from falling on the thick carpet.

She walked to a gilded arch, then motioned with one outstretched arm. "Our evening wear is here. May I show you a few things, or do you know what you want?"

"I just want to look around," Jamie muttered. It was humiliating enough that she had to find something to wear. She didn't need witnesses.

"Very well. My name is Monique. Please let me know if I can be of assistance."

She left them alone.

Jamie stared at all the fancy dresses. She didn't know where to begin. "What did you have in mind?" she asked.

Zach shrugged. "Something pretty. Are you going to be okay by yourself? I have to go talk to Monique."

She looked at him. "You're leaving me here?"

"Is that a problem?"

She would rather be in a roomful of snakes. "No problem," she said tightly. "I'll be fine." She'd been alone on mountaintops in hostile territory and survived. She could do this. Of course, on the mountaintop she'd had a gun.

She pressed her lips together when Zach actually smiled at her and walked away, leaving her in the torture house of beads and baubles. Damn him.

She fought against a feeling of helplessness. She didn't know what to do or what to buy. She didn't even know exactly what size she would wear in this expensive boutique. Were designer clothes bigger or smaller or the same? She vaguely recalled overhearing a conversation on the subject once, years before, but she couldn't remember the details. She hadn't been interested.

She circled one of the larger racks, trying to gather her courage. Thousands, millions, of women bought clothes every day. How hard could it be?

She focused on the clothing. There were mostly dresses. She saw a couple of pants outfits but didn't think that was what Zach had in mind. She stared at the different fabrics, some soft, some beaded, some sequined, some smooth. There were too many choices.

Finally she thrust her hand in and grabbed a dress. It looked short, maybe too short. It had broad, padded shoulders, a deep neckline and lots of hanging beads. What she liked most was the color. A pale cream at the top, darkening to the color of fire at the bottom, as if the garment were a flicker of flame. She walked to the three-way mirror and held the dress up to herself.

Her eyes changed to a muddy shade of gray. All the color left her face, and her mouth looked small and pinched. She stared in astonishment, then put the dress out to one side. The color returned to her face, and her eyes were once again a pleasing shade of hazel. With the dress close to her face, she looked as if she were coming down with malaria. Without it she was fine.

"Obviously not my best color," she said softly, and put the dress back. She felt oddly pleased, as if she'd just made an amazing discovery.

She reached for another garment. This was a two-piece outfit, a tapestry jacket with a long, soft, flowing purple skirt. Pretty, just as Zach had requested.

She returned to the mirror and held it up to her face. Her eyes deepened to blue, and her skin took on a luminous sheen. "Perfect," she said, and glanced around for a dressing room.

Several gilded doors stood at the far end of the room. Jamie approached them cautiously, bending over to make sure one was empty before pulling on the handle.

The dressing room was nearly as large as their bedroom back at the hotel. There were mirrors on three walls, a small vanity, a wing chair and a long rod for the clothing. She hung her single dress there and tried not to think about having to go out and find something else. Surely this was going to work. Then she could pay for it and leave.

She quickly stripped down to her bra and panties. The plain cotton undergarments looked out of place in the elegant surroundings. She reached for the skirt and stepped into it. The button at her waist was a little loose. Maybe she needed a smaller size. She glanced in the mirror and smiled.

The filmy skirt fluttered around her legs like Monet's water lilies come to life. The beautiful fabric made her feel special, feminine even. She looked at the hem falling halfway down her calves. What kind of shoes would she wear with this?

She didn't have a clue, so she pushed the question aside and shrugged into the tapestry jacket. It was also too loose. She buttoned it up the front and stared at her reflection. She looked boxy and formless in the thick jacket. Her head seemed to shrink, and she felt old.

"It's the fit," she said, frustrated that something so pretty on the hanger would look so ugly on her. She reached behind her and grabbed a handful of fabric, pulling the jacket tighter in front. It still looked bad.

She sank into the chair and dropped her head into her hands. She couldn't do this. She just couldn't do it. She didn't know how to shop or buy. She could spot jeans that would fit from halfway across a store, but real clothes were beyond her. She would have to tell Zach she was hopeless.

Her eyes began to burn, but she blinked the sensation away. This was a really stupid thing to cry about.

There was a knock at the door. "Jamie, it's Monique. Your young man suggested I check on you. How is everything?"

She opened her mouth to lie but instead blurted out the truth. "Horrible. I look like a geek."

Monique opened the door and stepped inside with a surprisingly kind smile. "No geeks are allowed in the store. Didn't you see the sign? Only beautiful women. If they aren't beautiful when they come in, they're beautiful when they leave."

She motioned for Jamie to stand up, then walked around her in a slow circle. "This is all wrong for you."

"I know."

Monique wasn't listening. "Very nice color, but the style, the shape. It hides what you should flaunt. This—" she touched the thick sleeve "—this is for the romantic type. The woman who is all soft lines and ruffles. Not you. Take off the dress and let me see what we're working with."

Jamie undressed quickly. Monique studied her for a second and sighed. "You work out, don't you? You're in fabulous shape. Flaunt it while you still have it." She patted her own narrow hips. "Time and gravity are not our friends. Stay right here."

She threw the tapestry jacket and filmy skirt over her arm and disappeared. Less than a minute later, she was back with a little black dress—*little* being the key word. It didn't look big enough to fit a dress-up doll, let alone a grown woman.

"It's too small," Jamie said.

"It stretches," Monique told her. "Trust me."

She set the dress on the hook, then tossed Jamie a black

teddy in silk. "The key to a good fit is the right foundation."

Jamie stared at the teddy. It had an underwire bra built in that looked more like scraps of silk cloth than actual support. But Monique was the expert.

Jamie put on the teddy. It was a low cut, as she expected. The silk came up over her nipples and stopped. The design was different than she was used to, forcing her breasts together and up, giving her more cleavage than was legal. So much for not having support. The rest of the undergarment slipped over her torso like a lover's touch.

"Are you sure about this?" Jamie stroked the soft fabric. It felt positively decadent. She loved it!

Monique just smiled.

Next came the dress. She pulled it on over her head. The stretch material clung to her like a wet shower curtain. She pulled the hem down and found it ended a good eight inches above her knees.

Monique stepped behind her and pulled up the zipper, then smoothed her hair down the center of her back. "You see. It's perfect."

Jamie stared at her reflection, not quite willing to believe what she saw.

The dress hugged every curve. She looked like a model, all long legs and cleavage. Her breasts threatened to spill out of the heart-shaped neckline. The black lace was see-through on her arms, but lined everywhere else. She looked like someone other people would turn to stare at.

"I'll take it," she said without thinking, then giggled.

"I thought you might. Do you have shoes?"

Jamie shook her head. "I don't have stockings, either."

Monique asked her shoe size and disappeared for a few minutes. Jamie stared at her reflection some more, unable to believe she'd actually found a dress she liked and that liked her. She turned around, admiring herself from every angle. She looked great and she couldn't stop grinning like a fool.

When Monique returned, she had several packages of panty hose and three boxes of shoes. She set them in the chair. "These are what I would usually give customers to wear," she said, pulling out black lace pumps with four-inch heels.

"No way."

"That's what I thought." She opened the second box. These were also lace, but a two-inch heel. "Could you survive in these?"

"I don't know. I've never tried."

"Put them on." Monique set them on the floor.

Jamie stepped into the shoes. She wobbled a bit, but it wasn't as bad as she thought. "I think I could manage."

"Good. When was the last time you wore panty hose?"

Jamie tried to recall. It had been years. No doubt her parents had made her dress up to go to some formal event in high school, but she couldn't put a date on it. "Um, I can't really remember."

Monique smiled. "I'll send you home with three pairs," she said. "In case you run the first couple putting them on. Now about your hair."

"My hair?" She touched the long strands. "What's wrong with it?"

"Nothing. It's beautiful. Curl it."

Jamie stared blankly. "How?"

Monique was a professional. Not even by a flicker of a lash did she let on that the question was strange. "Electric curlers. The drugstore on the corner will have them." She mentioned a brand to look for. "Don't worry about getting fancy. Brush your hair, then start rolling it up. You'll love the look, I promise. Do you wear makeup?"

Jamie thought about her failed efforts at the cabin. "I'm not very good at it."

Monique pulled a small pad from a pocket in her dress.

She wrote for a few minutes, then tore off the sheet. "This will get you started. You're going to knock his socks off."

"I hope so."

"Trust me."

Jamie smiled. "I do." Monique merely nodded as if this wasn't unexpected, but for Jamie it was a moment of revelation. She couldn't remember the last time she'd been willing to trust a stranger. Okay, this was shopping and not a matter of life or death, but she felt as if she'd taken a giant step on the journey to normal. She turned back to her reflection and grinned. Why had she ever thought shopping was a problem? She hadn't even needed her gun.

Jamie stared at herself in the mirror. She looked like one of those "before" pictures in the magazines. Curlers hung to her neck. The hot edges kept touching her skin. She'd finally had to drape a towel around her shoulders to protect herself from the heat. It had taken her about a dozen tries to get all the curlers to stay in her hair, but she'd finally managed.

She glanced at the bottle of foundation, then at the streaky mess on her face. Okay, so that wasn't going to work. At least the color had been better than the one she'd bought on her own.

She wiped her face clean with a damp washcloth and figured Zach had seen her bare skin enough to not be offended by it. She picked up a smoky gray eye shadow. The label proclaimed it to be foolproof. She wasn't convinced.

A diagram on the back showed where to apply the shadow. She closed her right eye and squinted with her left. The sponge applicator was made for small leprechauns with short fingers. She could barely hold on to it. But she managed to get a streak of the cosmetic across her eyelid, right at the crease. It looked a little stark, so she smudged it with her finger, then opened her eye.

Amazing. She couldn't really see the shadow, but her right eye looked bigger and mysterious.

"Cool," she said, then repeated the procedure on the other eye. She skipped the eyeliner. It looked way too dangerous. Next came mascara. She only clumped her lashes twice, but she'd bought a lash brush, which corrected the problem. She dabbed her nose, forehead and chin with face powder, then used a neutral shade of rosewood lipstick on her mouth.

She stared at her reflection. Not fashion-model beautiful, but not a half bad job, either. She was quite pleased with herself. Next came the stockings. She got the first pair on with no mishaps. The teddy went over the stockings. The dress slipped on easily, although she had to shimmy to reach behind herself to zip it up. She pulled and tugged until it was in place. Last she uncoiled the curlers from her hair.

She'd never done anything but trim it or pull it back in a braid, so she wasn't sure if it would even curl. Amazingly it did. Monique had told her to bend over at her waist and brush her hair from the underside, making that smooth but leaving the rest of it alone. The advice had sounded stupid, but Jamie did as she was told.

When she tossed her head back, curls tumbled onto her shoulders and down her back. Her eyes widened as she stared at herself. She looked great. She looked better than great. She looked fabulous.

Curls were everywhere. The slight disarray made her look sexy. The tight-fitting dress and abundance of curves added to the image.

Jamie fluffed her bangs, then grabbed the bottle of hair spray. She spritzed her curls in place, then slipped into her shoes. Where an inept thirty-year-old tomboy had been, stood a stunning, elegant woman. If Monique had been there, Jamie would have hugged her close and probably broken down in tears.

"Zach," she said through the door, then had to clear her throat because her voice had gone all husky. She tried again. "Zach, I'm ready."

She heard the rustling of plastic.

"Give me a second."

Nerves fluttered in her stomach. She couldn't believe what they were doing. When she'd come out of the dressing room prepared to buy the dress, Zach hadn't been around. He'd shown up a few minutes later with a plastic garment bag over one shoulder. He'd told her if she was willing to get all dressed up for him, he was willing to do the same for her.

"Okay, come on out," he said.

She put her hand on the doorknob, then paused as she fought a wave of shyness. She'd never gone to all this trouble with her appearance before. What if—?

Forget the "what ifs," she told herself firmly. Just enjoy the moment. With that, she opened the door and stepped into the bedroom.

The sun had barely set. She could see the faint colors of the sky through the sheers at the window. Zach had already put on the lamps, so the room was flooded with light.

"Jamie, I got you—" he said, and turned toward her. He held a gold box in his hands.

But it wasn't the present that captured her attention. It was the stunned silence and the look on his face. His eyes widened in shock, and his mouth dropped open, just like in the movies. He stared at her as if he'd never seen her before. As if he really liked what he was seeing this time.

"You're incredible," he said as his gaze dropped to her feet, then made a leisurely journey back to her face. "I always knew you were beautiful, but this—" He motioned to her dress, then her legs.

"You like it?"

His eyes got smoky with desire. "I like it a lot."

She did a little looking of her own. He'd rented a black tux with a plain white shirt. His cummerbund emphasized his trim waist, while the cut of his jacket made him look even broader across the shoulders.

"You look great, too," she said.

"Yeah?" He grinned. "Here's the first surprise."

He opened the top of the gold box and pulled out a delicate corsage. Baby red roses formed an elongated diamond pattern. He slipped the flowers over her hand and settled them on her wrist. Then he leaned forward and kissed her cheek.

"What are these for?" she asked, equally touched and confused by the gift.

"For all those proms and dances you never went to. Tonight is going to make up for them."

"I don't understand. I really don't mind that I missed them." The lie was automatic. Zach knew her too well to believe it.

"Of course you mind. But you're about to go to your first dance."

The tightness in her chest made it hard to breathe. Love filled her, warming her from the inside out. This was the reason she cared for this man. He was so in tune with her—he knew what she was thinking almost before she did. He understood about the hurts of the past and cared enough to do something about them.

A confession of her feelings hovered on the tip of her tongue, but she held it back. She didn't want to tell him before he was ready. For a long time, she thought he might never want to hear a declaration from her. But after this, she was starting to hope.

"Ready?" he asked, and held out his arm.

She placed her hand in the crook of his elbow and allowed him to lead her to the door.

* * *

The restaurant was one of the elegant, old-fashioned places with lots of wood and a small combo group in front of a postage-stamp dance floor.

They were shown to a table by the window. The city glowed beneath them, all bright lights and electric beauty. The night air was crisp, although the restaurant was pleasantly warm.

Jamie ran her fingers across the thick linen tablecloth, then touched the heavy silverware and delicate glasses.

"I adore this place," she said. "I want to live here."

"Wait until you try the food. It's even better than you'd expect."

A waiter approached and handed them heavy menus. He left with their drink orders.

Zach growled something under his breath.

"What was that?" she asked.

"I want a different waiter."

She glanced after the departing man. There wasn't anything extraordinary about him. "What did he do wrong?"

"He tried to look down the front of your dress."

She looked at the cleavage curving out of the deep neckline and laughed. "You're the one who wanted me to get all dressed up. So it's your own fault."

She didn't really think the waiter had been inspecting her, but it was nice that Zach thought so. She wanted to be special for him. For the first time in her life, she felt attractive and feminine. Maybe her goal of balance wasn't going to be as difficult as she'd thought. Maybe there was hope.

When the waiter returned with their drinks, they ordered, then sat back in their chairs and talked about their plans for the rest of their time in Denver.

"I'd like to see the Colorado History Museum," Zach said. "I've always liked the Old West."

"Me, too."

"Maybe we could do some more shopping."

She glanced at him over her wineglass. "Maybe."

"So it wasn't horrible?"

She shook her head. "Monique was great. I wouldn't mind going back to her store again. They had some more-casual stuff. As much as I love this dress, I can't wear it all the time."

"Too bad."

Their salads came and they ate. Later, after they'd finished their main course, Zach pushed back his chair and rose. "Come on," he said. "You owe me a dance."

"I couldn't." She tucked her hands behind the small of her back. "I've already told you I don't know how."

"It's a slow song. All we have to do is sway to the music. I promise I won't let you mess up."

She wasn't sure if she believed him, but he didn't look as if he was going to give up. A couple of people had turned to stare at them. Sighing, she got to her feet and let him lead her to the tiny dance floor.

Three other couples were already there. As promised, Zach didn't try anything fancy. He simply pulled her close and started swaying. His hands held her back firmly so she didn't feel like she was going to do something foolish. She wrapped her arms around his neck and leaned her cheek against his chest.

"This is nice," she said, absorbing his heat and the hard strength of his body.

"Hmm."

She raised her head. "What's wrong?"

"Look around the room."

There was a bar against the far wall. Several men were there without dates. A few of them caught her eye and smiled.

What on earth?

Then she realized what was happening.

"They're looking at me," she said, half pleased, half stunned. "At my legs."

"Not to mention other things. I want to rip all their hearts out."

She glanced up at him. Passion flared in his dark eyes. Passion and possessiveness. "That's the nicest thing you've ever said to me," she murmured. "Thank you."

"I mean it, Jamie. I wouldn't mind a little bloodshed right behind the bar."

She giggled, then leaned against his shoulder again. He pulled her closer. They touched from shoulder to thigh. Something hard brushed against her hip. She moved slowly back and forth, then pressed her lips against his neck.

"You're killing me," he whispered against her ear.

"And here I was trying to turn you on."

"That, too."

Someone tapped on her arm. Jamie turned and saw an older couple next to them. They were both short—the man was maybe five-six, and the woman barely came to his chin. They had gray hair and matching sets of wrinkles around their eyes as if they'd spent a lifetime sharing the same jokes.

"My wife and I were noticing the two of you," the elderly man said. "We think you're a happy couple and obviously very much in love. We're celebrating fifty years together this year."

"Congratulations," Zach said.

The woman smiled. "How long have you two been together?"

Jamie didn't know what to say.

"We met seven years ago," Zach said smoothly.

"So you're just beginning. I remember that." She patted Jamie's arm. "Don't let this one get away, dearie. The old saying is true. Good men *are* hard to find."

"I know. Thank you."

The older couple waved, then danced to the other side of the floor. Jamie felt a whisper of envy. What would it feel like to be them fifty years from now? They'd lived a normal life, laughing, loving. They might never have spent a night apart from each other.

"What are you thinking?" Zach asked.

"Just that they're very lucky."

"I'm lucky, too. After all, you're here." He tightened his arms around her.

"When did you get to be such a charmer?"

"I have a lot of secrets."

She laughed. "I'll just bet you do. Want to hear one of mine?"

"Sure."

She leaned closer and whispered in his ear, "I wouldn't mind if we skipped dessert and went straight back to the room."

His hands tightened on her back. "I thought you'd never ask."

Chapter 14

Zach unlocked the door to their suite, and they stepped into the darkness. Before he'd done much more than move into the parlor, Jamie was on him, her arms around his neck, her mouth searching for his. He gasped at the heat of her, the hunger in her kiss as she plunged into his mouth, then he bent his head and pressed his lips to hers. Passion exploded. He would die if he didn't have this woman now.

He managed to close the door and bolt it. The key dropped to the floor, but he didn't care. Jamie stepped out of her shoes. He tugged off his jacket. Their mouths pressed together again, open this time, damp, tongues searching, finding points of pleasure, pleasing.

He wrapped his arms around her and urged her in the general direction of the bedroom. The drapes were open with only the sheers pulled against the darkness of the night. Light from the street filtered in, allowing him to make out large pieces of furniture in the room.

Between kisses, between moans of pleasure, gasps of

lost air, between lips pressing and hands caressing, they made it to the bedroom.

She'd drawn the drapes in here before they'd left, so the room was completely dark. He felt along the wall and found the switch. When he pressed it, the lamps on either side of the large bed sprang to life.

Jamie stood before him, a pagan, barefoot goddess with her slinky black dress and tumbling curls. Her eyes were huge, passion making them brighter. Her mouth—already damp from his kisses—parted slightly. He could see the rapid rising and falling of her chest.

He took her hand in his and led her over to the bed. But instead of pushing her onto the mattress, he left her standing there. He brought her fingers to his mouth and kissed each sensitive pad. She tasted faintly salty with a hint of something sweet and forbidden.

He wanted her. Desire pulsed through him with every heartbeat. Between his legs, pressure built until he wanted to explode. He held back. He could no more rush this moment than he could force one of the nearby mountains to move. Their joining was inevitable—like the cycle of the moon. He wanted to enjoy every moment they had together, feel every caress, linger over every touch, every kiss. Something heady filled the night air, something that told him he was about to be shaken down to his soul.

He sucked on her fingers, one by one, then traced a damp circle on her palm. Her fingers curled in and stroked his cheek. She braced herself by placing her free hand on his chest.

He moved his mouth to the pad of skin at the base of her thumb. He nibbled there, making her catch her breath. Then he slipped lower, to her wrist. He could feel the rapid fluttering of her heart as blood flowed through her delicate veins.

When he released her hand, she swayed. He placed his hands on her shoulders and turned her so she was facing the bed with her back to him. The room was silent, yet he could hear music. It was similar to what they'd danced to at the restaurant. As if their physical dance was a mere continuation of what had gone before.

He gathered her hair in his hands, savoring the silky feel against his skin. He buried his face in the curls, inhaling the scent of her, then he tucked it all over one shoulder. As he slowly lowered the zipper, he leaned forward and kissed the side of her neck. She tilted her head to give him more room.

When the dress was unfastened, he pushed it down her arms, then over her hips. It pooled at her feet. With a quick kick, she tossed it to the side.

He rested his hands on her waist and studied her back. She was tall for a woman, with a medium bone structure. From here he could see the muscles she worked so hard to build and maintain.

They rippled as a shudder raced through her. He supposed there were some men who wouldn't find them feminine. Some people would experience her strength and be intimidated.

He reveled in her abilities. They were as much a part of her as the color of her eyes and the taste of her mouth. He alone knew the price she paid to be strong. He respected her determination, admired her dedication and ached for her pain. To him she was the perfect woman.

Contrasting with the honed body was a silky black wisp of lingerie. He pushed one of the shoulder straps down, then wrapped his arms around her waist and pulled her close. When she leaned against him, he rested his head against hers.

"You looked great tonight," he murmured.

"Thanks."

"All those other men wanted you."

She laughed quietly. "I think *all* is a slight exaggeration."

"Almost all."

"I might even believe that. I guess I have the dress to thank for that."

"It wasn't the dress, it was you."

She gave a snort of disbelief. "Then why haven't they been falling all over themselves for the past thirty years?"

"Because you haven't had the right attitude. It wasn't what you wore, it was how you wore it."

"It was the dress."

He turned his head and pressed his mouth against the sensitive skin below her ear. "I can see I'm going to have to find some way to convince you of the truth."

She reached her arms up behind her and touched his head. "I might prove to be a stubborn subject, but don't give up."

"I can be as stubborn as you."

"No one's that stubborn," she said.

She wove her fingers through his hair. Her position raised her breasts as if she were offering them to him. He cupped them in his palms and teased the taut peaks.

There was a contrast of textures and colors. Her pale breasts, the black lingerie, his tanned hands. The smooth skin of her breasts, the perfectly formed nubs of her nipples, the silk cupping her curves, the harder pads of his fingers.

He nibbled on her neck, then drew her earlobe into his mouth. Her fingers tunneled deeper, and she tightened her hold on his head. Using just his index fingers, he stroked the undersides of her breasts, feeling both the smooth fabric and her heat.

He pushed down the other strap. She dropped her arms, and the teddy fell to her waist. Now he could see, as well as touch. The creamy curves invited him to explore. He covered her with his hands, squeezing gently, watching her pale, plump breasts spill out of his grasp. He circled his palms over her nipples, moving quickly and lightly until her chest rose and fell with each rapid breath.

He turned her toward him and, as he did so, he sank to his knees. He raised his hands and continued to stroke her breasts while he nipped at her belly, her hipbone and the top of her thigh. He moved closer and gently bit the mound at the apex of her thighs. She sagged slightly, then braced her hands on his shoulders.

He glanced up. She watched him. Her hair tumbled over her shoulders, half revealing, half concealing her breasts. His fingers continued to toy with her nipples. He enjoyed feeling the tight skin and the erotic stroking of her hair against the backs of his hands. Within him blood heated as the need grew more insistent.

He dropped his hands to her buttocks and squeezed hard. She arched against him. He bit her again, frustrated that he couldn't see her and taste her there.

When he released her, she sank to the edge of the bed. He reached for her teddy and drew it off in one long motion, then pulled off her panty hose.

She was bare before him.

She half sat up, her weight resting on her elbows. Her eyes were the color of smoke, her lips pink and parted. She gave him a sultry smile that made him want to rip off his clothes and take her right there.

Instead, he settled between her thighs and used his fingers to part the delicate folds of skin that concealed her most sensitive place.

She was already swollen and ready. At the first touch of his tongue, she nearly came off the bed. Her knees drew back, exposing more of her to him. He cupped her hips, urging her to move in time with his strokes.

She tasted sweet. He circled that tiny point, then brushed it with the flat part of his tongue. She whimpered. Despite his need, despite the urge to plunge inside of her and find his own release, he focused on her and what he was doing to make her writhe on the bed.

It wasn't going to take long. He could tell from her increased breathing and the heat radiating from her skin. He could tell from her tensed muscles and a connection between them that defied explanation.

She tossed her head restlessly, murmuring sounds that might have been his name or pleas for him to continue. If he hadn't been otherwise occupied, he would have told her he had no intention of stopping until she'd reached fulfillment.

He concentrated on that small part of her body. He lavished it with attention, he adored it and circled it and forced her to the edge of surrender. Then he flicked faster, easing her into paradise, stroking her long legs as they trembled uncontrollably, continuing to please her until her gasps became whimpers and she was at last still.

It took them both a couple of seconds to catch their breath. Her feet settled on the floor. He bent over and kissed her belly. She sat up and pulled him to her. While they kissed, she reached for the buttons on his shirt.

Minutes later he was naked, stretched out on the bed. She knelt over him, brushing her mouth against his before moving lower to his neck, then his chest. His eyes drifted closed as he absorbed the sensations she created. The heat, the tingling, the passion-thickened blood coursing through him.

His erection throbbed in time with his heartbeat. One of her hands strayed down toward his thighs. He thrust his hips toward her. She held him gently, exploring him with delicate fingertips before grasping him and starting an up-and-down motion designed to drive him mad.

The pleasure between his thighs was so intense, it took him a minute to figure out what she was doing with her mouth. She moved across his chest in a seemingly random pattern, kissing one spot before moving on to another. A splash of hot moisture hit his skin.

"Jamie?"

She didn't respond. The hand between his legs slipped lower to cup him. He almost gave in to the pleasure and relaxed, but something teased at the back of his mind.

She moved to another spot on his chest, and he felt another splash.

He reached out and touched her under her chin. She ducked her head away. He raised himself into a sitting position and tugged on the end of her hair. She was finally forced to look at him.

Her face was still flushed and her lips were parted, but this time it wasn't from pleasure. Tears swam in her eyes. They slipped past her lower lashes and spilled onto her cheeks.

"What's wrong?" he asked, confused by her reaction to their lovemaking. "Did I hurt you?"

"No. Everything is fine. Really."

"Why are you crying?"

She shook her head. "I can't explain. You wouldn't understand."

"Try me."

She bit her lower lip. "I can't." Her voice was a whisper.

He stroked her cheek. He hated seeing her like this. "Please, Jamie. Tell me. I want to know what's hurt you. I want to make it better."

She touched a mark on his chest. He glanced down. It was an old scar. Another tear slipped free. She brushed it away, then placed her damp finger against the scar.

"I wish I could make that go away. I want to make them all go away. I know what they are. I know what they felt like. This one—" she pointed to a slender line by his ribs "—this is from a knife. There's a burn mark on your back. This is a bullet wound." She placed her hand on his thigh.

He stared into her eyes and wondered what he'd done to deserve her in his life. Why did she think he was worth even one of her tears? Other women had commented on his scars. They'd asked where he got them, if they still hurt. Sometimes he told the truth, and sometimes he lied. But Jamie didn't have to ask. She knew.

She knew that a knife wound didn't hurt at all. A sharp blade slipped through flesh as if it were thick cream. She knew how much blood there was, how the shock was the worst of it until you woke up in the hospital. Then it hurt like a son of a bitch. She knew that the pain of a bullet didn't come from the metal piercing flesh, but from the powder burn. She knew that bleeding from the inside wasn't especially frightening because you became disoriented quickly. She knew about staring at exposed flesh and watching the blood pump out in time with your heartbeat.

She knew everything.

He shifted her until she was straddling him. He pushed her hair back over her shoulders so he could stare at her body.

A thin white line stretched from the center of her chest, just below her breasts, around to her side. "Knife wound," he said. "Not very deep, but I bet it bled a bunch."

She nodded.

He touched a puckered oval on her thigh. "Bullet."

"Just missed the bone."

"Good thing." Flesh could survive a bullet; bone usually shattered.

She sniffed.

He cupped her face and brushed his thumbs under her eyes.

"Don't cry for me. I'm not worth it."

She bent forward and clung to him. "You are to me."

He swallowed hard. She knew too much. How was he supposed to hide from someone who could see into his very soul? The urge to run away was strong, but he forced himself to hug her close and murmur her name.

She rocked against him, reminding him parts of his body were growing impatient. She shifted slightly, rising up, then coming down on him, taking all of him in one liquid movement. He arched toward her and swore violently. She smiled her pleasure.

She rode him like a rodeo queen. Head back, hair flying, breasts bouncing, body alternately yielding and pushing him to completion as her paleness slipped up and down over his engorged organ.

She reached forward and they locked hands, fingers squeezing tight. He could feel her collecting herself again. He held back, wanting to watch her, wanting to see the flush of pleasure rise from her breasts to her face.

But at the first ripple of her climax, he found himself forced to follow with her. He thrust up and exploded, ripped apart by the pleasure, caught up in a moment of intimacy so intense, so purifying, he knew he would never be the same again.

Jamie snuggled close to Zach and absorbed his heat. She didn't know how long they'd been entwined together, sharing their bodies long after the lovemaking was complete.

She inhaled the musky scent of him and smiled. She could pick him out of a lineup blindfolded. All she would have to do was sniff some exposed bit of skin and she would know where he was. The mental image of her wearing a blindfold in front of a line of men made her giggle.

"What's so funny?" he asked, his voice husky and sensual.

"I was just thinking about how much I like the way you smell."

"That's amusing?"

"Sort of."

They lay on their sides, facing the window. Zach curled against her back, their legs tangled, his arm around her waist. She rested her hand on top of his.

"I had a great time tonight," she said. "Dinner was wonderful. Very romantic. I liked the dancing."

"Me, too." His voice rumbled in his chest. She could feel it vibrating against her back. "You're a pretty good dancer."

"I'm perfect if all we have to do is sway. Don't test me on anything more complicated."

"What about the rest of it?" he asked. "You know—dessert."

She turned onto her back and stared up at him. "Gee, Zach, we didn't have dessert. What are you talking about?"

He raised his eyebrows and waited.

She pretended confusion for a minute, even though she knew he wasn't fooled. "Dessert? Hmm...oh, do you mean the sex? Well, I can't possibly talk about it."

"But you can do it? Is that what you're saying? What, good girls don't actually discuss the act in polite company?"

"You're hardly polite."

He reached for her and started tickling. She shrieked and tried to scoot away, but he still had an arm around her waist. He hauled her hard against him and nibbled on her neck. One of his hands searched out tender spots on her tummy. She wiggled and squealed until he let her go.

He released her and smoothed the hair from her face. Affection shone from his eyes. She understood this man. She knew what he wanted and what he feared.

In his heart, he wanted to walk away from the agency

as much as she did. He wanted desperately to put it all behind him, but he was afraid. Being like everyone else meant facing the demons he'd locked inside for fourteen years. He would have to deal with everything he'd done, all he'd seen.

There were stories around the agency, of old-timers who retired somewhere quiet, as they'd always planned. Some were fine, but others lasted only a few months in the woods or by the shore. They either returned to the game and died in the field or took their own lives in that gray hour before dawn.

Zach wouldn't accept either fate. If he stayed in the game too long, he wouldn't be the best, and that would destroy him. If he walked away, then he had to wrestle the past and win. She felt confident he would be the victor, but how did she convince him of that? How did she find that magic combination of words to give him the strength to move forward? How did she convince him she loved him?

She stared up at his familiar, handsome face. She didn't have those answers yet, and obviously he didn't, either. So he advanced and retreated. Played at being strangers, then lovers. Held her in his arms, all the while believing he was going to be the one to walk away when this was over.

She smiled. "I really did have a good time today. Everything was great. Our run, the zoo. Even the shopping wasn't so bad."

"Told you," he said, then kissed her briefly and rolled onto his back. He pulled her along with him, settling her so her head rested on his shoulder.

"Remember that family at the zoo?" she asked.

"Hmm." His voice rumbled in his chest.

"They made it look so easy. That little girl was really cute. So much personality and so trusting."

"And all that leopard could think was snack time."

She brushed her hand over his chest, then tucked her fist under her chin. "Whenever I've thought about couples and children, I always thought it would be so complicated. But I'm beginning to see it doesn't have to be. I'm making it complicated because I don't understand the dynamics. Then I think of that old couple in the restaurant. I can't imagine what it would be like to be married to someone for that long. Yet they looked really happy together. So it can be done, if you're willing to work at it. There's no magic, there's just believing."

"What's your point?"

She ignored the slight stiffening of his body and snuggled closer. "I know why you're afraid, Zach," she whispered. "Despite that, it's still worth the effort."

"I won't pretend to know what you're talking about."

She sat up and shifted so she was cross-legged. The sheet pooled around her waist, but she didn't bother pulling it up. After all, he'd seen every part of her already. She had nothing to hide.

"I finally figured it out," she said. "I know what happened in the past. It took me this long to figure it out because I couldn't get beyond my own hurt to look at the bigger picture. I was so angry, for years I didn't care about your feelings."

He started to roll away. She placed her hand on his shoulder and held him in place. When he sagged back on the bed, she exhaled a sigh of relief. He could have defeated her physically. The fact that he didn't gave her hope.

"Seven years ago—"

"I don't want to talk about it," he said, cutting her off. "I don't have any magic answers for you. I'm not interested in finding a way back to the world you so admire." He glared at her but didn't move away.

"We have to talk about it," she said. "It's important." She paused to gather her thoughts. "Seven years ago, you told me I had to make a choice. Do you remember?" She didn't wait for an answer, but continued. "I could either be a good agent or I could have a normal life. I couldn't do both."

He glanced away without saying anything.

"You were right," she continued. "The agency requires a hundred percent commitment. I couldn't have done that kind of work if I'd been worried about a husband or a family. But no matter how much I used work to fill my life, I couldn't help but feel empty inside. For a long time, I thought it was just anger at you. I thought you'd led me on—got me to believe in you and care about you, then dumped me. I thought it was about your ego rather than my feelings."

His hand clamped over her wrist. His dark eyes filled with the truth. "I never meant to hurt you, Jamie. You've got to believe that."

She nodded slowly. "I do. I also know I made a mistake seven years ago. Why didn't you tell me the truth? Why did you let me walk away believing you were a jerk?"

This time he did roll away. He walked naked to the window and stared out at the sleeping city. The light from the small lamp by the bed didn't reach that far. Zach stood in shadow. A shiver of fear rippled through her, but she ignored it. She had to get it all out now. Something inside of her told her this might be her last chance.

"The choice wasn't between the agency and a real life," she said. "You were the choice. That's what I didn't get. Because you didn't ask me to stay with you, I thought you didn't want me. But the opposite was true. You really cared about me. You wanted me to demand to stay with you. And I didn't."

She drew her knees to her chest and wrapped her arms around her legs. "Of all the people in the world, you knew how important the agency was to me. You knew how hard

I'd worked to achieve my goal. You knew what I was capable of. So you let me go, because you believed it was the right thing to do. I had a chance to be the best, and you wanted to make sure that happened. At the time, I might have agreed with you, but now I'm not so sure you made the right choice."

"Don't do this, Jamie. You don't know what you're getting into," he said.

"Yeah, Zach, for once I do. For a long time, I thought I'd failed you in some way. I tried to figure out what I'd done that was so wrong. Then, when I started to realize what had really happened, I thought *I'd* been the one who had failed. Finally I got my answer."

She slipped off the bed and walked over toward the window. She stood behind him, close enough to feel his warmth, but not touching him. "Seven years ago, I wasn't right for you. I wasn't strong enough to deal with your demons, I didn't understand what you'd been through. I wasn't the right woman to love you."

She had to fight to keep her voice from shaking. This was harder than she'd thought. Continuing was the only option even though she really wanted to bolt for safety.

"I'm the right woman now. I know what you've been through because I've been there myself. I can help with the past. Together we can find a future. I'm the one you've been waiting for, Zach. I'm your other half. And I love you."

The silence was deafening. It throbbed against her ears like falling cabin pressure. She held her breath and prayed for a miracle. As the silence stretched on, she remembered she was dealing with a man who had sold his soul to the devil a long time ago. There wasn't going to be a miracle.

But she had to keep trying. This was the most important moment of her life.

"You asked me once what I would do if I could turn back time," she said. "Would I still do everything the same? I have my answer now. I would have done everything the same. I couldn't have stayed with you then. You wouldn't have let me be a part of your work, and I couldn't bear to have waited at home for you. I had to go out and make my own way. I had to use my skills, test myself. I had to grow enough to be your mate."

He spun on her with savage fury. "You're not my goddamn mate. I'm not a wild animal to be captured and bred."

"Yes, you are," she said softly. "You're exactly like that leopard in the cage. I don't know why I didn't see it before. It's more than your pacing at the cabin. It's the way you view life."

He grabbed her shoulders and shook her. "Stop it," he demanded. "Stop saying these things. I don't want to hear them."

She stared at him, unafraid. "You can't run away from this," she said.

"The hell I can't."

He released her and stalked to the bed. The lamp there illuminated his body. As always, his male beauty took her breath away. Love filled her and made her strong. They'd survived worse; they would survive this.

"I don't want to hear this," he repeated, and began pacing. "You can believe whatever you want, but that doesn't make it true."

"You can pretend not to hear my words," she said, "but that doesn't change reality. I love you."

He shuddered as if she'd struck him. "I don't want your love. Don't care about me. Don't you see? That's what all this is about. It's not that I don't want to love you, Jamie. I don't want you to love me."

He continued pacing, but she saw him from a great distance. It was as if she'd left her body and was floating above the room. His lips moved, but she couldn't hear the words. All that she heard was the thundering of her heartbeat.

He didn't love her now and he would never love her. Worse, he didn't want her to love him.

Something white cut through her. She identified it as intense, soul-burning pain. She'd been wrong about everything.

Awareness returned with a rush. His words continued to tumble out.

"Why do you have to make it more than it is?" he asked. "Isn't this enough?" He motioned to the bed. "It's a hell of a lot more than most people have." He stopped and stared at her. "All I wanted was a few laughs, kid. I'm sorry you got emotionally involved."

"I don't believe you," she said, forcing the words past stiff lips. "You need me to find your way back."

"I'm not going back."

"What are you so afraid of?" she asked, close to tears. "How can you keep on living like this? It's only half a life. There could be so much more."

He shook his head. "You seem to think I can't find my way into this world you admire. That's not it, Jamie. The truth is I don't want to. I'm simply not interested in the journey or the destination."

Chapter 15

The next morning, they drove back to the cabin in silence. Jamie was still in shock. She couldn't believe everything had disintegrated so quickly. One minute they had been lovers; the next they weren't even speaking. It would have been kinder if Zach had simply taken out a gun and shot her. At least that would have been quick. This way she was left to replay their conversation over and over in her mind. She could second-guess herself from now until the end of time, wondering what other words she could have said to make a difference. She could create other scenarios where she was able to make him see what was important. She could imagine a happy future that had turned out to be little more than a fantasy. But she couldn't change what had really happened between them.

She supposed the fatal flaw in her logic was her belief Zach would actually give a damn that she loved him. How naive. He'd never cared before. Why should this time be different?

She thought about trying to make conversation, but she couldn't summon the energy. It wasn't just her shattered spirit; she was also physically exhausted.

She hadn't slept the previous night. Zach had grabbed a pair of jeans and disappeared into the living room of the suite. She'd crawled into bed, curling up like a wounded animal. She'd stared into the darkness and tried to figure out how everything had fallen apart so quickly. She'd searched for an answer, prayed again for a miracle. There had been no answer but silence and the dampness of the tears on her cheeks.

She closed her eyes against the beautiful countryside stretched out on either side of the highway. She didn't want to see the trees or the mountains one last time. It was bad enough she'd lost Zach; she didn't want to have to miss their private world, too.

Time passed. A while later, she felt the vehicle turn onto a steep driveway. The Bronco rocked as it climbed. Then it came to a stop.

Zach got out without saying anything. He walked to the cabin. Minutes later he was back out, dressed in shorts and a T-shirt. He started running.

She opened the passenger door and stepped onto the hard ground. She knew where he was going and what he was going to do. He would run to the road and back. Down the driveway. She'd promised when he was able to do that, she would leave. Now he wanted her to go.

She thought about unloading the luggage in the back, but it was too much work. She could barely gather the strength together to draw breath in and out. Everything hurt. What had happened? Why was he doing this to her? What had she done wrong?

She made her way to the front stairs and settled there. It was a perfect late-spring day. Birds flitted from tree to tree. Soft green grass sprouted from rich soil. Wildflowers dotted the ground.

She inhaled the sweet scents of new life. Tears were so close to the surface, but she forced them back. As hard as she tried, she couldn't find an answer to the question of what she'd done wrong—and then she figured out why. She hadn't done anything wrong. None of this was about her. She was willing to risk it all for love.

Not Zach. He wanted to hold everything inside, regardless of what it cost him now or in the future. He chose to walk away.

The rumble of an engine caught her attention. She glanced up and saw a Federal Express truck pulling up beside the Bronco. A uniformed young woman stepped out and carried over a flat package.

"How you doing?" the woman asked.

"Fine, thanks." Jamie's response was automatic. She didn't think this stranger wanted to know how she was really feeling.

"I've got a package for Zach Jones."

"I'll sign for it." Jamie stood up and started toward the woman. "He's out running."

"I saw him. He's like a maniac, tearing down the mountain. I didn't know he was there and I was scared I might hit him. He just ran on by, like he didn't even see me."

"He probably didn't." She signed on the line indicated, then took the package. The return address was a familiar one in Washington.

Had Winston found him, or had Zach called in the night? Probably the latter. Winston wouldn't have known Zach was ready to return to work.

She waved at the woman as she turned her truck around. The sound of the engine faded, then there was only silence.

Jamie stared at the package. She knew what was inside. Information on Zach's next assignment. Where would he go this time? Would his life be in danger? Would he make it? She wasn't going to be around to rescue him again. He'd been in the field for nearly fourteen years. What if all his luck was used up? What if she never saw him alive again?

She sat there in the sunlight, trying to find answers. There weren't any. She could only exist through the pain and wonder if she was going to die of a broken heart.

Finally Zach came jogging around the bend in the driveway. He was breathing hard and covered in sweat. She knew what he was going to tell her. He'd reached the highway. It was time for her to go.

He stopped in front of her, then bent over and braced his hands on his thighs. Sweat ran down his face and neck. His T-shirt clung to him in damp patches. She couldn't bear to hear the words, so she spoke them for him.

"You made it," she said.

He nodded, still unable to speak. Finally he straightened. "You don't belong here," he gasped, then turned and walked back and forth in front of the porch. "I don't want or need you in my life."

She watched him. Through the pain and sadness, some small spark flared to light. Anger. It temporarily stopped the bleeding and gave her courage.

"I almost believe you," she said.

He glanced at her, obviously startled.

"You want me to crawl away broken and defeated, thinking I made a big fool out of myself," she continued. "It's not going to be that easy."

Under his quickly darkening stare, her courage nearly faltered. She reminded herself this was for all the marbles. There wasn't going to be a second chance. If she didn't risk everything, she would spend the rest of her life wondering what could have been.

"I've been sitting here trying to figure out what went wrong," she said. "What I did that was so horrible. Then I realized it was you."

"That's convenient," he growled. "Whatever works. You've had your say. Now go."

"Not so fast. I'm not done." She paused for effect. And because she was shaking. "You're a coward."

That got his attention. He raised his eyebrows. "Be careful," he warned, his voice silky with danger.

"I'm not afraid," she said. "You are. You are so terrified to feel even one emotion. You hide behind your work. You frighten people away. You won't dare get involved with anyone who might actually want something from you, especially if what they want is for you to feel something. You only slipped up once, and that was with me. Seven years ago, you got involved, even though you knew it was going to have a price. You were so scared, you were willing to do anything to get rid of me. That's why you made me choose."

She took a step toward him. He stopped pacing and stared at her. "Damn you, Zach. You didn't have the right. It wasn't your place to play God with my life."

"I did what I thought was best at the time."

She swore. "Go sell it somewhere else. No one here believes that. You talk as if you handled the situation well. I've got some news. You didn't. You were a complete jerk. You're nothing but a faker. You think you've managed your life pretty well. You think you're so tough, but there are ninety-pound weaklings with more backbone, more moral fiber and more courage than you can even imagine. Being able to take a bullet doesn't mean you're strong. Even a wild animal will face death bravely if the animal is motivated. Real strength is about giving something from inside. Giving something that matters, that actually costs something. It's not brave to risk it all when you have nothing to lose."

He turned away. "You don't know what the hell you're talking about."

"You're wrong. I've never been more sure of anything

in my life. And that's what makes this so hard." Her anger faded as quickly as it had flared, and she was left with nothing but the pain and emptiness. Still, she forced herself to go on.

"I know it all," she said. "I've been there, just like you. I've felt the pain and experienced the suffering. I've done things and seen things that aren't even human. I have nightmares. I'm afraid. But I'm still willing to put that aside for you. I'm willing to try. This is about us. Not the nebulous idea of a family, not for some unreachable dream of being normal. I don't even know what normal is. What I do know is that I would do anything for you. I would lay down my life. I would even walk away."

"Then just do it," he demanded, spinning toward her and planting his hands on his hips. "Get the hell out of my life."

"I will," she said, and nodded. She would do what he asked because there was no choice left to her. Funny, she hadn't thought it would end like this.

She pressed her fingers to her chest as if she could stop the bleeding. Her breath caught in her throat. "Oh, Zach, I wish you'd been honest with me back then. It would have made it all easier."

"I never lied to you."

"Yeah, you did. You let me hope that there was a chance, that you were capable of caring about someone. You should have told me a fling was all you were good for. You should have told me not to waste my time."

"Damn it," he yelled, and stalked toward the woods. When he was about twenty feet from the porch, he turned back to her. "Do you think I want it to be like this? Do you really believe this makes me happy?"

"Yes," she said quietly.

His shoulders slumped, and he rubbed his hand across his face. "What do you want from me?"

"I want it all. Don't you see? I'm the last person who's

going to come looking for you. I'm the last one who is going to care if you live or die. We could build a life together. We could be happy. We could be like that old couple, celebrating our fiftieth anniversary together. You can choose to spend your life in the dark like an animal, or you can join me in the light. You can try. I'm going to make it, Zach. With or without you, I'm determined to find what I want. I'm going to get some balance. I'm going to learn not to be afraid to show my feminine side. I know there are risks, but aren't they worth it? And wouldn't it be easier if we did it together?"

It didn't seem to matter how many times he knocked her down. She kept getting up. He didn't know whether to applaud her efforts or have her committed. Zach shook his head slowly. That wasn't true. In his heart, he admired the hell out of her. She had more courage, more conviction, more raw guts, than anyone he'd ever met.

He shouldn't be surprised. From the first day she'd shown up at the academy, he'd known she was special. She'd been determined to do whatever it took to achieve her goal. She'd worked harder, longer and smarter than any recruit he'd met before or since. He wanted nothing more than to be worthy of her, but he knew he wasn't. And if he tried to pretend, she would eventually find out the truth. This hurt for the moment, but in the end, it was the kindest act he could perform. One day she would understand that.

She might be willing to face the past, to look at the ugliness and move on, but he couldn't.

She brushed her face with the back of her hand. He hated that he'd reduced her to tears. "Please, Zach," she said, her eyes pleading. "If I've ever meant anything to you, if you've ever had a single hope that it could always be like this, then take a chance. I'll be there. We'll figure it out together."

She made it sound so easy. A single step of faith. No

big deal, right? Maybe for her, but not for him. He wasn't like her. Couldn't she see he was doing what was best for her? Didn't she understand the sacrifice involved?

"Don't make me do this," she said. "Don't make me leave you."

"It's best," he told her. "What you want is still possible. Find that life you so admire. Be happy. Get a husband, have some kids, drive in a car pool. I don't begrudge you that happiness, Jamie. You deserve it."

"But I don't want it without you." Her tears flowed faster.

He felt as if his belly had been ripped open. He fought against the pain. Why did doing right feel so wrong? "You want it any way you can get it. I know. My chance to go back was over a long time ago. I didn't take it. Sometimes I think I should have. I don't know anything else but my job. It's what I want to do."

"No. It can't be. Zach, no."

"All the wishing in the world isn't going to give me a second chance."

She studied him for a long time. Her eyebrows drew together and she sniffed through her tears. Then she seemed to come to some decision. "Seven years ago, you made me choose. You were wrong to do that."

She didn't know how wrong. Next to this conversation, it had been the most difficult moment of his life. But he'd known then she would never be happy if she didn't go out and experience all she'd worked for. He hadn't had the right to ask her to stay with him, so he'd let her go. He'd suspected then she'd been his last chance and he'd been right. Now it was too late.

"We can't change the past," he said.

"I know. But we can change the future. You made decisions without consulting me. You put yourself in charge of my destiny because you thought you knew what was best for me. What if you were wrong?"

"I wasn't."

"Maybe then. But you're wrong now." She drew in a shaky breath. Her dark blond hair shimmered around her shoulders. This was how he wanted to remember her. Proud. Beautiful. Strong.

"We both paid a price for that moment," she continued. "Now *you* have to choose. You can be the warrior or you can be the man."

"You still don't get it, Jamie. You're stronger than me. You always have been. The kindest act is to let you go."

"You're wrong. The kindest act is to love me. That's what this is all about, isn't it? You don't love me. You never have."

He wanted to speak the words. The lie. If he told her he didn't love her, she would leave and never look back. But he couldn't say it. He couldn't deny the one truly perfect part of his life. Loving her. He'd always loved her.

She walked to the porch and picked up a package. "You'll let me go, but you'll let me go wondering what could have been between us. That's cruel of you, Zach. I expected more. I deserved more."

He wanted to defend himself. Didn't she know how hard this was for him? He said nothing.

She held out the flat package. "This came for you. It's from Winston. Probably your next assignment. Tell me something. Is Winston omnipotent, or did you call him from Denver?"

"I called him last night."

"Good. I would hate to think he really does know everything." She glanced at the package. "This is the world you want. A world without love. Without me. Take it."

He stared at the purple-and-white envelope, but he couldn't reach for it. He wasn't ready to go back into that world. Tears rolled down Jamie's cheeks. He couldn't bear that, either. He turned and started to jog. Then he ran. Faster and faster until he couldn't see the cabin or hear her calling his name.

The canyon was less than fifty feet across, but the bottom was nearly a half mile down. Zach crouched in the underbrush and listened to the gunfire. It was closer than it had been just an hour before. The enemy had found the trail. There wasn't much time for any of them.

He functioned without thought, taking care of business, getting his men across the narrow footbridge. On one side of the bridge, the rope railing had been taken out by a shell blast. Two men were dead, a third injured. Their luck had run out. If they could just make it across, they would be safe.

He sent his second-in-command over next, then turned to scan the jungle behind him. Once everyone was on the other side, they would blow up the bridge. The enemy would be trapped with no way to get to them.

It wasn't supposed to be a difficult assignment. He'd completed a dozen like it. So why was this one so hard? Why was he hesitating? What had he forgotten?

Jamie.

Jamie! He turned around and peered through the thick underbrush. Something was wrong. He could feel it.

"Zach?"

Her voice. She was alive. He glanced up and saw her on the other side of the canyon. His men were gone; she stood in their place, exactly as he remembered her. Hair in a braid, jeans, sweatshirt. In front of her was a small blond little girl, about the same age as the child they'd seen at the zoo. Chubby pink cheeks, bright blue eyes and a pretty smile. He found himself smiling back.

"Come on," Jamie said, motioning him toward the bridge.

Zach couldn't move. His legs wouldn't cooperate. He couldn't get control of his breathing. He couldn't think.

The enemy moved closer. He had to destroy the bridge before they got across. Before they got Jamie. But he couldn't force himself to act. Something held him in place.

Fear. He could feel its coldness against his skin. He could taste it.

"Daddy, hurry," the little girl called. "Daddy, we need you."

"I can't. Run," he shouted as loudly as he could. Yet the sound seemed to float away on the wind. He knew they hadn't heard him.

"I'm not leaving without you," Jamie said, her voice echoing in the canyon.

"Daddy, please!"

The men were upon him. Dozens and dozens, all dressed in camouflage, heavily armed. They streamed past him, not even noticing him. He reached for his gun, but he was unarmed. He didn't even have a knife. He jumped in front of one of the warriors, and the man simply pushed him aside.

One by one they crossed the bridge and surrounded Jamie and her daughter.

He woke to the sound of a scream.

Zach sat up in bed. He was covered with sweat and panting.

Adrenaline raced through his body. He could feel the thundering of his heart. His legs twitched; his hands shook.

It was just a dream, he told himself. An ugly, vivid dream he wasn't going to be able to forget for a long time. But it wasn't real.

He stood up and walked to the window. He pushed up the glass and let the cold night air pour over his heated body. Dreams were a luxury he didn't usually allow himself. Everyone dreamed; he knew he did, as well, but he didn't allow himself to remember the dreams. This time he didn't get a choice.

The images were imprinted on his brain. When he closed his eyes, he could see the jungle scene, the trust in Jamie's eyes, the horror on the child's face when the armed men had approached. Instead of reliving it over and over, he stared up at the star-filled night and tried to think of other things.

Daddy, help!

She'd called to him, and he hadn't been able to respond. He'd let her down. He'd left her to die.

White-hot pain ripped through his already tattered soul. How could he have abandoned a child?

Daddy!

His child. His.

He clenched his hands into fists and leaned his forehead against the cool glass. He had nothing left with which to fight. He'd been drained of all strength. With a giant shudder, he released the last of the tension from his body and prepared for the onslaught.

His eyes drifted closed. He tried not to think, not to remember, but he didn't get a choice. The memories came at him, weaving and ducking like ghosts in a low-budget horror film.

Faces of the dead. Men he'd killed, those who had died under his command.

John Alder, age twenty-seven. Killed in a climbing accident near the southern border of the former Soviet Union.

David Weeks, age thirty. Murdered by terrorists in a rebel camp in Central America.

Ronnie Maple, Jeff Harrison, Graham Everett, Albatross. There were dozens of other names, and many more he'd never known. Enemies he'd killed himself, civilians, locals and those with the simple misfortune of being in the wrong place at the wrong time.

The ghosts of the dead surrounded him, mocked him, hurled their insults, and he knew they spoke the truth. His fault. *His* fault. The smell of death was everywhere. He could feel it on his skin and seeping through his body.

Forgotten moments roared back to life. Decisions he'd made. Times he'd been so sure he was right. How had he known? How had he been so arrogant?

The past was everywhere. He staggered under its weight, moved across the room and fell into the chair. This was what he'd feared. This was why he'd kept a tight cover on his emotions. Feeling anything, even affection or regret, unleashed them all. Sorrow, sadness, anger, rage, fear, horror. They forced him to the brink of madness and threatened to push him off the edge.

Daddy, help!

The voice of a child called him back to sanity. He turned toward the sound, but the blackness of the room smothered him. A child. New life.

A possibility? A second chance? A reward for doing the one right thing in his life—for loving Jamie?

But he'd had to let Jamie go. It had been the right thing. A noble act. A—

He pushed to his feet with such force that the chair shot out behind him and slammed into the wall. Zach stalked to the window and stared out at the heavens.

"No!" he yelled, then hung his head in shame.

She'd been right. He was a coward.

He'd let her go because he was afraid. He'd let her go because he'd feared he would never be enough. That once she knew the truth about him, once she glimpsed the horror and darkness he'd trapped inside, she would be repulsed by him.

He'd let her go because the dream of living a normal life, of loving one person, of trusting in the future, was beyond him. He didn't have that much left in him. He'd let her go because it was easier to deal with her anger and pain than with her contempt.

He'd let her go because, as the dream had shown so vividly, he would only end up destroying her.

You can be the warrior or you can be the man. You have to choose.

He'd chosen to let her go. Because he was afraid to be a man. He knew how to be a warrior. That part was easy. She'd been right. It didn't take much courage to risk it all when he had nothing important to lose.

Yet look how much she'd risked. She'd bared her heart, then begged him to accept her love. He'd trampled all over her feelings, yet she'd kept giving, kept offering. Kept loving.

If she knew the truth...

He pounded his fist against the window frame and acknowledged what he'd always suspected. Jamie knew the worst about him. She knew because those same demons lived inside her. She'd experienced the same life, she'd seen death, caused death, had made decisions and had to live with them. She wasn't afraid of the past or of him. She wasn't afraid to love. Did he really want to walk away from his last chance ever? Did he want her to go the rest of her life without knowing how much he loved her?

"No," he said, quietly this time, and headed for the door.

"Jamie?" he called.

He stepped into the hallway and listened. When he'd come back from his run, she'd been in her room. Was she asleep or out on the porch? Silence surrounded him. He wasn't sure how long he'd been asleep or even what time it was. Somewhere around midnight.

He knocked on her bedroom door, but there was no answer. He pushed it open and flipped on the light.

It was as if she'd never been there. The bed had been

tidied, and the dresser was bare. Her luggage was gone. Even the scent of her had disappeared.

He knew the truth instantly, but still he searched the house, hoping he was wrong. Naked, he stepped out onto the porch. The Bronco was gone.

She'd left him, just as he'd asked.

Chapter 16

Jamie cradled the cup of coffee in her hands. When she sipped the steaming liquid, it felt warm, but when she held the mug, her fingers couldn't absorb the heat. She knew what the problem was—she was turning to ice on the inside. All the hot drinks, warm showers and thick blankets in the world couldn't solve that problem.

She drew her knees up to her chest and leaned back in the wooden deck chair. She sat on the balcony of her San Francisco apartment. From here she could see across the bay. It was a postcard kind of morning. White, puffy clouds, people out on sailboats, warm air perfumed with sweet-smelling flowers. The kind of days families spent together, or lovers savored as they stole time to be in each other's company and make love.

Jamie sniffed a couple of times but refused to acknowledge the burning in her eyes. She was finished with crying. She'd done nothing else for the past week. Seven whole days of feeling sorry for herself. Seven days of tears, of second-guessing, of trying not to go back to the cabin and beg one more time.

The only thing that had kept her from hopping on a plane was the thought that Zach was already gone. By now he would be involved in his next assignment. While she didn't think he would forget her, she doubted he would allow himself to think of her often. He might miss her, but he wouldn't mourn her as she mourned him.

She still couldn't sleep at night, so she used the time to relive the weeks at the cabin. She replayed entire conversations, wondering what she could have done differently to change the outcome of the last time she'd seen Zach. There were no miracle answers, no moments of insight or revelation.

She'd left him again. She'd sworn to love him forever and she'd left him for the second and last time. It had been the right thing to do. She knew that. It had also been the hardest thing she'd ever done. Leaving him had been like cutting off an arm or a leg. He was a part of her very being. How long would it take the wound to stop bleeding?

She'd expected to feel pain. What she hadn't expected was the sensation of her emotional self draining away. And the questions. Had she left too soon? Should she have tried harder?

Jamie rose to her feet and shook her head. She'd run out of words and arguments. The bottom line was she couldn't make him love her and she wouldn't be with him if he refused to admit he cared. If he'd given her a hint it might all work out, she would have held on forever. In the face of his stubborn rejection, she'd had no choice but to go.

It was probably the kindest act. In the end, her love would have destroyed him. He wasn't ready to face his past and let the ghosts go. He had to do that in his own time. Until then, she would survive without him. Eventually she would figure out how to have a good life without the agency and without Zach. If he changed his mind, she wouldn't be hard to find. Not that she expected him to show up on her doorstep. The coldness in her heart told her he might never show up at all.

That meant she had to get on with her life, which sounded simple enough. If only she had a clue what she wanted to do. Not many of her skills were going to translate to the private sector. Not many companies needed employees well versed in the art of killing.

She walked into the living room. A cream-colored sofa sat in front of a bleached-pine coffee table. There was a gold-tone floor lamp in the corner and a stereo system sitting on the floor. She'd never used the fireplace. The walls were bare. She wanted to compare it to a hotel room, but hotels put a lot more thought into their decorating.

The bedroom was just as bad. A bed had been pushed up against one wall. That was it. No pictures, no furniture. In the closet, built-in drawers held her small collection of cotton underwear. Her clothing consisted of jeans, shirts and one black lacy dress.

"Pretty pathetic," she muttered, slipping off her robe and reaching for a pair of jeans.

She'd spent the past week immobilized by pain. She wasn't going to do that anymore. She had to get on with her life. The task seemed daunting, but that was because she was looking at it all at once. She would do better to break it into smaller, more manageable sections. At least there was plenty of money in her account. The agency had paid well, and she hadn't been around to spend much. She could go back to college or travel. She didn't have to find a job anytime soon.

But she did have to start living.

She pulled a sweatshirt over her head, then brushed her hair. After weaving it into a braid, she collected her keys and her credit cards, then headed out.

* * *

Jamie hovered outside the boutique. The fancy lettering on the window scared her. She knew she didn't look like any of the well-dressed customers that had gone in while she'd been lurking on the sidewalk. Yet the store had everything she'd wanted. Over the past week, in between crying jags, she'd called around to find a place that would fill her needs. Now all she needed was the courage to step inside.

She reminded herself that less than two months ago, she'd walked into an armed enemy camp and carried out a wounded prisoner. Compared to that, what was a little shopping?

Inside, the air was comfortable and lightly scented with roses. Jamie glanced at all the racks, trying to figure out what she needed first. The boutique had a wide selection of clothing, undergarments and accessories, including shoes. In theory, she could get everything she needed with one stop. That was her goal. Later, when she had more experience, she would venture out to a mall.

"May I be of assistance?"

She turned toward the voice and saw a small gray-haired woman standing in front of her. The woman couldn't be much over five feet tall, with a tiny waist and miniature feet. Jamie felt as petite and graceful as a giraffe. The urge to bolt was strong.

She sucked in a breath. Only the truth would work in this situation. "I need help. Bad. I've only ever worn jeans. I want to dress better, but I don't know what styles look good on me. I'm hopeless with accessories and makeup. I haven't done anything but trim my bangs and occasionally hack off a couple of inches of length on my hair."

The gray-haired woman smiled. "What's your name?"

"Jamie."

"Jamie, I'm Sandra and I'm going to change your life."

Four hours later, Jamie found out Sandra wasn't kidding. They started with casual clothes. Although Jamie liked the frilly blouses and fuller pants and skirts, they looked horrible on her. Fitted or tailored was better. Pants with tucked-in shirts, coordinated belts and flats emphasized her athletic build. For fun there were shorts, denim skirts and one scrap of black leather that barely covered her thighs. She tried on a couple of suits she just had to have, then they moved to dressier clothing.

Shortly after two, Sandra sent out for sandwiches. When they'd eaten, Jamie stripped and began trying on lingerie. Soon she had a wardrobe of lacy bras with matching panties.

Earrings had never been part of her style. She couldn't wear them on the job, and she'd never bothered in her off duty hours. But she allowed a young man to pierce her earlobes, then chose a collection of pretty earrings to wear when she could take out the diamond studs she now wore.

By three-thirty she was being escorted across the street, where Andre promised to work a miracle on her hair. Her skin was vacuumed, her pores cleansed, her feet pedicured and her fingers massaged. While this was done, Andre cut off six inches of hair, gave her a deep conditioning, then blew her hair dry over a fat, round brush.

A six-foot redheaded amazon beauty then explained the mysteries of makeup, chose a foundation that actually matched Jamie's skin and didn't streak.

By six Jamie was back in her apartment. She'd maxed out a credit card. Instead of feeling shocked, she was thrilled. "I should have done this years ago," she said as she scampered to the bathroom.

She walked into the room, closed her eyes, flipped on the light, then opened her eyes. A stranger stared back. A pretty stranger with thick, shoulder-length hair that swayed and bounced. Andre's cut had freed up natural waves Jamie didn't know she'd had. He'd trimmed her bangs and thinned them until they were wisps. Makeup highlighted her wide hazel eyes.

Color stained her cheeks and her mouth. Diamond earrings glinted at her earlobes.

In place of worn blue jeans, she wore a denim skirt, a fitted T-shirt with a suede vest hanging open. Jamie laughed out loud. She looked...normal.

She stared at the piles of boxes and bags all over the floor. She had shoes, makeup, clothes, lingerie, accessories. She was going to have to buy a dresser. Maybe even a nightstand and another lamp.

She ignored the packages and walked into her kitchen. Sitting in the middle of the round oak table was the plant she'd bought herself. *Coleus* something. The man at the flower shop had sworn it was about as hardy as they came. She couldn't kill it. She had detailed instructions about feeding and watering her new possession.

She'd never had a plant before. It implied permanence. That she would be staying here indefinitely. That she would be around enough to take care of it and talk to it. It made the sterile apartment more of a home.

She put a cup of water in the microwave to heat it for instant coffee, then leaned against the sink and stared out at the bay. The sun drifted toward the water, making the waves glimmer with gold. The emptiness inside was still there—it would always be there—but right now it was bearable. She hadn't yet learned how to forget, but eventually she would figure out how to go on living. Who knows, she might even get herself together enough to go to the trouble to make a pot of coffee for just herself.

The microwave beeped and the phone rang at the same moment. Jamie's heart jumped into overdrive. She reached for the receiver as her heart sent up a fervent prayer. Please, let it be Zach.

"Hello?"

"Sanders, you bored by retirement yet?"

The pain was so intense, she thought she might be dying. Not Zach. Foolish of her to think he would call. He'd made his choice and he was never going to admit he was wrong.

She sank to the floor and pulled her knees close to her chest. After taking a deep breath so her voice wouldn't shake, she said, "I'm fine, Winston. How are you?"

"I'm spending a lot of time wondering how I'm supposed to get anything done without you."

The microwave beeped softly to remind her about the heated water. She ignored it.

"You have lots of capable agents. I'm sure they can step in for me without any problem."

"You were a little more than capable. What have you been doing with yourself? I've been calling every couple of weeks, and this is the first time I've caught you home."

"I've been—" She squeezed her eyes shut. I've been falling in love with a wonderful man. I've been living the fantasy. I've been making plans and watching them disappear into dust.

"I've been adjusting," she said.

"Not easy, is it?" His voice was low and sympathetic.

"No, but I'm determined to keep trying. I'll figure it all out."

"Maybe you don't have to."

"What does that mean?"

"I used to be a field agent, just like you. After ten years, I tried to walk away."

The microwave beeped again. She opened her eyes and wiped the tears from her cheeks. "I didn't know that."

"Not many people do. The point is, I couldn't make it

on the outside. I needed the agency. It was in my blood. So I came back."

"Is that what this phone call is about?" she asked, then shook her head. "I'm not interested, Winston. I've made my decision and I'm going to stick to it."

"I'm not inviting you to go back in the field. I'm offering you something inside. A promotion. You'd be based here in Washington. Technology is changing and improving every day. We're going to be adding another department. I'd like you to run that."

She leaned her head against the cupboard door. "Would I be running agents?" she asked.

"Sure. You'd have a great team. The best. I'd let you pick them yourself."

That's what she was afraid of. "No, Winston. I don't want the best. I don't want to be responsible for sending other people into dangerous situations. I have to make a life for myself outside of the agency."

"What if you can't?"

She'd asked herself the question a thousand times. "If I can't, then I'll come crawling back and offer to work as your secretary."

"That would be great, but I'm not going to hold my breath. You've never failed at anything, Jamie. I figured you were going to refuse, but I had to try. Stay in touch."

"I will."

He hung up without saying goodbye.

She sat on the floor and listened to the silence. She could have asked. It would have been so easy to casually ask if Zach was back on assignment. After all, she'd been the one to save his life. Winston wouldn't have thought anything of the inquiry.

Where was he right now? The Middle East? Africa? South America? Was he even still alive?

That question kept her up nights. How would she know if something happened to him? Eventually information filtered down the agency grapevine, but she wasn't hooked up to that anymore. Five years from now, would she run into Winston and ask? Would he look puzzled and say, *Zach died years ago. Didn't you know?*

Would she spend the rest of her life waiting for Zach only to find out he was gone? Or would she just be waiting for a man who had no intention of finding her?

The microwave beeped, reminding her about the now-cooling water. She stood up and replaced the receiver, then reset the timer and started the machine again. She didn't have the answer to any of those questions. When Zach had refused to even try to make it work between them, he'd made his choice. When she'd walked away without a word, she'd made hers. There was nothing left to do but get her life together and move forward.

Winston stared at the report in front of him. Zach felt strangely out of sorts. Instead of waiting patiently, he prowled the well-appointed office, adjusting souvenirs on bookshelves and straightening already straight pictures.

"You passed the physical with no problem," Winston said, then flipped back a couple of pages. "You heal pretty fast for an old man."

"Thanks." Zach shrugged. "I owe it all to my clean living."

And Jamie. She'd taken care of him, fixing healthy meals, encouraging him to exercise. Together they'd worked out their own physical-therapy program.

"You want to know what the psychiatrist had to say?" Winston asked.

"Not really."

"He thinks you've got a death wish."

There's a news flash, he thought grimly. "What's your point?"

Winston lowered the papers to the desk. "Do you?"

Zach moved toward the desk and lowered himself into

one of the leather chairs there. He leaned back, then placed one ankle on the opposite knee. "Every assignment is a death wish. Going out in the field is inherently risky. Some people come back, some people don't. What your mental friend didn't like was that I'm not afraid to die."

Jamie had been right. It was easy to risk it all when he had nothing worth losing. That didn't take courage. Courage was standing up for a belief. Being terrified and doing it anyway. Risking heart and soul when there was every chance they would be rejected and trampled. Dying was easy—it was the living that had him stumped.

Winston flipped through more pages of a report, then nodded. "I have an assignment for you. High risk. Volunteers only. You interested?"

High risk. More than fifty percent probability of not returning.

There was no reason not to take it. He'd healed physically. His body was as strong as ever. But he wasn't whole on the inside. The ache in his chest never went away. Nights used to be worst; now the days were getting to him. He'd spent the past couple of weeks at the cabin trying to sort it all out.

But the cabin was no longer a sanctuary. Now it held Jamie's essence. The memories of their times together were a constant taunt.

Jamie loved him. He had no doubt about that. He loved her, perhaps more than he'd ever realized. His life was empty without her. He saw her everywhere, he heard her voice, he ached for her.

Yet he still hesitated. Because he didn't want to screw this up. He wanted to do what was right for both of them.

Should he just let her go, knowing that she would forget him and find some normal guy to make her dreams come true?

He closed his eyes against the image, but it came to

him anyway. The picture of her with someone else. Someone who didn't understand what she'd been through. How would this guy know what she was thinking? How would he know what to say when the nightmares came? How could he lovingly touch the scars on her body and heal them if he didn't know how they got there in the first place?

What about his dream? What about the child—the daughter—he'd seen? Would Jamie have that child with another man? Would the young girl call another man daddy, ride *his* shoulders, smile up at this stranger? Would Jamie give herself completely? Would she grow to trust this man as she had once trusted Zach? The image of that pierced him more deeply than any knife ever had.

No one would ever love Jamie as much, never love their child as much, Zach thought. Seven years ago, he'd let her go. How could he have done it again? Hadn't he learned anything?

"Zach?"

He looked at his boss. "Not interested."

Winston raised pale eyebrows. "There's a first."

"Prepare yourself for another one. I'm resigning."

Winston had the courtesy to look as if he'd just been shot. "Resigning? From the agency?"

"It's time."

It *was* time. He finally saw that. It wasn't all because of Jamie, although she deserved most of the credit. He'd finally come to the realization he could no longer live in the shadows. Even if she didn't want him, he wasn't going back. She'd shown him he still had a slim grasp on his humanity. She'd shown him about the healing power of love. Even without being with her, he would continue to love her, and that would be enough.

"I don't know what to say," Winston told him.

"Wish me luck. I'm going to need it."

"What are you going to do?"

"I'm going to live, or at least try to."

Zach shook his head. He didn't have a clue where to start. He wanted to find Jamie, wherever she was, confess all and beg her to take him back. What kept him in his seat was the realization it had been weeks and he hadn't heard from her. She was probably doing fine without him. She deserved better than he could offer.

"I can't believe I've lost two of my best agents in the same month."

"Who else quit?"

"Jamie Sanders."

"She did that weeks ago," he said.

Winston leaned back in his chair. "She officially left right after she rescued you, but a few days ago I tried to entice her back with a promotion and a desk job. She wasn't interested." He glanced at Zach. "I don't suppose I can talk you into it?"

"No. I've got better things to do with my time."

"Now *you* sound like Jamie." Winston dropped the file and stared at him. "I couldn't find her for several weeks. You wouldn't happen to know where she was hiding out, would you?"

Zach shrugged as if the matter didn't concern him.

"I see." Winston nodded. "Or I should have seen. Then again, I guess it's not my business." He wrote something on a piece of paper and handed the sheet to Zach.

"What's this?" Zach asked as he read an address in San Francisco.

"Just saving you some time." He rose to his feet and held out his hand. "I've enjoyed working with you, Zach. Stay in touch, okay?"

They shook warmly. "I'll be around," Zach promised, and walked out of the office.

As he waited for the elevator, he studied the address. God, he missed her. He'd never lived with a woman before. Hell, he'd never lived with anyone. Not since he was a kid. Somehow she'd woven herself into the fabric of his life. He couldn't escape her any more than he could escape his own skin.

The elevator doors opened, and he stepped inside. He'd created an impossible situation. Did he go to her and confess all? Did he risk his heart and soul knowing they might never be up to the task? Could he deal with the truth—that he could love her for the rest of his life and it still wouldn't be enough to make up for what he'd done to her? Would she take him back, knowing he didn't deserve another chance?

He stood alone in the elevator and realized this was what it would be like for the rest of his life. Empty space. He'd always lived that way—never letting anyone inside. Never having the courage to care. Only with Jamie could he be a part of something.

The elevator doors opened, and he walked out of the building and onto the street. Crowds of people surrounded him. He grasped the paper in his hand. He had nowhere else to go. He was too old and too broken to face the rest of his life alone. No matter what it took, he was going to convince her to give him another chance.

On the morning of the sixteenth day, Jamie awoke with a prickling feeling on the back of her neck. At first she didn't know what it meant. Then she didn't dare believe.

She showered, curled her hair and then carefully applied her makeup. She was getting pretty good at it. This time the eyeliner only smudged a little, and she corrected the mistake with a brush of a damp cotton swab.

Outside, the sky was clear, the sun bright. She dressed in shorts and a cropped T-shirt, then pulled out the coffeepot. There would be two for breakfast.

While the coffee perked, she went to her balcony and settled down to wait. The prickling might be completely wrong. There was no reason he would have changed his mind. She didn't believe in miracles anymore, but what else could it be? She didn't know how long it would take or why he was coming. She only knew he was on his way.

As she sat in the chair, she automatically slowed her breathing. Her mind was alert, listening to sounds. Her muscles tensed and released so they wouldn't cramp. She could sit like this for hours if necessary.

She didn't think it was going to take that long.

Forty minutes later, she heard an odd clicking in the hallway outside her apartment. Then a knock.

Her heart pounded like a jackhammer. Her palms grew damp and when she stood up, her legs trembled. She made her way to the door. Caution dictated that she look out the peephole, but she knew who was standing on the other side. She knew everything about him—how he looked, how he sounded, the taste of his skin, the sight of his pleasure. She even knew his deepest fears. What she didn't know was why he'd come back to her.

She opened the door. No one was there. Jamie frowned, then a whimper caught her attention. She glanced down. A golden retriever pup stared up piteously. Big brown eyes met her own, and the fuzzy tail started to thump against the floor.

Jamie looked for someone, but the hallway was empty. She stared at the pup. The animal whimpered again.

"What's the matter?" she asked softly, holding out her hand and letting the dog smell her fingers. She was rewarded with a wet kiss.

"Are you all alone?"

The puppy whined.

"Oh, you're scared." She crouched down and gathered the shivering dog in her arms. The puppy wiggled as if trying to get closer. It reached out and licked her chin. Jamie laughed.

"I knew you two would get along."

She started at the sound of a voice. Her eyes closed briefly as she absorbed the sound of him. A deep breath brought her his scent. He was still the best; she hadn't heard him approach.

She rose slowly to her feet. Zach stood in front of her in the hallway. He wore jeans and a dark blue T-shirt that emphasized his strength. Hunger filled her. Hunger fueled by love long repressed. She wanted to throw herself at him, but she couldn't move. She couldn't do anything but stand there and feel the pleasure of looking at him again.

"Hi," he said.

"Hi, yourself."

There was an awkward pause as she absorbed the thrilling sight of him. He gave her a quick smile. "You cut your hair. You look great."

She clutched the puppy closer, grateful she had something to keep her hands busy. She didn't want Zach to know she was shaking. "Thanks."

He swallowed. "You're probably wondering why I'm here."

In her heart she knew. Maybe she'd always known; maybe it was a miracle. But she needed him to say the words. Her battered heart and soul needed the soothing balm of his confession. "Why don't you tell me why."

He shifted his weight from foot to foot, as if he, too, were nervous. She nuzzled the puppy's soft fur. The animal had relaxed in her arms and was dozing off.

"What was that question you asked, the one about turning back time?"

She remembered the question. She remembered everything about being with him. Her heart tightened as she dared to hope. Surely he wouldn't have come all this way just to tell her he still wasn't interested.

They were standing half in, half out of her apartment,

but she didn't dare interrupt him to invite him in. She wanted to hear what he had to say first.

"If you could turn back time," she said. "If you could go back seven years, what would you do differently?"

His dark eyes brightened with a fire she'd never seen before. "I finally have an answer."

"Tell me," she whispered.

"I'd say I don't know how to be all those things you need me to be, but that I'm willing to learn. I'd say that I've never loved anyone before, and it terrifies me. But it's easier to be scared with you than without you. I'd take you in my arms and never let you go. I'd promise to love you for as long as I have breath, to the best of my ability. I'd promise to love you more and better each day. I can't live without you, Jamie. You're my whole world. I'm not the best guy around. You can do a lot better. I may never be normal, but no one can love you more than I do."

She threw herself at him. The puppy was in the way, and she couldn't wrap her arms around him, but it didn't matter. He caught her hard against him and pulled her close. The sleeping dog barely stirred.

"I love you," she said.

Then he kissed her, and she couldn't talk at all. Not that it mattered. The sensation of his mouth on hers was more perfect than any words.

His hands roamed her back. She leaned against him, not wanting the moment to end, not caring that she felt tears on her cheeks. It felt so right to be with him.

"Are you sure?" she asked between kisses.

"More sure than I've ever been. Are *you* sure? I'm bound to screw this up at first."

She smiled. "I don't mind."

Zach motioned to the puppy in her arms. "I bought a dog."

"He's pretty cute."

"He's a she. I've had her a couple of days. She doesn't

have a name yet. I thought you could think of a good one.'' Zach shrugged. ''I figured even if you didn't want to talk to me, you wouldn't turn away an innocent puppy.''

She looked at him and smiled. ''Stacking the deck in your favor?''

He didn't return her smile. Instead, his expression became very serious. He brushed the tears from her face. ''I would have done anything to win you back, Jamie. Anything.''

''I'm glad.''

The puppy stirred sleepily. He stroked her head. ''I'm a lousy single parent,'' he said. ''We need help, Jamie. We need you.''

She leaned against him. ''You've got me, Zach. For always. I still love you. Nothing can change that.'' She handed him the sleeping pup, then pushed open the door and invited him inside. ''I'm impressed by your commitment,'' she continued. ''I only had the courage to buy a houseplant.''

He wrapped his arm around her. ''I thought we could practice on the puppy, then when we've got this family thing figured out, we could try the real thing. That is, if you want to.''

''Kids?'' she asked.

He nodded.

She felt more tears against her cheeks. Zach understood everything. ''I'd like that,'' she said, her voice husky.

He set the puppy on the sofa. ''I think she's going to sleep for a while,'' he said.

Jamie smiled. ''Really. What did you want to do while she was resting?''

He cupped her face and kissed her gently. ''Live a mircle.''

Epilogue

Jamie paused at the front door to Jones & Jones Security. She glanced at her watch, shook her head, then stepped into the reception area. Running late, as usual.

"You've got forty billion messages," Amanda, the receptionist, said as Jamie walked by.

"They'll have to wait." Jamie started down the hall.

"Great suit," Amanda called after her. "Stop dressing so nice. You're making the rest of us look bad."

Jamie grinned but didn't stop moving. When she reached the door with a placard that said Zach Jones, Co-president she turned the knob and stepped inside.

Zach sat with his back to the door, facing his computer. The bursts of sound coming from the machine told her he wasn't working on a spread sheet. A large explosion was followed by an excited squeal.

"I'm back," she said, and moved toward the desk. She put her briefcase on the floor and unbuttoned her jacket. "I thought you were going to take the games off your computer."

Zach spun toward her and grinned. "They're not for me."

"You're hopeless," Jamie said, then lowered her gaze to the toddler sitting confidently on Zach's lap. "Has Daddy been letting you play computer games again?"

Three-year-old Alice nodded. "I'm winning, Mommy. We're gonna save the *universal.*"

"I'm sure the 'universal' is very happy about that, too." She shrugged out of her jacket and tossed it on the desk.

Zach picked up Alice with the familiarity of a father who fully participates in his child's upbringing. He settled his daughter on his shoulders, then came around the desk and kissed Jamie.

"You look tired."

"I'm exhausted."

He held on to Alice's pudgy legs with one hand. With the other, he stroked her cheek. "But you knocked 'em dead, didn't you?"

She smiled. "The meeting went very well."

"I know." He grabbed a paper from his desk. "They've already faxed over the signed agreement. We got the new account."

"Kiss Mommy again," Alice instructed.

Zach leaned close and brushed Jamie's lips with his. "The things I do for my daughter," he said.

"Hazardous duty," Jamie murmured. "Maybe we should see about getting you a raise." She reached up and took her daughter. Alice snuggled close.

"We missed you, Mommy," the little girl said.

"I missed you guys, too."

Theirs was a partnership that worked. Jamie sold the security systems that Zach designed. Their years at the agency had paid off, and they were one of the fastest-growing companies in the country. The signed contract was from a California bank with over two hundred branches. Nearly six months of negotiations had paid off.

"We need to celebrate," Zach said, collecting Alice and wrapping his free arm around Jamie's shoulders. "What do you want to do?"

She rested her hand on her pregnant belly. Their second child, a boy, was due in four weeks. "I want you to rub my feet."

"Done."

She glanced at her husband and her child. Five years ago she had left Zach at his cabin and thought she might have to spend the rest of her life alone. But he'd realized what they had together and he'd come back for her.

It hadn't been an easy road. They'd both had adjustments to make. The business had consumed them for a couple of years. But they'd always been together, growing stronger in love. They'd found their own version of normal. A dog, a cat, a beautiful, bright child with another on the way. And a husband who could make her heart race with just a smile.

As Zach and Alice talked and laughed together, Jamie remembered her question to Zach all those years ago. If he could turn back time, what would he change? When she thought about that now, she knew the answer. Neither of them would change one second of time. They'd found a miracle—their love.

* * * * *

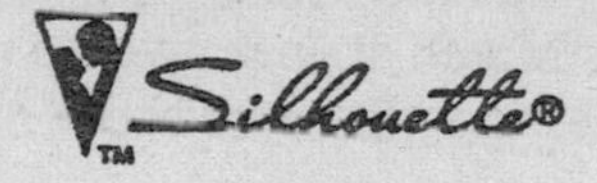
Silhouette®
TM